When Love grows doubt

The MacIntyres – Part I

Novel

Barbara Eckhoff

FOR JOANNE

Thank you for being a good friend and the best shotgun rider during our Police volunteer time. Thank you for encouraging me to translate my books. Without you, this project probably would not have come to fruition. Thank you for the great help and the tireless time you spent with it.

FOR RENATE

Who as a bilingual, was a great help in finding the right words. Thank you also for your good eyes that weeded out many mistakes and for the time you spent with the proof-reading.

WHEN LOVE GROWS DOUBT

The MacIntyres – Part I

Novel

Barbara Eckhoff

BOOKS BY BARBARA ECKHOFF

Um uns herum die Dunkelheit (German Edition)

Der Wind in meinen Federn (German Edition)

Wenn Liebe Zweifel sät (German Edition)

Wind of fate (English Edition)

When Love grows doubt (English Edition)

Prologue

The wind swept icily over the freshly covered grave. Despite the noon hour, it was gloomy outside and the sky held ominously dark-looking clouds. The mourners had long since retreated into the warmth, but the small, delicate figure standing over the grave with a flowing cloak was oblivious to all this.

Despite the warm winter cape with the fur-lined hood, she stood trembling infront of the mound covered with flowers. Her quiet tears were quickly dried by the wind, leaving red cheeks on her face.

Now everything was over. She had just buried her last hope. Who could help her now?

"Moira!"

She was startled when she felt a hand on her shoulder and heard the priest's voice.

"Moira, there is nothing more you can do for him! You will catch your death if you don't get warm. Come my child, Martha has a cup of hot tea ready, it will warm you up again."

With these words he put his arm around her shoulders and gently led her away from the grave towards the rectory. Moira silently let herself be guided. Inside the house, a comforting warmth from the heated fireplace welcomed her. Martha, the priest's housekeeper, handed her a hot cup of tea with a good shot of rum in it.

"This will warm you right up, my dear. You're half frozen!"

Gratefully, Moira accepted the cup, only now realizing

how cold she was. Her hands and feet began to tingle as the warmth flooded her body.

She looked out the window and saw that a storm was brewing outside. Perhaps she had better start on her way, so that she was home before the expected rain.

"I thank you for your hospitality, but I think I should be heading home now."

"You should have gone back with one of the others earlier, then you wouldn't have to go all the way alone. Oh, it's a shame. I remember when you used to drive up with your parents in the carriage. You should have kept it for yourself so you wouldn't have to walk home."

Moira had to think back to the time the priest was talking about. Yes, things had been different before. It seemed like an eternity when she could go through life without a care. When her father knew her so well, he could read her mind through the eyes of a parent and had promised her a rosy and secure future. But that was long ago. That time would never come back.

She was in trouble and the only one who could have helped her was now lying in the cold grave. Moira tried to suppress the tears that were welling up inside her again, but nodded and quickly said goodbye to the priest and Martha and headed back out into the horrible weather. A gust of wind caught her. She quickly held her cloak tighter to her body and hurried away with quick steps towards the village.

Normally she would have walked the path by the cliffs to her home. This was a shortcut, but in this weather it was not advisable. The narrow trail, which on sunny days gave a breathtaking view of the sea below, lined with warped trees and hedges on the landward side of the path, was now soggy and slippery in the rainy and windy weather. Thus, there was an easy danger of losing one's footing due to the strong gusts and falling down the cliffs. This had already happened in the past and for this reason Moira chose the longer, but safer way through the village. She had just heard the rumble of thunder in the distance.

How unusual at these temperatures, she thought, and took another step faster. In the village she saw no one on the street and so she hurried on in the direction of her home. As the first drops fell from the sky, she came down the long driveway. She paused for a brief moment in front of the burnt ruins of the large two-story brick house that had once been her home.

Then hurried past the ruins, over to a much smaller house whose lighted windows and smoke from the chimney seemed to invite her in. Just as the sky opened up and heavy rain dropped down on her, she reached the heavy wooden door and entered the comforting warmth of the house.

A few months later

"Moira! You have to come right away."

"What's so important?"

She was just checking her expense book when the door to the small room opened and Eileen, her only employee and friend at the same time, entered excitedly.

"Sir Dumfrey is driving up now. You should go greet him."

Moira pursed her mouth and heaved a sigh, but she rose from her chair and marched past Eileen, saying, "That's all I need."

She opened the front door just as Sir Dumfrey raised his hand to pull the bell rope. With a sugary voice and a beaming smile, Moira welcomed her uninvited guest.

"Sir Dumfrey, this is quite a surprise. You should have announced your visit, then I could have prepared something to eat. Unfortunately I can only offer you a cup of tea with some pastries."

Sir Dumfrey enclosed Moira's hand with his wet fingers and pressed a slippery kiss on it. Disgusted, she let it wash over her.

"My dear- Moira, you needn't trouble yourself. You know how you could make me happy."

Moira shuddered inwardly. Charles Dumfrey had paid his respects to her several times in the past months, and each time his visits had been accompanied by lewd innuendos. Twice he had already proposed to her and twice she had made him understand that she was not willing to marry him.

So what more did he want from her? Politeness dictated that she invite her guest in anyway, and so she led him into the small sitting room and asked Eileen to bring them a cup of tea.

Charles Dumfrey took a seat in one of the four small armchairs covered with dark red velvet and watched as Moira turned to Eileen.

The young lady was beautiful. Her petite figure was in a light blue muslin dress. Her slender waist was accentuated with a yellow belt, and with it she wore a white blouse and a tight, light blue jacket that stopped below her breast line. She had twisted her long brown hair into a bun. The rose complexion of her skin made her green eyes stand out.

She was young, just eighteen and actually too young for him, but he liked young, inexperienced women whom he could still mold to his liking and who were capable of satisfying his particular preferences. Moira had already turned down his marriage proposal twice, and perhaps it was time to show her that she had no choice. When she turned back to him and approached him, he began to speak.

"Moira, it always shocks me what poor conditions you must live in here. This," he made a sweeping motion with his hands, "is not worthy of you. Have you thought about my offer?"

Moira took a seat in the opposite armchair and let her thoughts run free.

"If by that you mean your marriage proposal, I'm afraid I'll have to turn you down again. I do not love you and I will not marry you."

"I am not asking you to love me either. Let's call it an agreement. I offer you a life at my side in my castle with all the luxury you deserve, and in return you give me the rights to your property. At the moment it lies fallow and decaying. Your house is in ruins and you have to live in a house which is not more than a barn."

"If my land is not worth much, why are you so interested in it? You are a rich man and don't need the house."

"Well, I was a good acquaintance of your parents, and it's just a shame how the property deteriorated after they died. Not that it's your fault. You are young and inexperienced and forgive me for saying so, but you are a woman and this is more of a man's business after all."

Moira was about to protest when Sir Dumfrey raised his hand placatingly and continued,

"I would like to have the fields tilled again and the house rebuilt so that everything is restored to its former glory. Now what do you think of my offer?"

Silently, she sat there for a while. It was a tempting offer, of course. How happy she would be if her home was rebuilt and the farmers could return. If everything would be like it used to be. But the price she would have to pay seemed too high.

She looked in Sir Dumfrey's watery brown eyes. He was at least in his mid-forties, was not much taller than herself, and had a bulging belly. His formerly black hair was streaked with silver and he wore a cologne that weighed too heavily on him and hung in her nose. His beige pantaloons were from an expensive tailor and the brocade vests he always wore were also made of fine fabrics; yet all his luxury could not hide the fact that she did not trust him.

His eyes always seemed to be on the lurk and something about him inwardly warned her to be careful. No, she would not sell herself for possessions. There had to be another solution for her to keep her land, and so she turned back to him.

"Sir Dumfrey, I am flattered that you seem to be

considering only me for your wife, but unfortunately I must again decline. Acceptance of this offer does not seem right to me and I ask you not to pursue me further."

"Well my dear. Your answer is unfortunate because I have thus granted you an opportunity to distance yourself from the debts of your parents. However, since you are still unwilling to consent to a marriage with me, I must inform you that I will demand from you the amount your parents owed me."

Moira thought she had misheard. What debt was he talking about? Her parents had been wealthy and had had no debts. There had to be some mistake.

"My parents had no debts, I would have known."

"I have with me the promissory bill that your father signed shortly before he died. He borrowed the sum of ten thousand pounds."

"Ten thousand pounds! That's impossible."

She was horrified. Why had her father needed so much money, and where had all the money gone? It could only be a mistake.

"May I see this document?"

"Certainly."

Sir Dumfrey pulled out a folded piece of paper from his vest pocket and handed it to Moira. She saw the incredible sum written on it and her father's signature. The date was a day, two weeks before the fire. She stared at the letter.

"I see you confirm the authenticity of the signature and I'm willing to give you the option of paying me back the amount in installments. Every month from now on you will pay me the sum of one hundred pounds."

"That...I can't do. Where am I going to get that much money. I don't even have enough to keep the orphanage open."

"You had a choice. With marriage, you would

have gotten rid of the debt all at once, so now it's your problem how to get the money together. You could, of course, transfer the land to me as compensation."

"Never!"

Annoyed, she jumped up. Sir Dumfrey rose slowly, came menacingly close to her, and said, "then we have nothing more to say to each other, and I expect the payments on the first of each month."

With these words he bowed and marched out of the room. Eileen, who had just come in with the tea, looked at him in surprise.

"Don't bother, I'll see myself out."

Feeling very pleased with himself, he boarded his waiting carriage, leaving two distraught women in the house.

Chapter 1

Scotland - Summer 1854

"**L**and ho!"

The call of the sailer in the lookout made the passengers step up to the rail. Robert, too, looked in the direction in which the sailor was pointing, trying to see something in the distance. On the horizon, a dark stripe stood out from the gray of the water and the sky was turning red from the morning sun. Although the early hour, there were already quite a few passengers on deck.

They probably longed for the end of the voyage as much as he did. At last, he was getting closer to the destination of his journey. It would now be another day or so before he could go ashore in Fort William.

Robert lifted his face to the sky and looked up at the sails inflated by the light wind. If the wind continued to blow like this, they would soon pass the offshore islands of Scotland and then shortly after reach the river delta up to Fort William. It was about time for Robert. Now that the harbour would soon be visible in front of him, he was eagerly awaiting its arrival.

During the last weeks and months of his journey, he had found out that he preferred solid ground under him and not these floating and swaying planks of a ship. In Boston, he had afforded himself the luxury of a single cabin, but in the course of the crossing to Scotland, he felt as if the walls had closed in on him and the cabin had become smaller and smaller.

He had probably already counted every nail in the wooden boards Robert thought to himself as he stared further out to sea and the gray stripe took more and more shape. The passage by ship had taken longer than expected.

They had left Boston with beautiful weather, but a few days later a violent storm had shaken them to the core. The subsequent calm had cost them two days. The ship had barely moved from the spot and had not been able to make up the time in the days that followed.

But now they seemed to have finally made it. Robert once again took a deep breath of the cool, but spicy air of the sea and descended a narrow and steep staircase into the belly of the ship, to his cabin. Once there, he looked around. He certainly wouldn't miss this room. Although the cabin was quite large, he felt like a prisoner in his own room.

How often had he counted the footsteps from his bed, which was at one side of the cabin and stood under a porthole that was now open to the small desk in the middle of the room. It had been only a few steps. He knew that he had booked a cabin with luxury amenities such as a small separate wet cell, in which he could complete his morning toilet.

All other staterooms were by far much smaller or even multi-bed accomodations. But for him, who had spent most of his life in the wilderness of the prairies, it was an ordeal. Robert went over to the small closet, opened it and took out the leather bag that was his only luggage. In Boston, the ship's boys had been astonished that he had gone on the long passage with only this small piece of luggage; but he had been on horse for a large part of this journey and therefore had to travel light.

Now that he had put his few shirts and pants neatly back into the bag, he had to smile inwardly.

Wherever it took him, he was accustomed to traveling with a large entourage, and he could imagine the big eyes they would make, when he stood in front of them with only this leather bag.

Two days later, the time had finally come. The carriage he had hired at the port of Fort Williams the day before, had been driving on his land for a few hours.

The Scottish weather was merciful to the newcomer and showed itself from its best side. The afternoon sun was shining and only small white clouds moved along the blue sky. Robert enjoyed the ride to the fullest. He had quickly disembarked in Fort Williams and had inquired with the harbor master, where he could get a carriage for hire. He had followed the description of the man through the lively alleys of the small harbor town and had quickly found a carriage rental.

The ride took him along surprisingly good roads past fields and pastures with cattle and sheep. They passed a number of small, picturesque villages. Then they drove a little inland around a large bay.

In a nice, small inn he had spent the night, and was gone very early in the morning. With rested horses, the carriage had gone further south and a few hours ago had passed the border of his property.

Now, as he glanced to the right and left out of the window of his carriage, he saw farmers working in their rented fields. Shepherds with their dogs keeping herds together and small settlements. People stopped in the street curiously looking after the carriage that passed them by.

The closer he got to his final destination, the

more the landscape changed. Where at first meadows and fields lined the path, there were now forests and small hills with lush greenery to be seen.

The air had also changed. The fresh scent of grain and meadow flowers had turned into the light spicy breeze of the sea. His path led him back to the water and the surroundings rose slightly. Just now he passed through the village of Shepherd, which was one of the largest villages that he was to administer from now on.

The settlement itself made a very neat impression and had its own church, several small shops, a post office and even an inn for travelers. From the village it was only a stone's throw to the sea.

The slightly outlying church, with the adjoining cemetery, gave one a view of the deep down lying sea.

After passing the church, trees and an adjoining dense forest lined the path and on the right, fenced meadows, on which there were large flocks of sheep.

His uncle had continued the family's long established sheep and highland cattle breeding and had profitably enlarged it during his short tenure. Robert would have to make some adjustments. Sheep and cattle were not exactly what he was a master at.

He was a horse breeder and planned to expand the small but fine breeding operation that his uncle started. There would be a lot of work ahead of him, but he had not come here to laze around.

As the carriage slowed down, Robert turned his attention back outside. They were driving down an avenue lined with old oak trees. The gravel crunched under their wheels. Behind the oaks lined large lawns with beautifully blooming rose beds and rhododendron bushes along the path. Small and large flowerbeds, as well as meticulously maintained hedges, let the large area shine as a magnificent garden.

In the air hung the scent of blooming flowers

and shrubs and freshly cut grass. At the end of the long driveway, the road opened up and revealed a view of a large, stately, two story Renaissance style castle.

Small turrets and battlements lined the right and left of the black roof. The white facade shone in the sun and almost dazzled the arrival of the visitor. In the long time of his absence, nothing seemed to have changed. The last time he had been here, his grandparents were still alive and he had been a little boy. He had romped through the many rooms.

With his little pony in the garden, he jumped over small obstacles and in the morning with his grandfather inspected the stables of the property.

Now his grandfather was long gone and his son had already been buried, and he was now the new owner. The carriage drove around a beautiful flowerbed and then stopped directly in front of the staircase that led up to the house. Immediately a boy rushed up to him and opened the latch of the door.

A small step was lowered, which would make it easier for the arriving guest to get out of the car. Robert rose and got out. The boy bowed deeply and let Robert go ahead. When he put his first foot on the bottom step, a number of servants rushed out from above and lined up in a row. A middle-aged gentleman dressed in a black tailcoat, came up to him. He bowed too and welcomed him.

"Welcome to Shepherds King, Your Lordship. I am Albert Gaines, the butler of your late uncle. Please forgive us that we were not prepared, but we did not know the exact date of your arrival. May I briefly introduce you to your household?"

With those words he pointed to the servants, who now all bowed. Robert continued up the stairs until he stood before Albert.

"It's a pleasure to meet you all, but I think I

should get my luggage first, so that the coachman can set off on his way home."

"Oh, that will be taken care of, by William, your Page."

Albert gave the boy , who was already standing in front of the carriage with Robert's bag in his hand a sign, and was about to turn back to the new lord, when he saw the uncertain look of the boy.

"Is there a problem, William?"

Somewhat disconcerted, the boy replied, "That's the only luggage, sir."

Astonished, Albert looked over at Robert, who just shrugged his shoulders and said, "I had to travel light and I hope to replenish my wardrobe here."

"Oh, but of course. We have an excellent tailor in the village and   I'll let him know right away that he must come to take your measurements. William, why don't you please take the bag up to the bedchamber. May I introduce now the others of your household, Lord MacIntyre?"

"Of course."

Besides Albert, the butler and William his pageboy, Robert was introduced to the housekeeper Harried. She had several maids under her control and if it did not deceive him, was the wife of Albert.

Also, he met the Chef, Gwyneth, who, with her industrious ladies, was from now on responsible for his welfare. Gwyneth with her somewhat large figure was the absolute image of a good cook. She tasted for herself what she cooked.

The performance was rounded off by Charlie Wethers, the gardeners' superintendent, and finally his young administrator with the euphonious name of Samuel Summerton.

Where Samuel had gotten the absolutely not Scottish first name , Robert didn't care. With his bright brown eyes and his pitch-black hair he corresponded to the typical appearance of the Highlanders and was therefore immediately sympathetic to him.

Two weeks later, Robert had settled in quite well.

Due to the abundance of tasks, his daily routine was tightly organized. Unlike his uncle, Robert was not willing to just hide behind his desk and leave the work to his employees. Every morning at daybreak, he went to the stables and took a first ride out to the sheep and cattle to see that everything was in order.

He enjoyed the ride in the early morning hours, over the meadows and fields, which were often covered with morning dew. Here he could greet the new day and let his thoughts run their course in silence. He felt at home with nature. Since he had gone to America with his parents, he had helped his father to raise a horse farm in the vastness of the West. For twelve hard and difficult years they dealt with the forces of nature and the Indians. They had achieved great success and had to cope with many setbacks. But now his parents' ranch had grown to be the largest in the area and the breeding was producing good yields.

Those formative years which were filled with hard physical labor, had made him who he was now. His parents had taught him that a person's origin did not matter, and so he had grown up with the children of the cowboys. Had grown up breaking horses and learning to become a good rancher. He had never thought anything of his lordly birth. In Wyoming, where his home was, none of that counted.

Robert rode the gray Arabian stallion, which he had chosen today, at a sharp gallop across the fields until the outlines of the castle were visible. At the stables Samuel was already approaching him. The young man, who was the same age as himself, had helped him in the last few weeks to quickly find his way around.

Together they had gone through the stock of sheep and cattle and Samuel had shown Robert the small, but nevertheless very fine breeding of Arabians and English Thoroughbreds, which his uncle had acquired in the last two years before his death. That's what Robert wanted to focus on. There was a lot to be done, but with the competent help of Samuel, they could build something here and he was looking forward to that.

"How did you like Majestic, sir?"

Samuel held the snorting stallion by the halter with one hand as Robert dismounted him.

"Very well. He's fast, but every now and then his temper gets the better of him. That needs some correction. The horses haven't been moved much, have they?"

"Well, your uncle was not a very good rider and preferred the carriage and I did not have enough time to take care of the training of the horses in addition to all the other duties."

"We will change that from now on. I will think about how we can redistribute the workload. My uncle started this breeding and it would be a pity not to pursue it further. Come to my office tonight after dinner and we'll talk about it."

"As you wish, sir."

Robert raised his index finger and with a smile on his face, he threatened Samuel with it.

"How many times have I told you to call me Robert, after all we have worked together?"

"Excuse me sir, I mean Robert. It's - I've never called my master by his first name."

"I am not your master. I want us to work together and you to disagree with me when my proposals, in your opinion, are not feasible.

If necessary, you should give me your opinion and advice. I would like to have a working relationship between two men on an equal footing. It would be nice if we could make that work."

Samuel looked at him in surprise, but then his eyes lit up and he nodded his head.

"Fine, now that we've settled the basics. I'll see you in my office tonight at 7:30 pm to discuss the details."

Robert was about to turn away to leave when he remembered something else.

"Rub Majestic down good and give him some more oats. He's earned it today."

"Yes - Robert."

With these words he looked at the young lord until he had disappeared from his view. Samuel did not quite know what to make of the past conversation. Did the young lord really mean it when he said he wanted to be treated by him like one of his own kind?

There had been much talk in the days after his arrival among the servants. Everyone who had seen the young lord, reported the same thing. Robert MacIntyre did not behave at all like a Scottish lord should behave. He wore clothes that emphasized his status and his manners were impeccable, but he by no means, kept the proper distance that the nobility kept to their servants in Europe. And so there were always reports of where the young lord had crossed the invisible boundary.

The gardener had to report that the lord had talked to him for half an hour about his family and had actually inquired about his well-being. The cook could report having caught him in the kitchen, making himself a sandwich.

When reminded that all he had to do was say something to Albert, he had replied that he would not make use of him for such a trifling matters. Such and similar stories had made the rounds in the first few

23

weeks, and if he had not seen him one morning mucking out the stable, he would have dismissed these stories as fantasies.

One thing could be said with certainty, the new Lord of Shepherds King was different from all the previous Scottish aristocrats , and he didn't know whether that was good or bad. For his part, he liked Robert very much, as he was now silently practicing to say, so that he would not be angry with him tonight.

"We'll see how it goes from here, won't we Majestic?"

With that, he turned his attention to the stallion in his hand and almost had to laugh when the horse nodded his head and whinnied.

"Well, come on then, I want to rub you down and have breakfast."

Chapter 2

Midnight had passed and everyone was in bed, except Robert. He had been tossing and turning in bed for hours and couldn't find any peace tonight.

The bright moonlight penetrated through the heavy curtains into his room. Annoyed, he went over to the window and glanced outside. Full moon, he thought sullenly. Every month the same.

He had been susceptible to it since he was a child. When the moon was round in the sky, he could not sleep. On those nights, he had only two options. Either he went back to bed and would continue to toss and turn from side to side for the rest of the night, or he got up and passed the time with something else, until his eyes would eventually fall shut.

Tonight Robert decided to do neither of these possibilities. He got dressed and quietly slipped out of the house, so that he would not wake anyone. The cool night air did him good and he decided to take a little walk. In the past weeks, he had been living here on the property, he had not been able to take a look from the cliffs to the sea. He knew that this part of his land extended to a bay, which could be reached by a narrow path. Since he could not think of anything better, he strolled off in that direction.

The bright moonlight illuminated his way and so he reached the cliffs with the bay below. The path ran further parallel to his fields and led directly to his nearest neighbors, the Fergussons. He had not yet had the opportunity to visit his neighbors, but immediately put it mentally on his to-do list. Indecisively, he stood there and listened to the steady sound of the waves crashing against the beach below him. Deeply he drew in the spicy air into his lungs. It was a beautiful piece of land which he owned here. Meanwhile dark clouds had appeared in the sky, obscuring the bright moon.

It was time to go home before it started to rain. He was about to turn back, when he suddenly jerked up. What had that been? Had he not just seen a flickering on the sea?

His eyes must have played a trick on him because no matter how hard he tried to see something in the distance, the sea remained black under him. Suddenly, words reached his ear.

Nervously he looked around to see if anyone came along the path, but there was nothing to see and the voices did not come closer. Cautiously he lay down on the ground and pushed his body to the edge of the cliff to peer over the edge down into the darkness.

"Shawn, give the captain the signal, so we can get started. We don't want to spend all night."

Robert watched as a small Lantern was swung twice. A short time later, another light flashed in the distance, on the water. What were these men doing down there and who were they? Curious, Robert remained on his belly and tried to see what was going on.

He did not have to wait long, because from below, words came up to him again. Apparently the men lulled themselves into safety, because they did not behave exactly quietly. Robert had no trouble listening to the conversations.

"Here they come. Is everything ready?"

"Yes, the others should be here any moment. The captain

is punctual this time, so it should go faster."

When Robert heard these words, he was able to jump up just in time to safely hide behind a bush, as he heard footsteps on the path and saw six men coming along. He kept absolutely quiet until he could be sure that no one was following and that the men had arrived at the cove. Quickly he crawled back to the place, which he had occupied before and could see two small boats, which were illuminated with torches.

Two sailors brought them to the shore. Immediately the eight men sur-rounded the boats and began to unload them. Unfortunately, Robert couldn't see what the load was and it was too risky to change his position.

Minutes later he observed how the two boats were pushed back into the water and shortly thereafter disappeared into the darkness. For a while he waited to see if more boats were coming, but it seemed to remain with the two down in the bay. The men were busily distributing the goods among themselves.

"Come on, come on men, hurry up. The cart will already be up there waiting."

"It's a miserable trek to get there. Isn't there any other solution?"

"Don't be a mule, the boss will reward you generously for this."

"Generous! Don't make me laugh! The few shillings aren't enough front and back."

"Now stop it and get on your way. The boss won't like it at all if we're late. And it would be better if you didn't show your displeasure to him, because he can get quite mean."

Robert noticed how the men on the beach moved away and seconds later a dancing light struggled up the cliff. In a moment they would pass his place and he needed a better place to hide.

He crawled behind a dense bush, which

protected him well from the upcoming light. The men, now lighting the way with the laterns, passed his hiding place not far from him. The danger to be discovered was great. Silently Robert crouched in the bush and could observe how the men went along the path, loaded with two barrels each on their backs.

He gave them enough of a head start so that they would not discover him, and then followed the group. The sky was now completely closed and the initially bright night surrounded him with a deep blackness.

What would Robert have given now to have the moonbeams light his way. At first he had seen in the distance still the dancing light of the lamps and had been able to orientate himself on the narrow path. But in the darkness he could not get ahead so fast in the unknown terrain, as he wanted and so the light suddenly disappeared. He stopped.

Below him he heard the thunderous roar of the waves as they crashed against the rocks , and it reminded him that he was in mortal danger here. He did not know the way and did not know how close he was to the edge of the cliff. The sea sounded very close and a misstep in the darkness could have meant his death.

Nothing helped, he had to break off the pursuit. He would look at the whole thing again in daylight. Perhaps he could discover something that would bring the solution to the riddle. Disappointed the mystery of this night could not be solved , he turned around and went back inland.

"Too late!
If there were any tracks here the storm of the last few days has washed them away", Robert grumbled to himself when he searched the beach three days later in

the early morning.

In the early morning hours of the same day, a heavy rain had started, which turned into a storm that lasted two days and the hope of finding clues had simply blown away. With the rain, the temperatures had dropped and the storm had torn off many branches from the trees. Still a strong cold wind was blowing and the sea churned up. The high waves hit the sand hard and washed away half the beach. It had not been exactly harmless to climb down the path here in this weather, but it had given Robert no peace.

He had to get to the bottom of it and now he was deeply disappointed that he had found no clues. While on his way home again without having achieved anything he thought about what had happened. It had been a full moon. What if the men came here only on these nights? He took it upon himself to lie in wait at the next full moon, because he was pretty sure that they would come again. It was only a question of when and until then he would memorize and explore this way at the cliffs exactly, so that he could walk it the next time in the darkness.

In the early hours of the morning a figure rushed through the dark alleys of the small village. Always anxious to save himself at any moment into one of the dark house entrances, in case another person should come across at this nightly hour. But no matter how often he stopped and listened, everything remained silent and only his own rushed breath was to be heard. Quickly he hurried on and turned around the next corner of the house, hurried down the alley and ran to the large oak tree that stood at the entrance to the village.

The branches of the old tree protruded far out

and thus forming a roof of foliage. During the day children liked to play under it, but tonight it would be the only witness to the meeting he had asked for.

"What is so important that you have summoned me here? I think I had made myself clear when I said that there was to be no contact with me."

He was terribly startled when he felt a hand on his shoulder and was almost ready to defend himself when he heard the voice and relaxed.

"I'm sorry, but I think it might be of interest to you that we have a problem."

He could not see the man across from him clearly, but he sensed that he was not edified by what he was saying.

"What kind of problem? Is there something wrong with the delivery or is the Captain giving trouble?"

"No, none of that. The new lord is snooping around the bay. The last time I made a delivery I had a strange feeling right away. As if we were being watched and because I couldn't get rid of this feeling, I went a few days later back to the beach and that's when I saw him there. He poked around but he didn't find anything, of course, but it's not good that he was there."

"Well, that's a new state of affairs. It was good of you to inform me. You go on as before. I will take care of the problem myself and I already know how."

Chapter 3

On this beautiful afternoon the children were playing outside in the garden and Moira envied them for still being carefree throughout the day. As best she could, she tried not to let them see how badly things were going. More than a protective roof over their heads, food and clothing, which urgently needed to be replaced, she could not offer them more from a material point of view. But how long could she continue to satisfy these simple basic needs?

The small vegetable garden yielded just enough for herself, and the payment she received for sewing from the tailor in the village paid for the flour she needed to bake bread. Twelve mouths needed to be fed, and even if she ate only the minimum, it was just enough for all of them not to go hungry. Moira sighed to herself as she rose from her desk chair and walked with heavy steps to the window.

Her gaze fell outside, but instead of enjoying the the beauty of the already coloring trees, her gaze went into the void. As if through a fog, the bright and cheerful voices of the children reached her ears. She would not be able to pay this month's installment to Sir Dumfrey. After all it was impossible ever to repay this large sum, and she knew that he knew it too.

This frightened her. What would happen if she could not pay? Would he put her in jail? Slowly, she turned her gaze to the sky, as if the solution to her problems was there.

"Oh father, what happened? Why did you need so much money and what happened to our fortune? What am I to do?"

Moira paused, for she sensed that Eileen had entered the room.

"Does it look that bad?"

Without taking her eyes off the outside, she said," Yes. I can go through my father's books many times, but his money is still gone, and our cash register is empty."

Moira turned around, crossed her arms in front of her chest, and looked at her best friend.

"It's over, Eileen. I have to dismiss you. I can't pay you anymore and to be honest, I don't know

how much longer I can keep a roof over the children's heads."

Eileen rushed to her friend's side, took her in her arms and and held her tightly.

"I'm not going to leave and you don't have to pay me. Together we'll make it work."

"No, we won't."

With a jerk, Moira defiantly freed herself from Eileen's embrace, took a step to the side and struggled with her rising tears.

"We won't. You don't know everything."

"What don't I know?"

"My father, just before he died, borrowed ten thousand pounds from Sir Dumfrey, and he demands repayment from me. I am to pay him a hundred pounds every month. So far I have been able to raise it, but now all the money is gone and I will not be able to pay this month. Perhaps it would be best if I agree to marry him and give him all the land."

Eileen shook her friend by both her arms and tried to get through to her.

"You will not do that, you hear me! You will not sacrifice your life to that creep. There will be another solution and we will find it together. Where did all the money go that your father borrowed? If we find it, you could give it back to Dumfrey."

Moira didn't know whether she should be angry with her friend for seeming to misjudge the situation or be happy that she was simply there for her.

"That's what I don't understand. My father was wealthy, he didn't need Sir Dumfrey's money. He always had it in his safe in the house, but after the fire I looked and the safe was empty.

I didn't find anything in the books about large expenditures. His money and the ten thousand pounds of Dumfrey's just disappeared without a trace."

"Could it have been stolen?"

"The combination of the safe was known only by me and my parents. Eileen, I just don't know what to do anymore. The garden doesn't produce enough for us to sell anything at the market and my sewing only covers the most necessary expenses. So what else do you think I can do other than to grovel at the feet of Dumfrey?"

There was a long moment of silence, and both women seemed to be feverishly searching for the saving solution, when suddenly Eileen cried, "I've got it! Why don't you go to see the new lord and talk to him? His uncle was going to help you and maybe he will too?"

"His uncle was my father's best friend. Lord Macintyre, however, did not know my father nor does he know our family. What cause, then, should there be for him to help me?"

"Perhaps because he is true to the word his uncle gave you? It would be worth a try."

Moira was silent for a while, thinking about what Eileen had said. Maybe she was right. He couldn't say more than no.

"What do the people from the village say about him? Did you hear anything?"

"Well, all I know is that he's been here since the summer, but he hasn't been to the village yet, apparently. In any case, the gossip there about him is only that which leaks out of the castle.
I hear he's young and handsome."

Smiling and with a twinkle in her eye Eileen nudged Moira. The latter had regained her composure and had to smile. Was Eileen trying to set her up?
"Aha. Young and handsome? And how do you know that, if he hasn't been seen much around yet?
Are you still seeing that Samuel?"
"You know about that?"

Eileen looked at her friend in amazement. Moira just nodded. A little embarrassed Eileen continued.
"Well, we love each other, and if everything goes well and Samuel keeps his well-paid position, I'm sure he'll ask me to be his wife."
"Oh, Eileen, I'm so happy for you."

"Well, it's not time yet, which brings us back to our problem. Anyway, Samuel says that Lord MacIntyre is so very different. Nice and approachable he's supposed to be and that's why I think you should talk to him."
"Maybe you're right. I'll think it over."
"You should do that and now come on, we'll make ourselves a nice cup of tea and sit down in the sun, too. Who knows how many times we'll get to see it this year. The Winter is already around the corner."

In the meantime, it had become mid-November and the dreary weather had Scotland firmly in its grip. Autumn storms were chasing the last sunny days and had not made it easy for farmers to harvest their crops in the dry weather. The trees had turned golden and were often the only glow of color on one of the gloomy November days. Robert hardly had time to get away from his home in recent months.

The management of this immensely large property had occupied his full attention and now that the year was drawing to a close, it was time to get everything ready for the coming winter. Despite all the work, he had been watching the full moon nights on the cliff and waited, but nothing more had happened.

The men had not shown themselves any more and so the whole thing had gradually been pushed into the background. Now he leaned back in his armchair, behind his heavy oak desk in the large office. He folded his arms behind his head and and allowed himself a little break. He closed his eyes, pushed through his spine and ran his hands through his thick black hair.

He hadn't been out of that room for days. The paperwork he hated had to be done and he had avoided it until the last minute. But he could not put it off any longer. The bookkeeping had to be done and the new leases for the coming year had to be prepared and sent to the farmers for signature. With Samuel, he still wanted to discuss the new horses he had in mind for the coming year in order to push the breeding further.

It seemed to him that the work was not getting less. Also in the village there were some things that had to be done, and he would soon have to spend time with the priest and the community representatives. Robert took a deep breath and was just about to return to his documents again, when there was a knock on the door and Albert appeared.

"I beg your pardon for interrupting, Mylord but Miss Fergusson requests a word with you."

"Fergusson?" asked Robert, not knowing at the moment

where he had heard the name before.

"Yes, your neighbor. She maintains the little Orphanage in town."

That was all he needed, to have such an old governess like that show up at his house to pay her respects. He had planned to visit his neighbors, the Fergussons, but work had kept him busy, so he had not yet been able to put this plan into action.

Now that his neighbor was obviously already standing in his house, his politeness required him to grant her the visit; but today really did not suit him at all and he tried to stall for time before he gave Albert a refusal.

"Albert, do you know what the lady wants?"

"With respect, I think she has come to collect the annual donation."

"Annual donation?"

Robert thought he had misheard. What was that about? But Albert explained to him.

"Your uncle has been donating to the orphanage every year at this time with a kind and generous amount of money."

"I see. Albert, would you please tell the lady that I'm very sorry, but I'm really not in the position to see her without an appointment. However, this year we are keeping tradition of my uncle and that she will receive the donation in kind and money. Please tell her that I will have more time after the Holidays and will visit her then."

"Very well, sir."

Albert was about to turn away when Robert addressed him once again.

"Oh Albert?"

"Yes, sir?"

"How much did my uncle donate?"

"The in-kind donations were related to flour,

salt, wool, and some beef, and the monetary donation amounted to two hundred pounds."

Robert whistled through his teeth.

"Oops, that's worth it for the lady. We'll definitely have to discuss that next year."

"Your uncle always cared a lot about the orphanage."

"Well, I have that impression, too."

With these words he dismissed Albert, shook his head thoughtfully and went back to his work.

Chapter 4

During the holidays, Robert had to struggle for the first time with gloom. He had always loved Christmas in Wyoming very much. At this time of year snow had a firm grip on the land there.

Despite the freezing temperatures and the snowstorms that made life there so difficult, he had enjoyed it every time, when the white splendor laid a stillness over the land. When the wildlife had retreated into their shelters and the people were drawn to the warmth of the fire. Those were the days when, at his parents home, his father had made the plans for the spring and his mother had lovingly supplied everyone with baked goods of all kinds. Here in Scotland it had also become frosty, but there was no snow anywhere to be seen, instead there was only rain and wind.

The days were gray and the sun let in only a few glimpses. In the house itself, the days before Christmas were hectic. Albert and his wife Harried had put up a Christmas tree in the large reception hall and decorated it, which had looked really beautiful. Gwyneth, with her kitchen staff, had prepared one delicious meal after another. Actually, Robert did not quite understand why he was so melancholy.

He had a whole court around him and yet he felt alone. To distract himself, he had thrown himself even more into work and in the meantime had finished all the documents of his deceased uncle that had been left lying around. In the process, he had made a discovery that astonished and also a little worried him.

In two title deeds of his horses, not only was his uncle listed as the owner, but also a Richard Fergusson. It concerned two noble Arabian breeding stallions, which, when he saw the purchase sum, he whistled incredulously through his lips. Each individual animal was worth a fortune. Good breeding stallions were expensive, he knew that, but this horrendous sum made him think.

Why had his uncle, who seemed to have little idea about horses, bought such expensive animals or had he simply been ripped off? And who was this Fergusson, did he know about horses? Was this the reason his uncle had taken him on board? Why had he not approached him, if he himself had invested so much money in these animals?

Samuel apparently knew about this second owner, which made Robert become even more suspicious. It was time to make inquiries about his neighbor. He did not want to continue to build up the breeding if it might end up in a legal dispute, so he wanted to make it his top priority to visit his neighbor after the holidays.

Sir Dumfrey was in good spirits when his carriage turned into the Fergussons' driveway. He had waited until the New Year to present Moira with a fait accompli.

His plan was set and the young lady would help him, and what was best about it, she had no choice. He had seen to that with the collection of the debt. Satisfied with himself, he leaned back relaxed, drumming with his fingers on the cardboard box that lay beside him and waited until the carriage stopped in front of the small house. A little later he was standing again in the small living room that he now knew so well. Eileen had led him inside and asked him to wait here for Moira, while she went to fetch her.

Now he had taken a seat in one of the small armchairs facing the door, the box lying beside him on the table. Like the spider in the web, waiting for its prey, he waited for Moira. But if he had assumed that she would come to the door like a frightened deer, it was not at all the case. Upright and proud, she now stood before him, as she began to speak.

"Sir Dumfrey, I had expected you earlier."

"So, then you know what I'm here for?"

"Well, you want to collect the installment, but I can't pay it to you, just as I did last month, All the money I have possessed, you have already received."

Since he expected that, he began to put his plan into action. Slowly he rose and walked around Moira without a word. Thereby he looked at her unabashedly from top to bottom and his looks were unmistakable.

Moira, who was not used to such lustful looks and was no longer sure what he was trying to do, felt very uncomfortable. She cursed herself that she had gotten into this situation alone without Eileen. She should have at least left the door open, but it was too late for that now.

"You are pretty, but quite chaste. You'll have to get rid of that if you work for me."

Astonished, Moira looked at him.

"Work for you? Why would I do that?"

"Why?"

Dumfrey came so close to her, that she could smell his bad breath. But before she could take a step back he grabbed her chin and held her tight. In a sugary voice, he continued.

"Child, you owe me a chunk of money and you're going to work it off."

"Never!"

Dumfrey's grip tightened even more and her jaw began to ache.

"Let go of me right now, you're hurting me."

Slowly he released his hands. Furious, she reared up in front of him.

"I will not work for you!"

"You will or would you rather go to prison because of the debt? I think that the choice of work is the better one. You will occupy yourself a bit with Lord Macintyre."

"Lord MacIntyre? I don't know that man."

"You will get to know him, and you will keep him so busy that he will not find time to meddle in my affairs."

"How will I do that? I have never met this man and why should he be interested in me?"

"Well, my dear. That is your problem. You would do well to do your job. I am not a patient man, and so far I have shown more patience with you than I ever have. You should appreciate that. I require of you to sweet-talk Lord Macintyre, turn his head and keep him from spying on the cliffs. You shall keep him busy, if it must be day and night."

Moira thought she had misheard. What Sir Dumfrey was asking of her was inconceivable.

"You ask me to offer myself to him like a whore?"

"Well, I wouldn't call it that, but it's to the point."

"What if I refuse to do this?"

"That, my child, would be very unwise, for then I would take this house and the land around it as my own, put the dear little children into the street and send you to one of the gentlemen's establishments in Edinburgh. I would get a nice little sum for you there. I assume you are still a virgin. That sort of thing is very much in demand there."

Moira was horrified and slapped Charles Dumfrey's face with her hand.

"How dare you!"

But Sir Dumfrey only laughed wickedly. Quick as a flash, which one would not have thought his figure capable of, he grasped Moira's wrists and pulled her close to him. Her breasts pressed against his chest, which he visibly enjoyed.

She, on the other hand, tried to resist and keep her distance, but she did not succeed.

"That, my dear, was a mistake. If you can't get Lord MacIntyre to stay away from the cliffs and from me, you'll be in Edinburgh before you know it. But if you do as told, your debts will be repaid. So you see, you have your fate in your own hands and perhaps, if you are good and he doesn't find out about your game, he might even marry you. Wouldn't that be a nice happy ending?"

Laughing, he let go of her, turned to the table, and picked up the box.

"Here, this is for you. In two days I'm invited to Lord McCormick's ball and you will accompany me. You will wear this dress for the occasion. A carriage will pick you up in time. Until then you have time to prepare for your role."

He pressed the box into Moira's hands, gave her a wet kiss on the cheek and turned to leave. When he got to the door, he turned to her once more.

"It goes without saying that you must not say anything about this conversation to a soul. After all, you don't want the lord to find outabout your intentions."

Smirking and absolutely satisfied with himself, he left the room and left a devastated Moira behind.

Chapter 5

Robert entered the entrance hall after his morning inspection ride, where he found Albert carrying two bags of clothes and the mail in his arms walking up the stairs to the second floor.

"Albert!"

The butler paused when he heard his name and turned to see Robert standing at the foot of the stairs.

"Yes, Mylord? The tailor has just delivered the new tailcoat and full plaid in your colors. In addition, I have received several invitations for you to attend this year's ball season."

"Ball season?"

Robert came up the stairs and walked with Albert toward his room.

"Yes, every new year begins with the ball season. The lords and dukes of the area invite each other to strengthen bonds of friendship and to broaden or deepen business interests. Your uncle has hosted one of these balls every year.

In view of the situation, we have not planned our own ball for this year, but Mylord should still participate in this forum to present yourself as the new master of Shepherds King. The first invitation would already be for the day after tomorrow with Lord McCormick. He owns the Lands around Loch Tay."

While Robert with Albert in tow, entered his room, he

wondered whether he should take part in it.

He had never been to a festive ball before. Such formal festivities had not existed in his homeland but Albert was right. He had to present himself to the others as the new lord if he wanted to do business with them in the future. So he didn't think twice and gave Albert the task of packing everything for his stay there.

Albert immediately set to work in Robert's closet for the right clothes to wear. Robert, on the other hand, got rid of his riding shirt to freshen up. For a brief moment he hesitated and stopped at the door to his bathroom. One question was still burning in the back of his mind.

"Tell me Albert, what do you know of Sir Fergusson?"

If Albert was surprised by the question he did not let it show, because he answered without equivocation.

"Sir Fergusson was for years a very good friend of your uncle. That is also the reason why your uncle has always supported the orphanage. Lady Fergusson started it a few years ago. Her daughter has now taken it over. You remember, just before Christmas she had been here."

"Yes, I remember. But you just said that he was a good friend of my uncle's - does that mean, that he isn't now?"

"Sir Fergusson and his wife were the victims of a fire almost two years ago. Their house was completely destroyed on that horrible night. To this day, no one can explain how such a catastrophe could happen.

The daughter survived the inferno because she had spent the night in the small orphanage next door. Since that day, she has been taking care of it."

Thoughtfully, Robert looked at Albert. He had not expected this answer. That was the reason Sir Fergusson had not contacted him. He had died before his uncle.

"How exactly did my uncle die, anyway?"

Albert hung the new tailcoat on a hanger in the armoire,

and laid out the matching pantaloons on the bed.

"Well, he was visiting friends in Edinburgh. Your uncle came home from a ball with a slight indisposition. At first we thought that he must have eaten something wrong, because he complained of stomach pain and nausea during the night. But it didn't get any better the next few days, so we had to consult the doctor."

Robert leaned with his naked chest against the door from the bathroom , his shirt forgotten in his hand. And listened to the report of his butler.

"And what did he find?"

"That's the strange thing. The doctor couldn't find anything wrong with him, except that he had an upset stomach. But your uncle could still not keep anything down. No solid food and also no water. The doctor prescribed medication but it did not seem to help, because he became visibly weaker and one morning when I went to his room to check on him, he was dead in bed."

"Did you hear if any of the other guests were also having problems or if they had eaten or drank anything unusual?"

"I asked the service staff afterward whether other guests had had any problems, but there was nothing known. Is there anything else you would like, Mylord? Otherwise, I would continue to pack your suitcases later and tell Samuel to prepare the carriage for tomorrow."

"Thank you Albert, that is all. Oh and please tell Samuel that I expect him in my office in half an hour. I would like to discuss with him his tasks while I'll be away."

"Very well, sir."

When Albert left, Robert was still leaning against the doorjamb. A fire in which two people had died and a death that had no explainable reason. Three people who knew each other and had even been close friends, had died in a short period of time. Was this a coincidence or was there more to it? Robert ran his hand through his pitch-black, short hair. He absolutely had to find out more about the circumstances of the deaths.

It was time to pay a visit to the Fergussons' daughter. He planned to do this right after the ball at the McCormick's.

Moira was amazed when she entered the ballroom. Countless couples were already crowded in the large, brightly lit room, whose walls were adorned with large candelabras with thick candles. The parquet floor had been polished to a high sheen and the light of the large, heavy chandeliers that hung from the ceiling were reflected in it.

On the left side of the room were several seats, which would later serve guests who wanted to rest between dances. The wall itself was decorated with portraits of old family members who had long since passed away. On the other side large patio doors invited you in the summer to stroll through the park-like garden. Now in winter they were closed with heavy red curtains. In the back of the hall, a small ensemble played soft music. Moira felt the hand on her arm that pushed her further forward.

The new impressions had almost made her forget that she was Sir Charles Dumfrey's company. Before she could say anything in reply, he had taken her to the hosts and was just about to introduce her as his hosts.

"Lord and Lady McCormick! This is Lady Moira Fergusson, my companion for this evening. This is her first time as a guest at a ball."

Politely Moira lowered her head a little, made a curtsy to the couple and looked up into the gentle eyes of Lady McCormick, who smiled encouragingly at her.

„Lady Fergusson, it is an honor to meet you. My husband and I were well acquainted with your parents. God have mercy on their souls. It's nice that today we have the honor of introducing you to the society."

As the two men talked, Lady McCormick took Moira aside.

"I know that on the first night of the ball everything is exciting and often frightening. One doesn't want to make any mistakes. Rest assured, though, we are not at court here and therefore it is quite casual. Enjoy the evening, I'm sure your dance card will fill up quickly."

"Thank you very much, Lady McCormick. I am actually very nervous. My parents were to introduce me to society this year, but it all turned out differently."

"Well, you have a very experienced companion with you. nothing will go wrong, my dear."

Moira wasn't so sure about that. If Lady McCormick knew for what reason she was here and that the so called Sir Dumfrey was in fact the devil himself, she would certainly not have been so friendly to her. A little later, Moira was standing among the other guests in the presence of this devil. While Sir Dumfrey was busy making conversation with the gentlemen present, Moira stood with the ladies and only noticed what they were talking about in passing, because her mind was somewhere else. Cautiously, she looked around.

Was Lord MacIntyre already in the room? Perhaps it was the young man standing a little away from her in his brown pantaloons, the jacket and the golden brocade waistcoat, constantly wiping his forehead with a white cloth. He seemed to be sweating heavily, although it was not too warm in the room .

47

Or was it rather the one with his artificial laughter and movements who tried to entertain a few ladies? He had to be here somewhere.

There were no more guests coming and the food would be served soon. So why didn't Sir Dumfrey introduce them to each other? She was about to address this question to him herself, when another guest entered the room. For a brief moment he lingered at the door, letting his gaze wander briefly over the room until he found the hosts and took long strides toward them. The manner in which the young, tall man moved, caused the people he passed to pause in their movements.

The looks followed him unabashedly, but he didn't seem to mind. Self-confidently he continued his way and greeted Lord McCormick with a slight bow, then immediately introduced himself to his wife with a formal kiss on the hand. Moira couldn't see more from her position, because in the meantime, the other couples had gathered closer around the hosts to see the newcomer. She was about to ask one of the ladies next to her if she knew the name of the gentleman, when Lord McCormick began to speak.

"My dear guests. Now that the last of them has found his way to us and gives me the honor of being my guest today, I would like to introduce to you all the new master of Shepherds King. Lord Robert MacIntyre."

A murmur went through the room when the name was mentioned. So, that was Lord MacIntyre. Moira didn't know whether she should be happy about the fact that he did not seem to be one of these dandies, or whether she should be afraid of him.

For the little moment, when she had had a clear view of him, he had not made the impression that he was easily fooled. Before she could think any further about it an arm hooked itself from behind her and a familiar voice whispered over her shoulder to her.

"Well, do you like him? I think you could do worse."
"You're a creep," Moira returned in a whisper.

Charles Dumfrey only laughed and joined her in the crowd of guests who had now been invited by the host to follow him into the dining room. Moira was only peripherally aware of the dinner. She ate like a sparrow and only talked to her seat partner on the left.

Sir Dumfrey was sitting to her right, seemingly enjoying the evening to the fullest. He seemed to be having a splendid conversation with the lady to his right. Moira, on the other hand, could not help but look cautiously in the direction of the young lord, who was sitting several seats away from her on the opposite side of the table. Lady McCormick was sitting on his right side and on his left a young lady of her own age, an absolute beauty in her eyes.

Whatever the three of them were talking about, it was a lively conversation and even the gentlemen and ladies from the opposite side joined in. Somewhat envious of not also being part of this group and to be able to talk so casually, she lowered her head and concentrated on the main course, which consisted of roasted pheasant with a truffle sauce.

The meal was a poem and deserved a little more attention from her, because since the death of her parents, she had not been able to eat as well, but she could hardly get down a bite.

Not only was the order from Sir Dumfrey a pain in her stomach, it also seemed sacrilegious to her to indulge in such a sumptuous meal, when she knew what Eileen and the children would find on the table tonight. In general, for the first time in her life, she had to lie to her best friend. Eileen had not understood why she had gone to the ball with Dumfrey today.

"After the way he has behaved, how can you offer yourself as an escort for the ball?"

Those had been her words and she had replied that he had asked politely and that she had agreed, because she hoped to be introduced there into the circles of the upper class, in order to find donors for the orphanage. With this white lie she had reassured Eileen, but she could not reassure herself.

The entire evening she had a sinking feeling in her stomach and she knew that it was her conscience, which could not be appeased. She threw a furtive glance again in his direction and this time was startled when he returned her gaze and nodded his head slightly to signal that he had taken note of her.

Embarrassed she immediately turned her head away, only to look at him a little later, realizing that he was still looking at her.

An hour later, the ball was in full swing. Most of the couples had arrived on the dance floor. After an opening polonaise and a square, they were just dancing a quadrille. The older ladies and gentlemen had taken their places on the chairs and listened to the music. Moira's dance card had filled up quickly.

She had danced the polonaise with the Kensington's son, who had stepped on her skirt twice. The square with a young man, whose name she had already forgotten; and was now dancing the quadrille with Flynn Haggert, who was more skillful in his dancing, but who talked incessantly about the various sheep shearing techniques, which he said he was a master of.

While Moira listened politely, asking questions now and then, so as not to appear disinterested, she risked a glance at Lord MacIntyre. He, who had not yet missed a single dance and was apparently regarded as a free prey by the singles, was immediately surrounded by a number of ladies.

Moira had to agree with them. In his tailored black tailcoat with a white shirt and starched collar, the matching black silk vest and the black pantaloons that accentuated his height, he looked stunningly handsome. She had never seen a man who appeared so self-confident without seeming arrogant. On the contrary, the ladies seemed to love him and the gentlemen listened animatedly to his words.

Despite his young age, he seemed to integrate into society. Was that the advantage of having the name MacIntyre, which was well known in Scotland?

The clan of Baron Killian MacIntyre was a large one and he owned large estates on the east coast of Scotland and Robert was his grandson. And now the possessions of this family would become even greater, as he would inherit the estate of Lord Kenneth Dunbar, the brother of his mother.

"Don't you agree the posturing that is being done around Lord MacIntyre is a little too much? Moira?"

"Excuse me? What did you just say?"

"I was just saying that I think the fuss being made about Lord MacIntyre is a bit too much. What does anyone know about him? Just look at how concerned everyone is about him. It's just as if he were the only man on earth."

"Are you jealous, Flynn?"

Moira couldn't help but tease this arrogant youngster.

"Not at all. My father's lands are at least as large, and it remains to be seen whether he knows how to manage such an estate."

"Yes, just like you," Moira replied promptly.

Flynn Haggert looked at her a little puzzled but Moira did not care. The music had just stopped playing, and before another boy asked her to dance, she apologized to

Flynn with the excuse of wanting to powder her nose. She gathered her skirts and was about to leave the room to get some fresh air, when she was held by the arm of Sir Dumfrey.

"Don't you want to finally put your plan into action? Think of what's at stake for you."

"Let me worry about how and when and now let go of me, I want to get some fresh air."

A little stronger than necessary, she tore herself away and hurried out of the hall. Robert, who had been watching the scene from a distance, wondered, freed himself with a pretext to his followers and left the hall as well.

"I hope you don't want to leave yet!"

Moira was startled to hear the male voice coming from the darkness. She looked around searchingly but couldn't see anyone. Then, the young lord suddenly appeared out of nowhere in front of her.

"I'm sorry, I didn't mean to frighten you, but I saw you leave the room and did not want to miss the opportunity to meet the lady who has been watching me all evening." Slowly he approached her until he stopped directly in front of her and looked at her.

"That – You noticed that? I'm very embarrassed. I'm sorry, I didn't mean to stare at you so openly, that's normally not my style at all."

Moira would have liked to sink into the floor. Had the other guests also noticed the stares? If so, what kind of person they must have thought she was, and what kind of person did he think she was? As if he could read her mind, he replied:

"Don't be too hard on yourself, and since you already know my name, it would be more than fair if you told me yours as well."

"Oh, yes of course, your lordship."

Moira curtsied and then said," My name is Moira
Fergusson. I'm your neighbor."

Astonished, Robert looked at her.

"You - are Lady Moira Fergusson? The director of the
Orphanage?"

"Yes, that very one. Your uncle was a good friend of my
parents."

Robert had to laugh inwardly. She didn't look
like an old governess at all and he was mighty glad of it.

"Has the hustle and bustle in there," he pointed toward
the brightly lit ballroom, "also become too much for
you?"

"I just wanted to get some fresh air."

"Will you allow me to escort you for a bit?"

"Gladly."

Together they strolled in silence through the
garden. Moira thought frantically about what she should
talk to him about. She didn't know him and had no idea
how she was supposed to manage to make him desire
her. Her experience with men was nil and therefore she
did not know which trivial topics would interest him.

In the hall, she had watched the ladies as they
had behaved toward him, but this seemed to her to be too
brisk an approach and she did not see herself in a
position able to use such tactics. Robert, on the other
hand, found her company quite pleasant for he liked her
reserved manner. It almost seemed to him that Moira
was afraid of him and that made him curious.
Something preoccupied the young lady.

The whole evening she had not really looked
happy. She had hardly eaten and had only talked when
necessary. Even now, she was behaving so very
differently from the other ladies in the hall, who were
constantly trying to catch his attention.

Moira seemed to him like a little wallflower, although she really did not have to be. She was not very tall and reached only to his shoulder, but her petite figure had all the attributes that he appreciated in a woman.

The crinoline dress, made of dark green silk, whose low neckline had been defused, but nevertheless revealed a glimpse of the base of her firm, small breasts. Her thin waist was tied with a black corsage ribbon and underlined her advantages. Matching in the same tone, she wore a long-sleeved jacket, which stopped below her breastline.

Her hair, which he thought had to be a chestnut-brown tone, was stuck in an elaborate updo, and he found himself thinking about how she would look, when the long hair was pulled back around her narrow face blowing in the wind. In general, he had noticed her face right away the first time he saw her at the dinner. She had a beautiful oval face. Her green eyes with the long, thick, black eyelashes and the shapely eyebrows had magically attracted him. From then on, he had not let her out of his sight.

Now that he was walking right next to her and her light perfume was in the air, thoughts came to his mind, about which he surprised himself and which he preferred to keep to himself, because he would scare Moira with them.

A quick glance at her side profile and at her beautiful, full lips, which she had opened a little bit in thought, made him start to sweat. He had to distract himself somehow in order to keep his thoughts under control.

"Miss Fergusson, I am truly sorry that I was unable to receive you earlier."

Relieved that he had begun to speak and that she no longer had to think about how nervous his presence made her, she replied:

"That was quite understandable. I'm sure, you have a lot

to take care of, and for that reason, I could not expect you to receive me without an appointment. I wouldn't have come then either if Eileen hadn't..."
"Eileen?"

"She's my friend and she helps me run the orphanage. She was the one anyway, who thought I should talk to you about the agreement that your uncle had made with me."
Robert stopped and turned to her.

"I had already made up my mind to go and see you after the holidays, but somehow something always got in the way. I would like to make up for it when we're back home the day after tomorrow. There are a few questions regarding my uncle that I'm sure you can answer, since you undoubtedly knew him better than I did. What do you think - we'd better get back inside before someone misses us."

Elegantly he held out his right arm to her and grateful that he had thought of her call, she put her hand on it and let him lead her back to the house. When they reached the steps to the terrace she let go of him to lift her skirt a little. From the inside cheerful waltz music drifted out to them.
"I know that your dance card is probably already filled, but would you still allow me to dance with you?"

"I would love to do that, but I'm afraid I haven't mastered the steps of this newfangled dance yet."
Robert leaned down toward her a little, which made her breath faster.

"Between you and me, I don't even know it yet. But how hard might it be to memorize the steps of the others and to imitate them. Shall we give it a try?"
Laughing, she agreed, and Robert was overwhelmed by her charm. She should laugh more often and Robert secretly resolved to work on it.

On the dance floor, the couples spun in circles. Swinging and in a tight dance posture they whirled across the floor. The voluminous dresses of the ladies and the tailcoats of the men bobbed in time to the music. Robert had already heard that at the Austrian court a musician with the name Franz Joseph Strauss Son had created a cheerful couple dance and caused a sensation. He watched the couples and now could understand why the tight dance posture had at first been considered scandalous, but the lively music had been convincing, and thus at every ball today at least one piece of this master was played. Robert looked over at Moira, glanced at her expectantly and held out his arm to her.
„Shall we?"

Smiling, she took his arm and together they mingled with the other dancers. A bit tentative at first, they became more and more confident in their movements, until he was holding her close to him, at the same pace of the others and whirled her laughing across the dance floor. Moira was easy to lead and adapted to his movements automatically.

He enjoyed it, to hold her in his arms, to look into her beaming eyes, while they were spinning in circles with a laugh. He hoped that the music would play forever. Moira had not had so much fun for a long time and that she owed it to Robert MacIntyre.

He had managed to put her worries behind her, even if only for a short time. How nice it would be if she could forget everything. If she could forget that she had to play an evil game with him. Satisfied that his plan was working, Sir Dumfrey watched the scene.

Chapter 6

Three days later, Robert rode his horse down the Fergusson's driveway. When he arrived in front of the burned-out ruin, he stopped. What might have caused such a fire that had left only the foundation walls.

It must once have been a truly beautiful estate, but now the beds were overgrown with weeds and the bushes and hedges were overgrown. Suddenly he heard children's voices, and so he steered his horse in the direction from which he heard them. In front of a small house, three boys were running around who immediately stopped playing and ran into the house when they saw the rider coming.

Even before Robert had dismounted from his horse, a young lady, who was about the same age as Moira might have been, came running out. She was wearing a simple brown work dress, which had seen better days. But except for the somewhat old dress she was neatly coiffed and made a sympathetic impression as she now approached him in a friendly manner.

"Good day, sir. What can I do for you?"

"My name is Lord MacIntyre, and I would like to see Miss Fergusson. Is she in by any chance? I know I'm without an appointment, but perhaps she might have a moment for me?"

"Lord MacIntyre! Why, of course. Come in, please. I am sorry that we do not have a groom who can take care of your horse and we can't offer you any other luxury but I am sure that we can offer a good cup of tea. If you would please follow me?"

With these words she turned and strode ahead into the house. Robert quickly tied his horse to a tree and followed the young lady.

Eileen seemed to be much more brisk than Moira. She had a pretty face with a light complexion and tiny freckles, and her reddish-blonde hair , which she wore in a long, braid down her back, gave him the impression that she had Irish blood in her. In the house, he was led into the small reception room, which was homey but without any particular luxury.

The furniture was old and some upholstery showed small traces of wear. Robert wondered what it must have meant to a young lady who had grown up and been educated in luxury with the prospect of a good marriage, now to live in these poor conditions, without really having a rosy perspective for the future at all. Robert was sure that the old rules of society still prevailed here in Scotland. No matter how wealthy you were born, if you had no more fortune, then you were excluded from society.

Robert was jolted out of his thoughts when the door opened and Moira appeared in the doorway.
Friendly, but more reserved than she had been when she left the McCormicks, she approached him.
"Lord MacIntyre, this is a surprise to see you again so soon ."
She meant it sincerely, he could tell. She hadn't really expected to see him again after the ball.
"Miss Fergusson, I told you that I'd been planning to visit you for a long time. But if it is not convenient for you today, then I'll be glad to come back some other time."
"No, no. Everything is fine. Please have a seat. Eileen

will be right back with a cup of tea and some pastries."

Robert sat down on the same red velvet chair where Sir Dumfrey had sat only a short time ago and she was glad that this time it was much more pleasant company. When Eileen had served the tea and Moira had poured him a cup, she took a seat opposite him. She handed him the plate of pastries, and he took it gratefully.

"Lord MacIntyre, what can I do for you? I'm sure you've come to see the orphanage and I would like to show you around and give you a tour."

Robert chewed the rest of the delicious cookie and took a sip of the still too hot tea before he answered.

"The first thing I would appreciate is if you would just call me Robert. I am used to being called by my first name only, and stiff titles don't mean much to me."

Moira was taken aback by this statement. So far she had never met a nobleman who would voluntarily renounce the mention of his title. On the contrary, there was one or the other who pretended to be one without having the legitimate claim.

"May I ask you a question?"

"Yes, of course - Robert."

"I saw the ruins of the fire. Would you tell me how it happened?"

Moira wrestled with herself. She did not like to talk about that night back then, yet she began to tell him.

"I'm afraid I don't know any more details than that. It was the time when quite a few of the children here had fevers and I was here more days to take care of them than I was in my parents' house.

On this unspeakable day, my parents had a visit from Sir Dumfrey for dinner. You saw him at the McCormicks's ball. I was there with him. I think he was a business associate of my father's, and he was there that night for dinner. Shortly afterwards, however, I excused myself because I wanted to spend the night with Eileen and the children. Then, in the middle of the night, we were struck by the smell of burning wood and the crackling of the fire.

When I arrived at the house, everything was ablaze. The servants had been able to save themselves and were already trying to extinguish the fire, but it was too late for my parents. The flames had already eaten through to the roof truss."

She paused, because she had to fight back the rising tears. Robert felt the need to take her in his arms and comfort her. He assumed that probably no one had ever done this before.

The pain in her eyes was unmistakable. He was just about to apologize to her for having had started the subject when she continued.

"The next morning we found their bodies in the burned-out bedroom. Everything we had owned had been destroyed in one night. The little that could be saved is in this house here and since that night I have lived here with Eileen and the children. Eileen is the only one I have left. Since my father's money had also disappeared, I could no longer pay the employees and so it did not take long until one after the other looked for a new job and left."

"Your father's money disappeared? How did that happen?"

"The safe was empty. My father did not trust banks and therefore had everything in his safe. The safe survived the fire, but it was empty. The family jewelry as well as the cash assets, everything was gone. To this day I don't know what my father did with it."

"Is it possible that things might not have been above board?"

Moira looked at him in amazement.

"You think someone stole it? But only my parents and I

knew the combination."

Robert was silent. What if someone had extorted the combination and had set the fire to cover up the crime? There had to be more than one source of fire that had ignited such an inferno. But for the time being he kept his suspicions to himself. He did not want to give Moira any more painful thoughts. Moira, on the other hand, continued in her narrative.

"Maybe I should have left then, too, but I just couldn't bring myself to abandon the children. You must know that my mother started this home and it would have been a betrayal to her if I had given this up."
Moira sighed.
"So I've been trying to save every shilling I can get my hands on, to keep a roof over the children's heads and give them an education, so they can have a future. Your uncle helped me with his donations, but unfortunately he died much too early."

Robert leaned forward in his chair, put his hand on her arm and smiled encouragingly. He had made a decision.
"Moira, I'd like to help you. Maybe you can show me around so I can get an impression?"
"Yes of course, come on."

She led him through the house. He saw the small room with the chairs and tables that served as a classroom, where Eileen was giving a mathematics lesson. The dormitory was provisionally divided with a curtain in the middle of the room, so that the boys and and girls were visually separated from each other when they slept.
Moira must have felt she had to say something because she explained, "When I first moved in here after the fire and the main house was no longer in use, we had to make changes.

Eileen and I moved into the girls' room together and out of the boys' room we had to make the dining room because the kitchen was too small for all of us. I had actually planned to have an annex, but we don't have the money at the moment."

She didn't tell him that she would probably never have the money.

"You don't have your own room?"

"No."

Moira led him further through the house and everywhere   Robert took a closer look, he saw deficiencies that needed to be fixed. There was the water stain on the ceiling, because the roof was leaking, some windows lost their frames because they had become crumbly, doors were squeaking, the children's clothes were old and patched and even Moira wore a dress that was not worthy of her.

It was far from the one she wore the evening at the McCormick's and yet she wore it with an elegance that seemed to him hardly possible. Moira, on the other hand, seemed embarrassed that he saw her like this, for when she thought she was unobserved, she fiddled with her blue work dress. When they got outside and she led him in the direction of the ruins, a question burned on his lips.

"Was your father a horse breeder or was he well versed in horses?"

"My father could ride well, but we did not have more than a few work and riding horses. Would you like to see the stables? They're right over there."

"Mmm. I saw some pastures on the way here. I'm assuming that this is your land. What did your father keep there?"

"We had sheep, but after I didn't have any money to pay the employees, I could no longer manage the work alone and had to sell the flocks. Since then the land has lain fallow. For a long time I resisted selling the land and Sir Dumfrey had already made me an offer, which I rejected at the time, but I believe that soon I will have no other choice."

Slowly they strolled on over her land. It was not a large estate, but it had two good pastures right by the bay abutting his land, so he was considering whether he should make her an offer to sell them, but he kept silent. Some things made him wonder. Why had her father been a partner with his uncle, when he knew as little about horse breeding as his uncle did?

And what does Sir Dumfrey want with the two pastures at the bay when he owned no other land far and wide? Many things did not make sense. When they had finished the tour and had come back to his horse, Robert inwardly tipped his hat to Moira.

The estate was in a neglected condition and the small house was also in desperate need of some repairs, but considering the situation, she had tried to make the best of it.

She had a great burden on her slender shoulders and was almost in danger of breaking. Her will and ambition to breathe new life into the estate was remarkable, but without money and help she would not manage to.

"Well, Robert. Maybe you can imagine what it once looked like here. The roses were in bloom and the hedges were neatly trimmed. The main house was whitewashed and in the summer my parents had several parties here and the guests would stroll across the lawn. Your uncle was also a welcome guest here and my father was very good friends with him."

"Yeah, I've heard that before. Maybe you can tell me about it on my next visit, when I can come by again. I would like to know more about him. I only knew him until I was ten years old, and I don't remember him very well."

"Yes, I would like that very much."

Robert said goodbye to her, kissed her hand elegantly, then mounted his horse, nodded to her once more in farewell and gave his horse the spurs. Moira looked after him for a long time.

She was still standing there when he could no longer be seen. In her mind she had put the back of her hand, that he had kissed, to her mouth and it went through her head, how it would probably feel if his lips had touched her mouth. Robert did not ride home right away, but steered his horse in the direction of the village. He could, of course, let Albert do the things he wanted to do, but in this case he felt the need to do it himself and so he rode directly to the clothier.

Chapter 7

"**E**ileen! Eileen!"

Eileen poked her head out of the classroom when she heard Moira's excited voice in the hallway.

"Yes, what is it?"

"What's that hammering about on the roof?"

Eileen called out to the children that she would be with them in a moment and then closed the door behind her. Beaming with joy, she took Moira by the hand and pulled her excitedly to the front door.

"Come, you have to see this for yourself. Oh wait, first this."

She half pushed Moira in front of her into the reception room. Once there, Moira couldn't trust her eyes. The small sideboard and another table, were piled up with bales of fabrics in different colors.

Disbelievingly, she went closer and let her fingers glide carefully over the beautiful fabrics She felt the material and the desire to sew new clothes from it arose. But then she came to her senses again. Abruptly she turned around and looked into the happy eyes of Eileen, who seemed to be thinking the same thing.

"Who's this from?"

Eileen, smiled at her as she paused at the door.

"You must have made a great impression on the lord the day before yesterday. He had these bales delivered very early this morning and the roofer has also been commissioned by him."

"Roofer? What Craftsmen."

"Well, the ones who are on the roof and later on will repair the windows. Oh Moira isn't that fantastic?"

"Fantastic? Not at all."

With those words, Moira stormed past Eileen who didn't understand why Moira reacted so angrily. Outside, she stood rooted to the spot when she saw three men standing on her roof, hand in hand, inspecting every single shingle and replacing the bad ones in the process. How could he presume to order repairs?

The house was not his and how was she supposed to pay the men. Furious, she turned around and almost collided with Eileen, who had stepped quietly behind her.

With an angry, "How dare him!", she stomped back into the house, tearing off the winter cape from the hook and was about to go out the door again when Eileen stood in her way.

"Where are you going?"

"I'm going to tell that cocky lord where he can stick his bolts of cloth."

"You're not going to do that."

"You bet I will. Put the bales of cloth all back together and clear the way."

"Not until you calm down and listen to me."

Impatiently, Moira bobbed one foot and looked at her friend waitingly.

"Now, come on, say what you're going to say."

"Why don't you calm down first? I don't understand why you're so upset. You know as well as I do that these repairs are urgently due if we don't want the roof to fall on our heads. Also in winter it's always drafty, so we've always sealed the windows with cloths, that shouldn't have slipped your mind.

And with the fabrics we can dress the children well. We need all these things urgently and I think he saw it the same way. So it's more than nice that he took care of it."

"Oh, yeah? You forgot a little, tiny thing in your list," Moira pressed her   forefinger on her thumb and held both close to Eileen's face," what do you think I'm going to use to pay for this? I don't want to
more dependent than I already am."

With these words, she pushed Eileen to the side and stomped off in the direction of the street. Eileen thought about it for a moment before she called after her, "What do you mean dependent?"
But Moira no longer heard these words and Eileen watched her shake her head. She hoped Lord MacIntyre would bring her back to her senses.

"Moira! Nice to see...."
Moira rushed past Albert as he opened the heavy front door for her.
"Is he in his office?"

Albert was so surprised by this attack that he was startled and moved to the side. He regained his composure relatively quickly, however, and replied in his usual distinguished manner.
"If you are looking for his lordship, he is not in the house."
"Where is he, Albert?"

"Well, you can wait for him in the reception room while I send for him, if you   tell me what the urgency of the matter is."

Upset, she blustered at Albert that she would tell the lord herself. Albert, who had experienced much in his long career as a butler, knew when it was better to back down. Whatever the young man had done to Miss Fergusson, that she reacted so violently, was the lord's own affair. So he replied, "He's in the stables. Shall I take you there?"

But he did not get an answer, because Moira had already stormed out of the house. She knew her way around the property from her previous visits and went straight to the stables. Shaking his head, Albert closed the door again and hoped that the lord would get along with Miss Fergusson.

She saw him at the end of the stable alley with the young man Eileen hoped to marry one day. She remembered that his first name was Samuel. Robert MacIntyre was standing with his back to her and both men seemed engrossed in their conversation, for they had not yet noticed her.
While she was walking down the long alley, a few horses poked their heads out of the stalls with curiosity. Some began to whinny and announced her to the men even before she reached them.

Robert turned to her and greeted her with a bright smile, but when she approached, he saw her angry face, his smile immediately disappeared. Before he could say anything he heard Moira scolding him savagely.
"Lord MacIntyre, how dare you interfere in my affairs!"
Samuel, who was looking at him with an astonished look and an open mouth as Moira addressed the lord like a fury, was glad when Robert told him that they would talk more later. Grateful not to have to witness this controversy he quickly disappeared out the back door and left Robert to his fate.

"Moira! How nice to see you at such an early hour. I see the delivery has already arrived at your house."

He threw her a disarming smile. Moira, on the other hand, wished she were a man, then she would have smacked the grin off his face.

Nonchalantly, he stood there before her in his white shirt, the sleeves which he had pulled up to his upper arms and whose upper buttons stood open. His pitch black hair was slightly disheveled and gave his face some boldness. He had a striking face with high cheekbones and thick eyebrows. But the most interesting thing about his face were his bright blue eyes.

She had never seen before such an intense blue , which now looked at her somewhat mischievously, and drew her under their spell. Suddenly it occurred to her that she might be overreacting, but she still had to put him in his place and therefore replied angrily:

"Yes, and I want you to cancel this delivery."

Astonished at her words, he said:

"Why? Don't you like the fabrics?"

"Yes, but...."

"Well, then everything is fine, why all the excitement?" he interrupted her, gently put a hand on her back and turned her around so that she could walk next to him. Somewhat taken aback that he had cut her off, she tried again.

"It's not okay at all. You can't just order supplies and repairs for something that is none of your business."

Abruptly, Robert stopped and looked at her thoughtfully.

"Can't I?"

"No, you can't."

"Moira, I had told you that I wanted to help you, and the work I had commissioned is urgently needed. That you know as well as I do, so why do you resist so vehemently?"

"Because it's my business and I'll take care of it when I think it's necessary."

"Well, it has been necessary and I don't understand why you're so opposed to me taking a little of the burden you have loaded on your pretty shoulders. Don't be so stubborn."

Moira was fuming inside. How could she explain her situation to him in a plausible manner, without telling him anything of the agreement she had made with Dumfrey. In her situation, she didn't need anyone else to whom she owed something. The water was already up to her neck without him.

"I'm not stubborn! I simply can't afford to take your help because I can't pay for it."

So, now it was out and she was more than embarrassed to have to confess to him that she was as poor as a church mouse. Ashamed, she turned away and patted one of the horses who had curiously followed the conversation.

For a while, none of them said a word. Robert had already thought something like this, when he saw the somewhat neglected condition of the house, so he had ridden directly into town to order the most necessary things. Under no circumstances had he wanted to enrage Moira with his advance.

It had rather been meant as a spontaneous assistance. Moira was a proud woman and he was trying to fathom how he would have felt in her position if someone had simply gone over his head. Slowly, he turned to her and looked into those beautiful green eyes that were now looking at him through a wet veil.

He pulled a clean, white handkerchief from his pocket and dabbed her tears with it. Then he spontaneously pulled her into his arms.

He noticed how she stiffened and did not press her, but then she gave in and her anger seemed to be gone.

"I'm sorry, I didn't mean to hurt your feelings."

Moira trembled inwardly, but no longer out of anger. A completely different feeling flooded her body. At the moment, when he had pulled her tenderly against him and held her in his arms, she had felt as if a weight was falling from her shoulders.

It seemed to her as if his strong arms would give her support. The pleasant scent of his aftershave enveloped her and she caught her hands on his chest. Robert's heart was beating up into his throat. Even through the fabric of his shirt, he could feel Moira's hands precisely.

The same blissful feeling he had felt when dancing set in and he did well to put some distance between them again, otherwise he would have kissed her.

"You don't have to worry about the payment. You are welcome to consider it as a down payment, if that's what you really want."

Moira thought she had misheard.

„Down payment?" She would certainly not sell herself to another man. Already she noticed again, the anger rising in her and Robert noticed it, too, because she had immediately left him and looked at him furiously.

"Down payment? For what consideration from me?"

Appeasingly, Robert raised his arms.

"Not a down payment from you - but from me."

"I don't understand what you mean."

"Come on. I want to show you something."

Chapter 8

Robert took Moira by the hand and pulled her over to the house. As he stepped through the the front door, Albert came out of the kitchen and walked up to him. In passing, he turned to the surprised butler.

"Albert, I do not wish to be disturbed at the moment."

Reflexively, the latter replied, "Very well, Your Lordship."

But Robert did not seem to want a response, because he had already disappeared into his study with Moira. Albert shook his head and thought more to himself what the young people of today thought about this behavior.

Robert, on the other hand, let go of Moira's hand, gestured for her to make herself comfortable in one of the armchairs at his desk and then closed the door behind them. Moira, who had been in this room during his uncle's lifetime, noticed that not much had changed since his death.

The heavy oak desk still stood in the same place, directly in front of the glass front, but it was packed with folders, documents and other worksheets that Robert had been working with. On the right and left, wall-high shelves adorned the room. They were crammed full of books that had been accumulated over the centuries of history of the Dunbars.

On the right side of the room, there was a small, secret alcove, which Robert now approached and walked towards. He pushed away the wall of books in front of it. Behind it was a wall safe, which he opened and took out two documents. With these documents in hand he took a seat on his desk. Without further ado he began to speak.

"Since you are the heiress of your father, I would like you to look at this."

He handed her the two documents and meanwhile continued with his execution. Moira glanced at the two purchase contracts.

"I found these contracts while going through my uncle's papers. It clearly states that your father is co-owner of these two horses with forty percent. What I don't know is why my uncle made this purchase with your father, who as you told me, had as little idea about breeding as my uncle did."

Robert leaned back in his chair, rested his arms on the armrests and let his head rest on his hands, while he watched Moira study the papers.

"I don't understand this either. And then this horrendous sum. Is that a reasonable price? I had no idea that horses could be so expensive."

"Well, the price also seems quite high, and I believe at this point that our old masters have been ripped – off. Breeding stallions have their price, especially if the pedigree is first class, which I have already checked and can say what it says is true. Nevertheless the price was quite high. However be that as it may, I would like to know from you whether the signature on the contracts is your father's, so we know if the contracts are legal."

Moira took another close look at the signature carefully and there was no doubt.

"Yes, it is."

She handed the papers back to Robert and while he put the documents back in the safe, several thoughts went through her head. The date of the sales contracts was a date which was a few weeks before the fire. Had her father invested his entire fortune in two horses? If so, that would have been unbelievably stupid not to have reserves.

Was that why Sir Dumfrey had come into play with his money loan? Had her mother known about the risky investment? It really made little sense to her that her father, who had always been very businesslike, had gotten involved in such a risky business.

"Something is bothering you, Moira. What is it?"

Torn from her thoughts, she looked into those incredible blue eyes that now looked at her questioningly.

"What do you think about this whole thing, and what do you intend to do now? Are you going to sell them again?"

Secretly she was already thinking that her share of the sale would be enough to cover Lord Dumfrey's debts and thus be free.

It would be the solution to her problems. But the words of Robert put a spoke in her wheel.

"No, I don't want to sell the horses. They wouldn't bring to market what they were bought for. We would take a big loss. My uncle and and your father have bought the animals for breeding and that is exactly what I intend to do. The only way we can recoup the cost is through the breeding."

"When I hear you talk like that, you seem to have a clue. Do you know anything about horse breeding?"

"I've done nothing else all my life. My father is the second son of Baron Killian MacIntyre and he moved to America with my mother and me. We emigrated to America twelve years ago. There he raised horses on a farm in the deep west. It took us a long time to make it what it is today one of the largest breeding farms in the area. Ever since I can remember horses have always played a big part in my life, and yes, I think I have enough experience to start a breeding business here."

"Well then the only thing left to figure out is how we're going to deal with these two contracts."

Smiling, Robert looked at Moira. She was bright and she wasn't stupid. She was a woman quite to his liking.

"Well, there are two possibilities. First, I will pay you off as soon as I start to see success and I could free you from any ties right now or you will become my business partner and we will do the whole thing together. That would mean for you that you also share forty percent of the costs."

"I'm afraid I don't have the money to share in the costs, nor do I know anything about breeding, so the only way would be to sell my shares."

"That's right, and yet I've already told you that I would like to help you and here is a chance for you to make money again if we are successful. I admit there is a risk involved. If we are not successful with the breeding, logically, there would be costs and no profit to anticipate the answer to your question... You have two very good pastures on the bay that we could put to good use. I'd be willing to waive any further expenses on your part. This would keep the land in your possession and be leased, so to speak, to the breeding business and you would get your share as soon as successes are posted."

"Now this is all a little unexpected to me and I'd like to think about it."

"Of course. Consider my offer."

"I do have one question, though."

"Go ahead"

"Even if I let you use the pastures, you will do worse than I. So why do you want to do this? As you have found out, I had no idea about these contracts. You could have just kept it all to yourself and never tell me about it."

Robert looked at her in silence for a while. He seemed to be thinking about how he should answer. Then he said in a firm voice.

"Moira, I'm a man who plays his cards close to his chest and lies are not my style. I like you and I believe that I am also acting in the interest of my uncle, who also wanted to help you. That is why I offer you this partnership and it is up to you to accept it or reject it. My offer remains so and is not connected with any further conditions. Take the time you need, and in the meantime, I would be delighted if you would join me for dinner the day after tomorrow."

"I will consider your generous offer and I will gladly accept the invitation."

"Very well. I will send a carriage for you."

When Moira was on her way home, her thoughts revolved around the conversation she had just had with Robert. Should she accept his offer and become his partner? That would mean that they would see each other more often. This thought made her feel joyful, because he was an interesting man, who had long since aroused more than just business interests in her. When she arrived at home, the roofers were already done with the roof and were working on the windows. It was actually a nice gesture on his part, and in retrospect she could not really understand why she had reacted so violently. In the hallway there was a letter for her, which must have just come today.

She took it with her into the reception room and stopped in front of the fireplace to warm up a little from her walk, when she opened the letter and started to read with trembling hands, the only sentence it contained.

Meet me tomorrow at midnight at the
large oak tree at the entrance to the village

There was no return address on the letter, but Moira knew who it came from and immediately got a bad feeling. She quickly crumpled up the letter, threw it into the open fire and watched as the flames consumed it.

It was just before midnight when she arrived at the oak tree. No one seemed to be there yet and so she was startled when a voice behind her said:
" You're right on time, very good. I had already feared that you might have changed your mind."
"What do you want from me."
"Well, I understand you've been invited to dine with Lord MacIntyre the day after tomorrow."
"How do you know that?"
"You don't have to care about that. I don't want him to show up at the cove during the night and you will see to it that he doesn't."
"What's happening at the cove? What are you doing there?"
"It's none of your business, and it's better for your pretty nose if you stay out of it and only do what I tell you to do. You'll give him, before you leave the house that evening, this powder.
Put this in his last drink, "Charles Dumfrey held out a small can to her. Moira took it in her hand and opened it.
"What is this? Poison?"
"No," Dumfrey laughed maliciously.
"Such drastic means are hopefully not necessary if you do what I order you to do. It's a sleeping powder."
"No, I can't do that. This man has done nothing, and it is

not lawful."

"And how you will do it. Think of what's at stake for you. The whorehouses in Edinburgh are far from the finest. So don't make a fuss. He'll just sleep through the night like a baby."

Reluctantly, Moira took the can and put it in the pocket of her skirt. She was about to turn to leave when Dumfrey grabbed her by the arm.

"Do not think that you can betray me, I have my spies everywhere and would know immediately if you did not solve the matter to my satisfaction. Do we understand each other?"

Moira nodded and hurried away as fast as she could.

Chapter 9

Robert felt an inner restlessness. The last two days he had been thinking a lot about Moira. Even during the nights he had dreamed of her. He had felt her hands on his body and imagined how it would be to kiss her. They had only known each other for a few days and yet she had left an impression on him that pleased and frightened him at the same time.

He liked her - liked her a lot, in fact, and if he wasn't careful, he was well on the way to falling in love with her. Not that he minded that but until now he didn't know if she felt the same way. He believed that she had enjoyed it when he had held her in his arms in the stable alley a few days ago, but it could also have been that he had imagined it as his own desires arose.

In any case, she had accepted his invitation and would arrive in a few minutes. Like a little boy just before Christmas, he could hardly wait to hear the carriage in the driveway.

He took the black suit jacket off the hanger, put it on, and then went down the stairs into the vestibule. Just as he passed the last step he heard the carriage as it stopped on the gravel in front of the door. Albert, who at that moment had come out of the kitchen, opened the doors and was about to go to the carriage, when Robert went to help Moira out himself.

When he opened the hutch of the carriage and folded out

the footstep, he reached his hand inside the carriage and a gloved delicate hand seized it immediately.

Then Moira's smile appeared. He took a step back and let her get out of the carriage. My God, she is beautiful, thought Robert, as he saw her in front of him. She was wearing an eggplant colored taffeta dress, with a black velvet blouse that was cut like a cadet's uniform. Her hands were in black, short leather gloves and around her shoulders she was wearing a matching cloak to protect her from the chill of the night.
Her hair had been styled into the same artful updo that she had worn at the ball.

Robert was so fascinated by the sight, that he almost forgot his manners and remembered in time that he now greeted her with a formal kiss on the hand. He looked her deeply in the eyes. Moira, on the other hand, felt hot and cold. Those blue eyes seemed to penetrate right into her deepest inner self.

She had been feverishly thinking about what to wear tonight. This ensemble was her favorite and it was the only passable dress that had survived the fire unscathed. Since then she had never had the opportunity to wear it again, and for tonight it seemed almost inappropriate; but Eileen had taken it out of the closet as a matter of course and said that it should be this and no other. Well, she didn't have a better one anyway.

Only the green dress from Sir Dumfrey, but she never wanted to wear it again, because it reminded her of the pact with the devil she had made. The little can in her Skirt pocket weighed tons tonight. At least it seemed so to her. Robert, on the other hand, brought her such a radiant smile that she tried to forget her worries and and reservations.

The evening passed faster than she thought and Moira had to admit to herself that Robert fascinated her more and more every minute. They had been talking well all evening. Moira had told him about her childhood and laughingly they had realized that they had probably met here in their childhood days at one of his uncle's summer parties.

Fascinated about the paths that fate often forged in life, they had laughed heartily about it and made jokes and Moira had realized that she had not felt so at ease in a long time. That evening she had come to the realization that Robert was by no means only the Scottish aristocrat that many saw in him. No, he was a man who seemed to have many facets.

When they had finished their tasty dinner they made themselves comfortable with a liqueur and Moira had a question burning on her lips.

"Robert, now that you know everything about me, including the fact that at the tender age of ten, I had a small weakness for Ian Roames. Which I really never told anyone."

She looked at him smiling and this flash, which arose in her green eyes, seemed to drive him out of his mind. It was hard for him not to go over to her and take her in his arms to kiss her. Moira seemed to feel nothing of his arousal, for she went on and brought him back down to earth with her question.

"Why don't you tell me something about your life in America. That must have been very exciting and thrilling. What is it like there? I've never traveled far. I can't imagine living far away from Scotland."

"I didn't choose it myself either. Neither of my parents came first in the line of succession and so one day they decided to seek their fortune on the other side of the Atlantic. I still remember the crossing as if it were yesterday, although it is now almost thirteen years ago.

To save money, my parents had only bought third class tickets, so we ended up below deck in a kind of dormitory, which was full of people.

I had only known those as stable boys or maids. I thought I was better than them, had a better education and had grown up on the sunny side of life.

So it was not long before I got into a fight with a boy when I demanded that he sit somewhere else. This boy saw it quite differently and our discussion ended in a scuffle, where I got the short end, because the boy was much stronger than me and had probably already boxed in his lifetime more than I had done.

My father caught me at that time by the collar pulled me away, lectured me with the words: "What I would think of my person before God and that I should never again judge a person only by his origin." On top of that I got such a beating that I couldn't sit on the seat of my pants for two days. At that time, I was very mad at my father, but today I'm glad to have been taught that lesson, because he was right. I don't care about titles, they don't mean anything anyway.

I have learned to judge people by their ability and not where they come from. It does me no good to own a lot of land if I don't know how to farm it."

Moira sipped her liquor.

"That's a wise view."

"No, that's the view you get when you work hard all your life. I've seen my father work together with my mother from sunrise to sundown to fulfill their dream of owning their own ranch and as best I could do, at my young age, was to help out. Today, they can proudly say that they have made it and I hope to be there again one day."

Astonished, she looked at him.

"You don't want to stay here forever?"

Robert leaned back thoughtfully.

"Honestly, I don't know yet. I have come for my mother, who is the rightful heiress. She transferred everything to me because she wanted to continue to stay in America. Whether I will stay forever, I cannot say today. It may be foolish, but some days I feel lonely and then I miss my family."

Moira could understand that well. She often felt lonely too, even though the house was full of children and Eileen.

"I know what it's like to feel alone. I miss my parents every day and the children and Eileen are there, but they are not a substitute."

"Yeah that's exactly how it is."

A melancholy atmosphere grew between them, which no one really knew how to break through. Somehow a transparent bond was built between them, because they could understand each other and that led to a familiar togetherness. In order to re-enter somewhat safer waters again, Robert turned to Moira.

"Your glass is empty. May I give you another refill?"

"Yes, I'll have another small liqueur. Why don't you tell me what it's like over there? Is there nothing but wilderness?"

Happy to have a neutral topic again, Robert poured liquer in both their glasses again and began to talk about America. He told her that on the east coast, the places like, for example, Boston, New York and Washington were quite large. That in the south there were large farms, called plantations, and were mainly run by French emigrants.

The products of these plantations ranged from cotton, tobacco and sugar cane to nuts and sweet, juicy fruits called peaches and oranges.

Moira listened intently as he talked about his life on the ranch in the west of the Great Country: Of Indians who had roamed across the prairie and who had spread fear of being attacked by them, or how they had warded off a night attack by deserters from the nearby fort .

She glanced at the small grandfather clock behind him on the dresser, when he had ended and she realized again that she still had a job to do tonight. It was getting late and she would have to leave. Dumfrey did not want Robert near the bay tonight but how was he so sure that Robert was planning to do this at all?

She touched her skirt pocket and felt the small can. She didn't want to hurt Robert. He was a nice man, and how could she ever look him in the eyes again if she administered this sleeping pill to him. Moira wondered if she should dare not put the powder in his drink, but then her fear of the consequences won out.

"I would gladly pay a penny for the thoughts that are going through your head right now, Moira?"

She cringed, could he be reading her mind? No, certainly not, she reassured herself. She tried to smile.

"I was just thinking about how good it would be to be a man. It seems to me that a man is always allowed to do what he likes, while women are always patronized. I wish I could move far away, too."

"Mmm. Well at the moment I'm quite happy that you are not a man," Robert said to her mischievously. Was he flirting with her? Moira blushed and quickly busied herself with her liqueur glass. Robert smirked; it looked as if he had upset her a little. He would have liked to continue the amusing conversation, but it was late and he still wanted to go down to the bay tonight, because it was a full moon and he hoped to finally see the men again, who were up to some mischief on his property. But before he said goodbye to Moira, he still had one more question in mind.

"Moira, have you had time to think about my offer in the last few days?"

She nodded.

"Yes, I have, and I would like to be your partner. Maybe you could also teach me some things so I could help you?"

"I'm glad you accepted my offer. Let's have a toast to the future partnership"

„Yes, but then I really have to go. It's late now."

"The carriage will take you home again, of course. I'm just going to tell Albert that he'll drive them up. In the mean time, why don't you pour us a little drink, so that we can toast our partnership."

With these words he stood up and Moira poured another toast. It was her opportunity and yet she hesitated. Nor could she let it go, but the fear of Dumfrey seemed to cloud her mind, and so she quickly pulled the can out of her skirt pocket , poured the white powder into Robert's glass and swirled it a little so it would dissolve.

Then she let the can disappear in her pocket again and waited for his return. When Robert entered the room again a short time later and approached her, she thought that the deed must have been written all over her face. As best she could, she tried to regain her informality of before, but when he now raised his glass, she winced inwardly. Perhaps she should have clumsily knocked it out of his hand, but she did not move.

She let it happen that he welcomed her as a partner and then emptied his glass. A few minutes later, she was sitting in the carriage that was to to bring her home safely, and began crying out of despair over what she had done. Robert, who was unaware of all this, had gone into his study, because there he could pass the time until his departure. The evening had been beautiful and if he had not intended to ride into the bay today, he would certainly not have let Moira go.

He had enjoyed this evening, but now he wanted to concentrate on his project. For months nothing more had happened and he had wanted to give up, but somehow he had the feeling that the villains would try it again tonight. It was now shortly after ten and it gave him the opportunity to read some documents.

But as he took the first sheet, he was overcome by a leaden tiredness. He rubbed his eyes with his hand and tried to read on. But the letters blurred before his eyes and the eyelids became heavy. Strange, he had not drunk so much alcohol and yet he was suddenly so tired. Maybe it would help if he closed his eyes for a moment.

Chapter 10

"Robert? Robert!"

He woke up as he was rudely shaken.

"What?"

"Finally! Have you been here all night?"

With difficulty, Robert tried to open his eyes and was astonished when he looked into the brown eyes of Samuel, who was bending over him and shaking him vigorously by the shoulder.

"What - what do you mean and what are you doing here?"

Gradually, his awareness seemed to return. It took him a moment to realize that he was still sitting at his desk, in his evening suit. Suddenly, he was wide awake. He was going to go to the bay after all.

He straightened up in a flash and surprised Samuel, who looked at him in amazement.

"What time is it?"

"A little after seven. I came here because I was worried. Normally you are already on your morning ride and when I came into the stable and your horse was still there, I came here to see what was going on."

"After seven already? How is that possible? I only came here for a little while last night."

Robert couldn't believe what Samuel was saying. He had been here all night at his desk? This had never happened to him before.

"Must have been a busy evening."
Samuel nudged him amicably in the shoulder.

"The last time I couldn't remember how I got to bed, was at the wedding of Glenn Harrods, the potter, and I must confess, I'd had a good portion of the wine. However, the awakening the next day was not so great. My skull wanted to burst. How are you?"
"I haven't been drinking that much. I can't explain it."

Robert ran his hands thoughtfully through his tousled hair. It's too bad that he had such an attack of fatigue that night. Now he had missed the chance to finally get behind the secret of this gang, but perhaps all was not yet lost.
"Samuel, saddle my horse, I'm going to change. I want to go for a ride."
"Will do!"

A little later Robert was in the bay. His horse tied up at the top of the cliffs and walked down the small path. Unlike the last time, it had not started to rain during the night. On the contrary, it was a sunny spring day and the temperatures were quite mild.

The sea below was calm and only very gentle small waves beat against the beach. The narrow path that led into the bay was stony, and if people had used it that night, no traces would be found here. But he was lucky. The beach was full of footprints leading from the path to the water and from the water back to the path. He had known it. They had been there and it annoyed him even more now, that he had not been. How many men?

He could only guess, but he was sure by now that they were smugglers. They had waited here in the darkness on the beach and then pulled several boats ashore. Thanks to the low wave action and the tide, he could still see the deep drag marks in the sand where the men had pulled the boats ashore. Robert walked over to the cliffs. Perhaps there was a cave where they hid their contraband. But as much as he inspected everything, there was no cave or anything else like that. They must have transported the goods away.

Quickly he ran back up the path, grabbed his horse and continued on foot along the path that the men had taken the last time and where he had lost their tracks. Now in broad daylight, the deep boot prints were quite visible. The men seemed to be quite sure of what they were doing, if they did not cover their tracks.

After a while the path had widened and the footprints had ceased, but now he could make out grooves running parallel to each other and he saw deep hoof prints. His life in the wilderness had taught him to be able to read such tracks, and he inwardly thanked Henry Whittler, his father's old cowboy, who had taught him these tasks.

Here - they had loaded everything onto a cart. Before he followed the tracks, he got on his horse and looked around the area. He had left his property and, if he was not mistaken, was on the Fergusson's land. Curious to see where the trail would end, he followed the tracks. Robert was quite surprised when the path suddenly divided.

A much narrower path led further along the cliffs in the direction of the village and the wider part led inland. Robert followed the tracks which were clearly visible and stood a little bit later on the grounds of the Fergusson. The ruins of the fire loomed before him like a memorial and the tracks showed him the way.

They had driven around the house, had broken through the hedge on a small path and then had taken the road into the village. Shortly before the first houses came into sight, the track got lost, because too many carts and carriages were driving there. Disappointed at not getting any further, he turned around and rode back to the ruins. Why had they chosen this road?

Weren't they afraid of being discovered on the estate? It is true that the tracks did not pass the small house where Moira lived, but rather on the other side of the old mansion; nevertheless the risk of being discovered was quite high.

Something was nagging at him. Why did the smugglers take such a risk? Or perhaps they did not need to be afraid because there was an accomplice? But Moira had told him that she would be living there alone with the children and Eileen, and he couldn't really think of Eileen as a member of a Gang of Thieves. It just didn't make sense. Maybe it was a former employee of her father who was up to mischief here.

While he was still thinking about it, he hadn't even noticed that he was riding down Moira's driveway, and stopped in surprise when he saw her appear in front of him.

"Good morning Robert! I didn't expect to see you this morning."

Moira could not believe her eyes and was relieved when she saw him coming down on his horse. He was doing well. Thank God, what she had done last night had apparently left no consequences. She resolved inwardly to never do that again. There had to be another way to get rid of Sir Dumfrey.

"Good morning Moira." Robert tipped his hat to her and stopped his horse. "I was just looking at your pastures and rode the cliff trail while I was at it. I had no idea it ended here on your property.

"Yes, it can actually be taken right off the street, if you know the somewhat hidden entrance through the hedge. A few of our employees used it as a shortcut, so they didn't have to walk up the long driveway when they wanted to go into the village. At that time it was still equipped with a small gate, which disappeared at some point. I think the hedge will soon become so overgrown that it won't be able to be used."

Moira seemed to have no idea that the small trail was no longer as small as she had assumed and was being used by thieves. Even now he could not think what that might mean, because Moira had asked him a question.

"What do you think? Are the two pastures suitable for the horses?"

"Oh, yes, absolutely. I'm going to talk to my caretaker about it and then we can get started with the business."

"That sounds wonderful and so exciting."

She was so delighted, her face radiant with a smile, that made his pulse beat faster.

"Moira, I enjoyed last night very much and if you did too, I would be delighted if you would be my guest again."

"I would be very happy to, but this time you must do me the honor of being my guest, if you could be content with the modesty of my house."

Robert leaned down to her and came closer with his face. Again she looked into those unbelievable eyes, which seemed to look at her tenderly.

"I thought I told you yesterday that I didn't particularly care for all the luxuries. I openly admit that I like you and I don't care whether you live in a palace or in a tree house. So if you want to invite me, I'll be glad to come. Just let me know when, and I'll be there."

"I'll let you know."

On impulse, Robert leaned even further toward Moira and breathed a kiss on her cheek.

"Looking forward to it."

Then he tapped his hat in greeting, turned his horse around and rode back down the driveway. Moira's heart leapt inwardly for joy. He had told her for the second time that he liked her and he was flirting with her. How happy would she be if she could enjoy his courtship of her, but she was not stupid. She knew, that if he ever found out that she had deceived him, she would be dead in his eyes.

Chapter 11

His hands slid contentedly over the oak barrels as he walked around the sparsely illuminated vault.

The last shipment had finally arrived. The fine Jamaican rum would bring him a lot of money in the pubs and taverns along the harbor in Edinburgh. Down here, in this cellar, the barrels from three deliveries were stored and waited to be transported.

A small fortune, if he was not mistaken. His plan was ingenious, and he was not far from his goal. Soon he would be one of the powerful of this country.

His opinion would be valued and he would enjoy great influence. For more than two years he had been working on his plan and now it seemed that it was going to happen faster than he had planned. Unconsciously all acted according to his will.

The young MacIntyre had apparently fallen for Moira's grace and beauty, as he seemed to be seeing her regularly in recent weeks and months. His informant told him that they met for meals, went for walks, or went for rides together. It was probably only a matter of time before the lord would ask her to marry him.

But how could he resent him. He himself wanted to possess her and would achieve this in the not too distant future. But first she had to become Lady MacIntyre, even if it would mean that Robert would have his hands on her body first.

This was the price he would have to pay for his success. Time was working for him. In the coming week he was expecting another delivery and it was necessary to tighten the thumbscrews on Moira. The good woman probably thought she was free from him, already, since he had not been in touch for a long time. Well, next week she would have to be used again and he smiled smugly at his perfidious plan. Nobody was as ingenious as Charles Dumfrey.

"Samuel, what I've been wanting to ask you: Have there been any cases of smuggling around here in the past? Have you heard anything about it?"

Robert was with Samuel in the stable and was examining the first mares that had become pregnant from his breeding stallions. A start had been made and he hoped that the next few months would go well and that the mares would give birth to healthy foals.

Right now they were in the process of planning to turn one of the two pastures at the cliffs to an all-mare pasture, so that the pregnant ladies could tend to their foals in peace and quiet, with good grass and fresh air. Robert's thoughts suddenly turned to the nocturnal activities in the bay. The only explanation he could tell himself was that he had a picnic date with Moira later on and the tracks led across her property.

"Smugglers? Here in our area? No, I haven't heard anything about that. Why do you think there are smugglers? I ask, because your uncle asked me exactly the same question shortly before his death. At that time I could only give him the same answer as I can give you now."

Surprised, Robert looked at Samuel.

"My uncle asked about that, too? That is strange."

"That's what I think too. So, what happened to make you ask me that?"

Samuel looked expectantly at Robert, but he did not let on. Could he dare tell Samuel about his observations in the bay? Or could it be, that he was in cahoots with them? Samuel needed money.

He had seen him here in the stable a few days ago, standing in a close embrace with Eileen. Without wanting to, he had witnessed a conversation between them, through which he now knew that Samuel had money problems.

The two were in love and wanted to get married but Samuel could not afford to marry Eileen at the moment. Eileen had then left in disappointment and Samuel had also been unhappy about the situation. Robert had planned to talk to Samuel that day about a raise because of his good work, but had not yet had the chance to do so. Now he remembered this conversation and he wondered whether Samuel would be desperate enough to join such a gang?

For the time being, he decided to keep it to himself until he had gathered more information. The mere fact that his uncle had apparently also witnessed activities at the bay made his death appear in a different light.

Could it be that things had not gone right there and the supposedly natural death had not been one at all? In order not to give Samuel further speculation, Robert resorted to a white lie.

"I read a book about this area and it was about smugglers. Apparently my uncle read the same book," Robert grinned at Samuel.

Samuel was apparently not so easily deceived, because he watched Robert for a while, but then he just nodded and said nothing more about it.

"OK, we're done. Please ride over and inspect the fences at the pasture, so that everything is in order when we bring the mares tomorrow. I won't be here this afternoon."

"Are you meeting Moira?"

"Yes, it's a beautiful day and I've invited her to the picnic."

"She deserves it. The last few years haven't been particularly good for her. Eileen and Moira work very hard to support themselves and the orphanage."

"Samuel, I was an unwilling listener to your conversation with Eileen the other day and I know that you would like to marry her."

"Yes, we've known each other forever and we love each other, but..."

Robert interrupted Samuel.

"That's exactly why I want a chance to talk to you. Unfortunately, we have to postpone it, because I have to go. Let's have the talk in the next few days," with that he cheerfully patted Samuel on the back and turned to leave.

Samuel called after him: "Say hello to Moira from me," then Robert hurried out of the stable.

Half an hour later he was sitting on his little Landauer, which was pulled by a strong, brown English thoroughbred gelding and was looking forward to the afternoon. In the back he had a fully equipped picnic basket, which Gwyneth, the cook, had stocked with many delicacies; a good bottle of red wine, two glasses, a fluffy blanket and a surprise for Moira, which he himself wasn't yet sure, how she would react to it. Eagerly to finally get to her, he slammed the reins down on the horse's backside.

Moira could hardly contain her excitement. All day long she had been looking forward to this moment.

Robert would be there soon and they would spend this beautiful spring afternoon together. He had invited her to a picnic and the weather seemed to be graciously accommodating with them.

The temperatures were quite warm for early May and the sun was already high in the sky. A light breeze made the spring flowers dance happily in the flower beds. Moira had made herself a dress from the fabrics that Robert had bought for her. She had sewn herself a dress from yellow muslin fabric. In keeping with spring, the fabric also featured small meadow flowers. She wore a white long-sleeved blouse with it. Her head was adorned with a yellow sun hat with a broad brim and a chin strap, which was now loosely tied. Nervously, she stood at the door.

She was alone at home. Eileen had gone to town with the children to deliver the sewing work they had done for the tailor, and also to get bread from the baker. Moira couldn't wait to see Robert again. In the last few weeks they had seen each other more regularly, and each time it had been harder for her to say goodbye to him. When they were together, she could forget her worries and feel happy.

She enjoyed it when their bodies touched as if by chance, or when he kissed her forehead and cheek goodbye. Moira had found herself the last few times wishing that he would kiss her. What would it be like to feel his lips on hers? She was so unsure.

Was it sacrilegious if she longed for more? She dreamed that his hands would touch her everywhere? Did he feel the same way? He had never made any effort to get close to her. So far, everything had proceeded with decency where no one could have any complaints about it and yet she longed for more. Much more.

Moira heard the carriage coming and even before Robert had brought the horses to a stop in front of the house, Moira was out of the house and ran to meet him beaming with joy.

Robert, with equal fervor, jumped off the wagon, greeted her with a bright smile and a kiss on the cheek and helped her onto the carriage. When he had taken his seat next to her, he looked at her with a look that went right through Moira. Her heart was beating up to her throat and she realized that she had fallen head over heels in love with Robert MacIntyre.

"Ready?" Robert asked her with a grin.

"Ready!" replied Moira with a laugh, and immediately he turned the carriage and trotted off again.

From the small hill on which they had stopped, they had a breathtaking view of the distant sea on one side and of the slight hills of the hinterland on the other side. Robert had found this place on one of his rides and had chosen it for the picnic.

A bunch of small trees brought the necessary shade and so he spread out the large blanket on the grass. Moira was completely enchanted by the view, she closed her eyes, spread her arms and turned like a child in all directions, as if she wanted to see the whole world. Robert, who was quietly observing this, had to control his soaring heart. How he would have liked to just take her in his arms and close her mouth with his. Her well formed lips seemed to literally scream for him. He cursed inwardly. If he had not been brought up so well, he would have long since tasted her lips and and let his hands glide over her body as he imagined night after night.

His desire for her grew day to day and he could hardly hold back from approaching her. He noticed how his thoughts began to dominate his body, and before it could become more than embarrassing for him, he had to create a distraction somehow.

"I hope you brought an appetite. Gwyneth has been very kind to us and has filled the basket as if an entire cavalry would have to be fed from it."

Moira turned laughing, and came toward him. Robert, you're in trouble, he thought to himself, as she sat down on the blanket in front of him and began to take the delicacies out of the basket. He quickly took a seat next to her and distracted himself by opening the bottle of wine. For a while they sat next to each other in silence and ate from the delicious meat pie, fruits and bread. The atmosphere between them seemed to be different today than usual.

The impartiality of the last encounters was lost. Robert glanced furtively at Moira, who was sipping her wine and looking off into the distance. His hand slipped into his vest pocket and clutched the small box. He noticed his pulse quickening. What was so damn hard about showing his feelings for her?

Why couldn't he just ask her? He loved her and wanted to be with her. She was the woman he had been looking for and he wanted to hold on to her for the rest of his life. He knew that she also liked him, but was it love with her, too?

What if she laughed at him and thought he was crazy. After all, they had only known each other for about half a year and yet he was so sure that she was exactly the right one for him.

Moira must have noticed the expression on his face because she looked questioningly at him with her green eyes. Come on, say something, Robert encouraged himself.

He felt like a little schoolboy, but in all his life nothing had ever been so important to him as the impression he made on Moira. So he tried to be casual with her again.

"It's nice here, isn't it?"

Was he mistaken, or did a disappointed look just flit across her face? If so, she quickly regained her composure and hid it.

"Yes. The view you have from up here is really breathtaking."

"Just like you are."

Moira paused in amazement. Had he really just said that? Robert seemed magically attracted to her, for he bent to her and let his hand slide over her cheek. Her soft skin was warm and he noticed how Moira stiffened under his touch. Becoming brave, he let his hand play with a strand of hair that had come loose from her hairstyle. Without giving an objection, Moira let herself feel these strange sensations. Her heart beat faster and the vein on her neck throbbed violently. Would he kiss her now?

Since they had arrived here, she had the feeling that something important was going to happen today. The atmosphere between them seemed to crackle. She didn't dare move, possibly destroying the intimate moment when she felt his hand in her hair.

Slowly, she lifted her arm, carefully took off her hat, and placed it next to her in the grass. Robert took this as an opportunity to let his hand deepen into her hair. Suddenly she noticed how it was loosened and fell in soft waves over her shoulders.

"You should always wear it like that."

Her breathing was intermittent, her lips became dry and she was no longer able to speak. Somewhat anxiously she watched as his face came closer. When his lips touched hers tenderly, a tingle flowed through her body. An indescribable happiness surrounded her and she heard herself, as if from afar, groan. When the pressure of his kiss intensified, she closed her eyes and allowed the wonderful feelings that overwhelmed her take over.

Robert had only wanted to touch her briefly with his lips, but the sensations had struck him like a thunderbolt, demanded more and so he had deepened his kiss. He had changed his position slightly and now took her tightly in his arms. His lips closed hers with an intimate kiss. Moira seemed to enjoy it, because she let herself fall. She returned his kiss and opened her lips for him. Immediately he penetrated her with his tongue and took her in possession.

In both of them the fire flared wildly. Moira held on to him convulsively and Robert closed her tighter in his arms. Over and over again they kissed and with each time the desire for more grew. Suddenly Robert shifted his weight and carefully pushed Moira backwards to the ground; where she now laid under him on the blanket. The weight of his upper body, which lay half on top of her, held her captive. She should have stopped him but somehow she couldn't.

She enjoyed being touched by him. To feel his warm breath on her face and his lips on her mouth. Under no circumstances did she want him to stop now. Time should stop for her. Full of passion he kissed Moira again and again.

He had been surprised at the vehemence with which the feelings had been kindled in him when he had touched her with his lips. And now he was on fire. He wanted more, wanted to touch her all over her body, caress her and he did not want to let her go anymore.

Breathing heavily, he paused for a moment and had to smile, when he looked into Moira's disappointed face. The words that had seemed hard to say at the beginning of the day now bubbled out of him.

"Moira, I love you."

Her face lit up and to his relief, she replied, "I love you, too."

Robert rose and helped the astonished Moira to her feet, then he knelt with one leg in front of her. From his pocket he pulled out the small box and looked up at her.

"Moira, I know we haven't known each other very long and yet I feel as if I've known you all my life. I love you and it makes me happy when we're together. When we part, I count the hours until we meet again. You are the woman I see by my side all my life. Will you marry me?"

Robert opened the box and held out to her a beautiful sapphire ring. He looked at her expectantly.

Moira could hardly believe her luck. She had fallen madly in love with Robert and here and now her secret desires and wishes were coming true. Overjoyed, she threw herself into his arms and thus brought him down. Tears of joy ran down her face, and before the stunned Robert could say anything, she pressed a kiss to his lips and laughed and exclaimed, "I do, I do, I do."

Chapter 12

For the next two days, Moira's thoughts were occupied with the upcoming wedding. She was overjoyed. In the morning she woke up with a smile on her lips and hummed happily all day long. Eileen, who at first had not known the reason and had wondered greatly about Moira's state of mind, had been delighted when she learned of Robert's marriage proposal.

"You see, everything will be all right now. You can pay Sir Dumfrey the money back and the work at the orphanage can continue, or what does Robert want to do?"

"I don't know. I haven't talked to him about it."

Eileen, who had known Moira long enough, suspected there was more to it.

"But that you owe Sir Dumfrey money, he already knows that, doesn't he?"

Guiltily, Moira looked to the floor. Eileen stood up in front of her and put her arms on her hips.

"You didn't tell him! Moira, you need to tell Robert the truth. How are you going to pay Dumfrey back the money, if it doesn't come from Robert, and what will your husband-to-be say when he this matter hanging over your head?"

Annoyed, Moira interjected to her friend,

" I know. I just haven't had the chance yet, to talk to

Robert about it."

"Then you should do that right away, because you shouldn't go into a marriage with secrets."

Eileen was right. Robert had to know about it and would certainly help her. She resolved to tell him about it on her next visit, on the next evening. In order to steer the somewhat unpleasant conversation in other directions, she started to make plans for the wedding with Eileen. Robert wanted to marry her as soon as possible, but he had social obligations and so the wedding would not take place for several weeks.

Tomorrow they were going to go through the guest list, so that the invitations could be sent out. Also, quite a few arrangements should be discussed regarding the feast day. Robert's small court had been thrilled when they were informed of the Lord's wedding plans. In the next few days, the cook wanted to offer the couple a few menu suggestions and Albert and his wife Harried, the housekeeper, had immediately started planning the guests' accommodations.

Such celebrations cast their shadows far ahead and so it was not surprising that the normal daily routines were almost neglected. Moira, at least, felt that way and Eileen indulged her. Admiringly, Moira now stroked her fingers over the noble fabric.

She would soon become Lady MacIntyre. Her guests belonged to the high aristocracy and a suitable dress was needed. She had found in the village this wonderful bale of silk, a few pale pink florets for the collar, white lace for the veil and an elegant pattern, straight from Paris. Eileen and she would spend the next few days and weeks creating a gorgeous gown for her. Just as she was daydreaming about how Robert would happily embrace her on her wedding day, there was a knock at the door and Eileen entered.

"Moira, a letter has just been delivered here for you."

"Excuse me? Oh, I see, thank you. I'm sure this will be Robert's first draft of the guest list he was going to send me. I should take a look before tomorrow night to possibly add someone else."

But even as she received the letter, she froze. Quickly, before Eileen could notice anything, she forced herself to take the letter and had it promptly disappear into her skirt pocket. The apprehension was for naught, however, as Eileen was baking a cake in the kitchen and thus hurried out immediately. Alone again in the small reception room, she reached into her skirt pocket and pulled out the letter with trembling fingers.

She had recognized the envelope right away. The same paper and the same writing on it. Just like the last time. Moira was willing to throw the unopened letter into the fireplace, but she knew that would not solve her problem either. Therefore, she tore the yellowish paper apart.

With engraved handwriting the letters were written, but what she read made all cheerfulness die in her. She had thought it was over. For weeks she had not received any more news and she had been glad about it.

Yes, she had almost pushed him out of her mind. But now he was back and wanted to meet with her again. Could she allow herself not to go? He wouldn't let her go until the matter had been cleared up, she was quite sure of that. She would tell him that she would pay back the money and so Moira decided to go to the meeting one last time.

He flipped the gold cover of his pocket watch back on, then let it disappear into the pocket of his brocade vest and bent impatiently out of the window of his black carriage.

She was long overdue, and he wondered why she had not come. Could it be that she had not received the letter? But his messenger had confirmed that he had delivered the letter to the house. She was hopefully not foolish enough to believe that if she ignored him, she would be rid of him.

This could be very dangerous for her. Just as he was about to give his coachman a signal to depart, he saw her dainty figure approaching him. Without a word, he opened the door and let her in. Immediately the carriage began to move.

"You are late and I was just about to leave."

Quite out of breath, Moira took a seat opposite him. As the carriage started, however, she pulled up from her seat and was about to rush out of the the door, when Dumfrey rushed forward, held the door shut and and pushed her back onto her bench. Outraged at this treatment, she shouted at him.

"Stop the carriage at once. I will not go with you anywhere."

"Relax, we have things to talk about. I understand that Lord MacIntyre actually proposed to you. I'm happy for you."

Self-confident, he leaned back in his carriage and did not take his eyes off her. She was beautiful, and when she was angry, her eyes sparkled dark green.

He noticed how his body reacted to her closeness and he longed to let his fingers glide over her soft rose skin. She must have walked briskly because her pulse was fast and her firm breasts rose and lowered. Who should stop him here and now from approaching her?

His coachman was secretive and outside there was not a soul on the road who could hear them. He would only need to apply a few practiced moves and he would have her in the position where he could give in to his urge. She would anxiously beg him to leave her alone, but he would take her against her will, hard and again. He liked it when they were virginal and tight and when they trembled with fear, so he could exert his power over them.

Over time, he had discovered his preference for this and went to special establishments to get his satisfaction. But gradually it was too boring to take the girls willing to give him pleasure. It was much more satisfying when he got himself young girls from the street. Often it was maids he lured into his carriage with flimsy excuses, and then he had fun with them.

He did not have to worry about charges, because a few pennies settled his deed in most cases. In addition, he saw to it that he never poached in his own environment, but always where no one knew him. Moira, who had not missed the lecherous look of Dumfrey felt noticeably uncomfortable, but she tried not to let it show.

"Don't you feel well? You're starting to sweat."

"Uh what? No, it's just quite warm today."

Dumfrey wiped his forehead with his lacy handkerchief and concentrated on what was really important. If he would have liked to lay a hand on Moira, it would have been a mistake that could not be repaired and so he decided to put his needs behind and set his goal once again before his eyes. His time with her would still come.

"Where are you taking me?"

"My coachman will just drive us around a bit. It's more inconspicuous than if my carriage stood by the side of the road. You will have another mission tomorrow. Here is the tin of powder."

Sir Dumfrey drew from his coat pocket a similar tin as the first time and held it out to Moira. She, however, made no effort to take it. Instead she tightened herself and looked him firmly in his small gray eyes.

"I will not give my future husband any more sleeping

powder. I plan to ask him for money tomorrow night to give you your money back. That would pay off my parents' debts and we will have nothing more to do with each other."

He had almost counted on something like that, but she didn't count on him. Patronizingly he withdrew his hand with the can, and before she could react, he sprang up and clasped her chin with his hand. He squeezed so hard that she groaned in pain and almost fell to the floor in front of him. Moira tried to free herself from the strong grip, but she had no other choice than to let Dumfrey have his way. Quietly, but with a dangerous undertone in his voice, he hissed in her ear:

"Honey, it's not just about the money anymore. Have you still not understood this?

The money was merely a means to an end. I don't want MacIntyre anywhere near me, and you're going to take care of it as we discussed. And if you still do not understand, I tell you when it's time to stop or something terrible will happen to the children and to your girlfriend.

Don't make the mistake of underestimating me. I have my eyes and ears everywhere and whoever resists me, has regretted it."

Charles Dumfrey pushed Moira back onto the bench and knocked with his fist against the carriage roof. Immediately the carriage stopped. He opened the door and held the small can out to her.

"Go and do your work."

Moira grabbed the can with a pale face and got out of the carriage without another word to him. Immediately the door was closed again and the carriage rolled away. She looked around briefly and realized that she was not far from her home. With the can in her hand, she dragged herself home. She felt sick to her stomach. Being able to tell Robert about the debt now was out of the question. She would be putting at risk the lives of those who played a major role in her life.

How on earth was she supposed to find a solution for this, she was all alone and could not confide in anyone. This meeting had to remain her secret so that no one would be harmed, because she was sure that Dumfrey would carry out his threats. She had seen the determination in his eyes.

Robert had been sitting and working in his writing room all day. Now he was overcome with the urge to go for another ride, and although it was late and most of the inhabitants of his castle had already gone to rest, he enjoyed riding his horse across the fields.
At such times, he fondly remembered his home in Wyoming when he had spent days out in the wilderness and nights under the stars.

The moon shone brightly tonight and lighted the way and so Robert allowed his horse to gallop faster over the meadows. His thoughts wandered from the work he had just finished to Moira, whom he would see again tomorrow evening. Soon she would be his wife and he counted every hour he had to be without her. How had it been possible that she had conquered his heart in the shortest time?

He saw her in front of him, smiling lovingly at him with her emerald green eye and how her body felt against his when he held her and kissed her. For nights on end, he dreamed of what it would be like when she lay with him.

Gradually these thoughts became torture for him, because until his wedding day he would be allowed to see her, touch her and kiss her, but he could not allow himself more if he did not want to destroy her reputation. Once again, Robert cursed softly to himself. He didn't give a damn about all these rules of decency but his status here did not allow him to violate them.

He had no alternative but to press ahead with the preparations for the wedding to take place as soon as possible.

Tomorrow evening they would discuss everything and he would tell her that he had chosen a date in three weeks. Unconsciously, Robert had ridden to the hill where he had proposed to Moira. He stopped his horse and looked into the distance. The moonlight fell on the distant sea.

Tomorrow was another full moon, it occurred to him. I wonder if the smugglers would come again? Nothing had happened in the last few months, so why should they come back tomorrow of all days? And yet, he suddenly had a feeling that this was exactly what was going to happen, and so he decided to lie in wait again the next night.

He wanted to finally understand what the men in the bay were doing and finish them off. Satisfied with himself, he slammed his heels into his horse's flanks and let it race home at a brisk gallop. He was racing around a small wood and almost collided with an equally fast carriage on the road. Luckily he pulled his horse around at the last moment.

The two carriage horses shied for a moment, giving the coachman the arduous task of taming them, and cursing, he cracked the whip on the backs of the two black horses until they continued on their way at the same rapid pace. Robert, who was reining in his horse a short distance away, looked around to see what had just come into his path and was astonished when he saw the completely black carriage with the two black horses standing on the road.

The coachman had some difficulty in calming

the frightened animals, but then they continued on their way without giving a damn about him. Who in the world was here at this time of day with a completely unlit carriage? There had been no monogram on the door, as was usual and yet it seemed to him as if he had seen the carriage and the driver somewhere before.

Since it would not occur to him, however, he now directed his own horse, which was apparently a little irritated by the moment of fright, home.

"You did a good job," soothingly Robert patted his stallion's neck.

"Let us now start on our way home at a slower pace, or we'll both break our necks."

While he steered his horse now in a light trot, his thoughts drifted back to the mysterious carriage. Who had the carriage transported and where was it going at that rate? Or better yet, where had it come from?

When he lay in his bed a little later, he could find no rest. The feeling did not let go of him that he had known the carriage, but he just couldn't think of it, and so he pondered it until the early hours of the morning before tiredness finally set in and he fell asleep.

Chapter 13

Yesterday, she had hardly been able to wait to finally see Robert again. But today she hoped that the evening would never come. She had been lying awake all night, racking her brains about how she should behave tonight with Robert. Now she already had a severe headache and dark circles under her eyes.

"If Robert sees you like this today, I'm sure he'll think twice about marrying you,"

Eileen joked the morning she saw Moira.

"You look terrible. He must be haunting your head all night and thus robs you of your beauty sleep. Bad boy."

Eileen nudged her mischievously.

Moira, who was in no mood to joke, only grimaced, which immediately triggered another headache.

"Eileen, I'm not feeling well at all today. I have a terrible headache."

Concerned, Eileen put her hand on Moira's forehead and said,

"You're not going to get sick now, are you? There's nothing to do today that I can't do alone. Why don't you lie down for a little while, so that you'll be back on your feet tonight. You look really terribly tired."

Without a word, Moira just nodded and dragged herself out of the room. She felt as if she had heavy weights on her legs.

Eileen was a treasure. She would never do anything that

would endanger the life of her friend or the children's lives. It was only a sleeping pill and if Dumfrey didn't want Robert to be in the bay tonight, for whatever reason, then she would give him this powder again. Nothing had happened the last time and so Robert would wake up tomorrow and at most be annoyed that he had again not managed to get into the bay.

While Moira went back to bed, she wondered what Dumfrey was doing in the bay in the first place. Maybe it was time to find out more about it. Was that the solution to her problem? The more Moira thought about it, the better she liked the idea of investigating. Tonight she would do again what Charles Dumfrey asked her to do, but after that she would find a way to bring this matter to an end.

Still clothed, she lay stretched out on her bed and glanced at the bright stain on the ceiling, which was caused by the lighted oil lamp on her night table. Silently and in thought she let the past evening run through her mind.

Robert had welcomed her with a passionate kiss and the memory of it now made her smile dreamily. In general, they had eyes for each other during the whole dinner. His bright blue eyes had looked at her lovingly and one or the other moments of desire had been seen there, which had made her shiver pleasantly.
Unlike Dumfrey's lustful eyes, which always terrified her, Robert's looks left her in a state of longing. Moira tried to imagine what it would be like to be married to a man. What was required of a wife?

She wished her mother was there to tell her how she should behave toward Robert. They had been busy with the guest list after supper, had laughed and joked around. Robert, at the mention of some relatives on his father's side, had recounted anecdotes and memories from his childhood so vividly that they had hardly stopped laughing.

Again and again he raised his finger in admonition, pulled his mouth to a snout and pinched his eyebrows so that this sight alone had been enough to make her laugh. He had then imitated in a disguised voice one of his distant uncles, who had always told him to drink a fresh glass of milk every day to grow up and be strong. God, they had fooled around like children and she had felt liberated and happy.

Would it always be like this with him? Would he always make her laugh and would she be so happy?

"You get a beguiling little wrinkle when you laugh. Right here," he had said and then kissed her on the left temple.

"And here."

Where he had immediately kissed her temple on the other side. He had taken her in his arms and held her. Their eyes had met and there it was again, the moment in which she longed for more than just kisses. Robert had then taken her by the hand.

"Come!"

Without another word, he grabbed the the wine and two glasses and had gone out with her into the garden. It had already been dark, but a few torches had illuminated a narrow gravel path that led to a small pond. In the water, which was surrounded by higher hedges, grew water lilies.

On one of the large leaves sat two frogs, which were singing in the stillness of the night. Robert drew them over to a park bench that stood on the shore and settled down. Moira, who had never seen this place before found it very romantic. Moira had hardly taken a seat next to Robert, when he had held out a poured glass of red wine to her. They both sipped their wine.

"At last we are alone. I should have had the idea of bringing you here much sooner. It's nice here, isn't it?"

"Yes. Funny how the frogs croak."

Had she really said something so stupid? She could literally feel the atmosphere charged up between the two of them. With her lips dry, unconsciously she ran her tongue over to wet them. Robert took the glass from Moira's hand and placed hers and his on the floor and turned back to her. Her heartbeat quickened as she read the passion in Robert's eyes.

"Oh, Moira, I love you, and it's driving me crazy to be near you without being allowed to touch you."

Moira, not understanding what he meant by this, only replied," But you do touch me. You kiss me and..."

She didn't get any further, because Robert had closed her mouth with his. Demanding and urging, he drove with his tongue over her lips until she opened them and allowed him to enter. Carried away by his passion, she closed her eyes, clung to him and returned his kisses. Suddenly his mouth wandered along her neck to her collarbone.

An indescribable tingling sensation gripped her body and a moan escaped her mouth. While Robert did not stop running his lips over her tender skin, he changed his position on the bench and pulled her to him.

He pushed away the disturbing hoop skirt with his hands which immediately puffed up behind Moira's back. "What a foolish fashion!" came to his mind as he struggled with the monster and at the same time simultaneously tried to continue kissing Moira.

He would have loved to rip her clothes off. That was what he would have liked to do most at the moment anyway. He was on fire. He wanted to touch her all over her body, caress her, kiss her and taste her, love her and give her love. Moira, who automatically tensed when she realized, she was sitting on Robert's lap, didn't know how to act. She had never been so close to a man before. "It's all good. Just relax and enjoy it."

He breathed little kisses on her neck and saw her cartoid artery throbbing wildly. Her cleavage rose and fell violently. In a burst of ecstasy, he pressed his lips to the naked base of her breasts. Moira cried out with desire and he closed her mouth with his lips.

His hand wandered up her back and deftly opened the clasp of her top. With both hands he slowly pulled the top down a little and exposed her upper body.

Two flawless firm breasts stood out, their pink buds perkily raised by the coolness that now enclosed them. Robert swallowed hard at the sight. He noticed how he became hard and his body tensed. Moira, who had realized too late what was happening to her, straightened up and wanted to turn around ashamedly. But Robert lovingly took her face in his hands and kissed her. Then he said:

"Please don't. You are so beautiful. I love you. Can you feel how I desire you? Can you feel it? I want to explore your whole body, caress and fondle you. I want to kiss you and love you. I hurt every single day that I can't have you. Moira please, let me touch you and I promise you that I won't do anything that you don't want me to do."

Somewhat frightened and wide-eyed she looked at him, but something in her told her she could trust him. Even though her mind told her caution, her body spoke a completely different language. She had enjoyed his touch and the deep feeling that burned inside her. She herself had become curious, demanded more and so she just nodded and let him. Robert kissed her and rekindled the passion between them. His hands ran over her naked back and slowly found their way to her breasts, which they enclosed tightly.

They filled his hands perfectly and the feeling Robert experienced was indescribably beautiful. But when he pressed with his thumb and forefinger one of the firm buds, he was surprised about Moira's fierce reaction. She cried out passionately and dropped her head down into her neck.

He kissed her tense larynx and continued to rub her breasts with his fingers, until he felt her hands on his chest. Quickly he stripped off his jacket and vest and began to undo the buttons on his shirt, when Moira stopped him. Breathing heavily he put his hands down and waited. With trembling fingers she slid over the fabric until she stuck one finger into the open cuff and felt his skin underneath.

Robert drew in a sharp breath. More courageous by his reaction, she opened one button after the other. Robert could have torn the damn shirt off his body, he was so impatient, but he did not want to scare her off and wanted to feel her hands on his skin. Wanted to see the passion in her eyes. After a time that did not want to end she stripped off his shirt and exposed his upper body. Admiringly she looked at the sun-browned skin. His upper body was hard and muscular.

The well-proportioned muscles were tense and the tendons on his arms stood out. A light fuzz of black hair adorned his chest, and when she let her gaze wander a little lower, she saw that his belly was flat and firm. Robert was in good physical shape and had not an ounce of fat on his body Moira, who seemed to be engrossed in the exploration of the male torso, did not catch Robert's longing looks. Breathlessly he breathed to her: "Touch me, Moira. That, which pleases you, pleases me."
Carefully she let her fingers slide over his upper body. The softness of the chest hair surprised her and so she played with some of the little hairs. It cost Robert a great deal of self-control. But any impetuous advance would

now be a mistake and would destroy Moira's trust in him. He wanted to gently show her the erotic world of love and wanted to explore it together with her.

She was passionate and he was sure that they would have a lot of fun together in bed. Slowly, he leaned forward and found her mouth. He pulled her closer to him, so that he could feel her naked breasts on his skin. Suddenly Moira froze, she abruptly straightened up and pushed him away a little; put a hand on his mouth and listened into the darkness.

"Did you hear that? I think there's someone there."

Excited and looking around, she tried to discover what had caught her attention. Robert, on the other hand, did not want the evening to end; when it seemed to get interesting and he just said succinctly:

"It was probably an animal, which rustled in the bushes."

But Moira was not so sure. She suddenly felt as if they were being watched and it reminded her of Sir Dumfrey, who told her that she was under observation. A little stronger than she had intended, she pushed Robert back, slipped off his lap and pulled her top back up. With her hands, she held it in place and turned her back, with the silent invitation to close the back fastener again. Robert, understanding that the evening was hereby ended, sighed and stepped behind her to close the dress. Then he turned her around and took her in his arms.

"Moira, it would have been only an animal."

"And if it wasn't? I have shown myself indecent here and I've done things that don't befit a lady. I want to go home, Robert."

"I'm sorry. I didn't mean for the evening to end like this. I enjoyed it very much, and I think you did too. There's nothing wrong with indulging in love. And when we're married, we'll pick up where we left off today."

Moira felt how the blush rose to her face. Continue?

Was there more? Perhaps she had encouraged him too much today. Whatever it was that had made that noise behind her, reminded her that she still had a job to do. She reached into her skirt pocket and felt the small can. How was she supposed to give him the powder now? But then her eyes fell on the two glasses of red wine and a thought came to her.

"Robert, I want to go. Please put on your shirt and take me back inside."

Robert, not wanting to press Moira further, turned around and bent down to pick up the clothes he had carelessly thrown to the floor. Moira used that moment to pour the powder into his glass. When he turned to her again shortly thereafter, clothed, he took her face tenderly in his hands.

"I hope you are not too angry with me. I love you."

"I love you, too, Robert. It's been nice, but it's time for me to go home now."

"Let's at least have that glass of red wine together."

She agreed, and inwardly held her breath when she saw that the powder had dissolved and he emptied his glass. Now she was lying here on her bed and had a guilty conscience. She had told him that she loved him and yet she betrayed him. This had to come to an end. Abruptly she sat up. Dumfrey had said that Robert was in his way because he was doing some villainy in the bay and Robert had apparently somehow caught on to him. He couldn't be there tonight, but she had the opportunity. Maybe tonight was her chance to find out what was going on there. Firmly determined, she got up from the bed, took her cloak, sneaked out of the house and hurried away towards the bay.

Chapter 14

Fearfully, she flinched at every sound. She knew the way in and out, but in the darkness and at this time of night everything was different. Normally she was not particularly jumpy, but her inner tension was reason enough for it. Suddenly, a dancing light appeared in front of her and seemed to be approaching her.

Panic-stricken, she looked around. What should she do now? If these were the villains, they would see her in a moment. She did not have much time to look for a hiding place. The light had disappeared, but she knew that the path made a bend and if they kept the direction, they would reappear in front of her any second.

What was she to do? Under no circumstances did she want to run into the hands of those who were coming. Hastily she looked around and saw a large tree standing slightly to her right. If she huddled against it, she would be hidden behind it.

She was not yet two seconds behind the tree crouching when she heard voices and footsteps. What the scoundrels said, she couldn't understand, but she listened to the footsteps and was terribly frightened when she heard them close to her.

Moira held her breath. Don't make a mistake now, she thought to herself. Silently and with bated breath she crouched against the tree. She did not dare change her position, because any noise would have warned the men. Suddenly the voices stopped and small beads of sweat formed on her forehead. Unfortunately, she could not see anything from her position and it seemed too dangerous for her to look. Then she heard the footsteps moving away.

Relieved that she had not been discovered, she waited a few more seconds before she carefully rose from behind the tree. She was about to come out of hiding when a hand grabbed her and yanked her around. A scream escaped her.

"Miss Fergusson! What are you doing here?"

Surprised to see a woman here before him, the man held her with an iron grip.

"How do you know my name and how did you know I was here?" stuttered Moira as she realized that she had fallen into the hands of the criminals.

"It doesn't matter. The boss told us that something like this could happen and my feeling that we were being watched has never been wrong. He's not going to be thrilled about it when I report to him that you are spying on him. It would be better for you to keep your nose out of his business and now get up and go forward."

He pushed her rudely in front of him, until she reached the path. But if she now believed that he would release her so she could hurry home, she was mistaken. She saw in front of her the glow of light that seemed to be waiting in a few hundred yards, and wondered what was going on there. She couldn't see the man who had grabbed her in the darkness and now continued to push her along the path, but she was sure that she had heard the voice before. To figure out who he was she tried to make him talk.

"What's going on here, anyway?"

"None of your business," he growled.

"And what's going to happen to me?"

"You will know soon enough. Now shut up and see that you keep moving forward. I don't have all night to worry about your chatter."

Moira resigned herself to her fate and continued on her way in silence. Even though he was more rude to her today, she was sure that the man behind her was the coachman of Sir Dumfrey. Just as she was wondering what the realization now brought her, they reached the gang, who were already busy with loading a cart with barrels. So that was it. Here Dumfrey was smuggling some barrels ashore. How long has he been doing this? "Hey, who do we have here?"

One of the smugglers had left the group and was now approaching her. Just as he tried to touch her with his hand on her chin, with Moira wanting to retreat in disgust, he was rudely pushed back.

"Make sure you finish. We've been held up long enough."

"It's all right. We're done, boss. Everything's loaded," the man replied, trying to diffuse the situation.

"Good," replied Dumfrey's coachman, turning to Moira.

"If I am to give you any good advice, go home and forget what you have seen today. It would be better for your well-being."

Thereupon he passed her and left her in the darkness behind. The men, however, all climbed onto the carts and continued along the road. Moira did not dare move and looked at the ever-shrinking cart until it disappeared from her sight. Such bad luck. This evening had not gone at all as she thought it would. While she now knew what was going on, unfortunately, Dumfrey would also learn that she had not kept her end of the bargain and it did not make her position towards him any better. She would have to think carefully about her next step.

A good night's sleep was out of the question. Since Moira had gone to bed around two in the morning her thoughts had been wandering back and forth. She wondered if Dumfrey would do anything, now that he knew that she had not kept to the agreement. He had specifically warned her not to meddle in his affairs.

Had she put everyone in danger with her appearance tonight? Annoyed with herself, she had to admit to herself that she had been too dilettantish.

Full of worry about what he might be planning now, she had spent the rest of the night tossing and turning and was glad when the morning dawned and she could finally get up. During the morning hours she had been able to distract herself with work, but when it was afternoon, her restlessness was so great that she could not shake the feeling off that something was wrong.

She had expected to receive a letter from Sir Charles today, asking her to meet again, but even the realization that this was not the case did not reassure her. Robert had not yet shown his face today either. He rode by almost every day to steal a kiss.

Was it perhaps that, which made her worry? Towards late afternoon she could stand it no longer and ran over to the castle. Was she mistaken, or were the residents looking at her strangely today.

Moira was friendly as she passed the gardeners, maids and stable boys, but something was not right. She could literally sense it. It seemed to her as if they all knew about what she had done yesterday.

That she had poured a sleeping powder into their master's wine. Moira closed her eyes briefly and scolded herself for being a fool. It was only her guilty conscience that was bothering her.

She hurried up the stairs and pulled the doorbell. After

what felt like an eternity, the door opened and Albert appeared. He looked tired.

"Oh, Miss Fergusson, I'm sorry, but his lordship cannot see you today."

"Isn't he in?"

"Yes, he is, but he is indisposed."

"What's the matter with him?"

"We're at a loss. Gwyneth is already reproaching herself, for it seems he ate something that didn't agree with him. You had dinner with him last night, didn't you? Did he perhaps ingest something that you did not eat? You're feeling well, aren't you?"

"Yes, I'm fine and I don't understand. What did he have, exactly?"

"He can't keep food or drink down and he has chills and an elevated temperature. We have already called the doctor, but he couldn't find anything either and has only prescribed strict bed rest."

"My goodness, that sounds bad. How can I help? I don't understand it at all. After all, we ate the same thing. It can't be the food. Maybe I should check on him? Can I talk to him?"

"I'm sorry, but he's just fallen asleep and the doctor said that he should have rest at all costs. I would hate to wake him up. But I can let you know when he is feeling better."

"Yes please do Albert. I'm very worried. I will check on him again tomorrow if it's all right and tell him that I was here."

"Of course."

Just as Albert was about to close the door, Moira thought of something else.

"Oh, Albert. Do you think his lordship would mind if I borrowed his carriage for a while? I've got a few errands to run and it would be much easier with a carriage."

"I guess that's all right, since you'll soon be mistress here yourself. Tell Samuel, he will prepare it for you."

"Thank you and please let me know immediately, if there is any change in his condition."

At the stables, she met Samuel, who had just treated an injury of one of the workhorses. When he saw Moira coming down the aisle he paused in his work and rose.

"Moira, what a surprise. Have you heard the bad news yet?"

"That Robert is sick? Yes."

"You're all right, though? Albert thinks it might have been the food."

"I don't think so. We ate and drank the same thing yesterday and I have had no problems with it. He must have caught something. I just hope he recovers quickly, I'm very worried."

"Yes, I hope so too. It's all quite strange."

"Samuel, can you get Robert's carriage ready? I was going to borrow it, because I have to run a few errands. Albert said that would be all right."

"Sure, I'm sure Robert won't mind. Wait outside, I'll bring it right over."

"Thanks."

She then went back outside and waited impatiently for Samuel to drive up in the little buggy. What on earth had happened? Why was Robert suddenly feeling so bad? Could it have something to do with the sleeping powder she had given him?

It was the only thing she could think of that only he had ingested. She hoped that she was not to blame for his condition, and she wanted to get some clarity.

It was time to talk to Charles Dumfrey. When the carriage pulled up a little later, she did not waste another minute, but climbed aboard and trotted the horse. Her path led her directly to Dumfrey's estate. Even if he had not allowed her to visit him, she had to speak to him. His mansion was a good half-hour in the opposite direction from the village. The long driveway, lined with old trees, was deserted. Here no one was working outside in the garden. Nor did he have any animals that needed to be cared for. What Dumfrey did for a living was not widely known.

It was generally assumed that he was born rich and managed his fortune well. As Moira approached the house, her trepidation grew. The dark walls with their pointed towers looked more like a castle than a manor house, and in the late afternoon hour casting wide shadows ahead.

A dark raven flew close over her as she stopped in front of the house. That's fitting, Moira thought to herself as she stepped down from the buggy. She looked around and then climbed the five steps to the front door. This place, like its owner, exuded something threatening. "What are you doing here? Didn't I tell you that I never want to see you here?"

Dumfrey angrily pulled Moira into his writing room, pushed her rudely inside and closed the door behind them. Moira, who had lost her courage a little at first, now straightened her shoulders and turned around angrily.

"I need to talk to you and I need to now."

"Oho, are you giving the orders here now?"

He looked at her with amusement, folded his arms in front of his belly and leaned back against the door. Moira clenched her fists inwardly. He was such a creep, but she had to have certainty.

"Robert is in a very bad way and I want to know why."

He appraised her with his eyes.

"I suppose that's what happens, you don't feel well if you've ingested poison."

He let the words pass his lips. Poison? What poison? Gradually Moira seemed to understand, because he could literally see how her thoughts began to circle and how the color slowly drained from her face. This sight alone had been worth the whole thing.

She reproached herself. God, his plan had been ingenious. Self-satisfied, he looked at her. Now she was his and would be at his mercy forever and ever. What did it matter now that she knew what he was doing in the bay. She could do nothing with this knowledge without delivering herself to the knife.

"What, what have you done?" came from Moira's mouth, who was beginning to understand what had happened.

"I didn't do anything. YOU gave him the powder."

"You made me believe that it was a sleeping powder and that nothing would happen to him."

Moira's voice seemed to roll over as she half leaned on him in a hysterical voice.

"What a monster you are."

She slammed both her fists into his chest as hard as she could, but in her desperation and the tears that were now running down her cheeks, it was easy for him to grab her and hold her tight.

"Stop it! You have nothing to fear yet. You just have to go on as before and no one will ever know anything. The dose was not very strong and he will survive. I just had to get your absolute cooperation, and I have it now."

With a jerk, she pulled away from his grip and would almost have fallen over backwards if she had not found a foothold at the last moment.

"What was it?"

"Arsenic."

Shaking her head and not knowing what happened to her, she heard herself ask.

"You made me a poisoner, why? What have I done to you that you would do this to me?"

"I needed your cooperation, and lately I've had the feeling that you didn't really want to hear me. So I resorted to a measure that would give me your full attention. I have learned that you were at the cove last night. Didn't I tell you to stay out of my affairs? And did you? No. But it will not do you any good. You are now a criminal and if anyone should ever find out that you tried to poison your fiancé, the rope is waiting for you. You can see for yourself that it is only to your advantage that no one finds out about it. So go ahead and marry him and wait for new instructions from me and until then, don't show your face here again."

"I can't marry him. How can I ever look him in the eye again? I can't be with him. I just can't, and what good will it do you by me marrying him?"

"You can and you will marry him, or you will lose your head faster than you like. And I warn you, do not think that his love for you will be enough to forgive you for this deed. If he finds out, he will hand you over to the authorities. He is a proud and truthful man."

"What kind of devil are you?"

"I can live well with that appellation. Go now and leave me alone."

Without another word and with a bowed head Moira left his estate. What had she done? She had almost become a murderer. Why hadn't she asked Robert for help from the beginning. Now it was too late. Now he could never know. How could she face him again? How was she ever going to love anyone again? What if Robert died because of what she had done? Dumfrey had said that he would not die, but he had lied about many other things as well. She looked up at the sky. Quietly she turned to God.

"I am ready for my punishment, but please don't let Robert die."

Chapter 15

He didn't know if it was day or night. Rain pattered against the windows from outside, and the room was in darkness. No light penetrated through the closed curtains from the outside, only in the fireplace burned a small fire and threw a narrow light beam on the floor. It was the first time in a long time that he woke up and did not feel like throwing up.

Slowly he realized that he was in his own room. The large mahogany bed with the four posts stood in the middle of his bedchamber, on a small pedestal. Opposite was the fireplace, whose fire slowly threatened to go out. He felt warm and slipped the white sheet off his legs. Dressed in his undergarment only, he lay in his bed. Someone must have undressed him, because he could not remember doing it himself.

What had happened? Never in his life had he felt so ill. Even now he had no real impetus to get out of bed, but his mouth was dry and his lips were chapped. He was thirsty. Carefully he tried to get up and swung his legs over the edge of the bed. Immediately, a queasy feeling set in, admonishing him to slow down.

With deliberation he pushed his upper body off the bed, but as he was about to take the first step off the pedestal, his eyes went black and his legs buckled. At the moment of the fall, he looked for support on his nightstand, but his weight knocked it over and he fell to the floor along with the oil lamp that had been standing on it. Quick steps hurried down the hall and his door was pulled open. With a horrified look Alfred looked at him, as he tried to get up again, which he could not do without help.

Albert rushed toward him.

"My lord. You must not get up yet."

Albert grabbed Robert under the arms and lifted him up again so that he was standing on his feet. Slowly he sat him back on the edge of the bed. While he fluffed the pillows and placed them against the headboard, he watched Robert closely. His face was ashen. He looked like his death.

"Come on, get back in bed. You are still too weak to get up. Are you feeling a little better?"

He rested Roberts body in the pillows and covered him with the white sheet again.

"I'm terribly thirsty."

"That's good. I'll get you something in a minute. How's your stomach? Still feeling unwell?"

"No. I feel weak and worn out, but I don't feel sick anymore. Only thirsty I am."

"I'll go get you something. Please stay in bed."

When Albert returned a little later with a large glass of cool water, a little bit of color had returned to his face. With shaky hands, Robert held the glass of water in front of his mouth and before he could spill any of it, Albert supported him as he drank.

"Just take small sips, Sir. Don't let your stomach rebel again."

But Robert drank hastily like one dying of thirst. Then he leaned back into the cushions, exhausted.

"What time is it?"

The butler picked up the oil lamp from the floor and placed it back on the nightstand, where he had put the water glass so that Robert would have it handy next to him and said, "It's almost six o'clock in the evening, Mylord. You should try to go back to sleep. The rest will do you good."

"How long have I been lying here?"

"Almost three days. Gwyneth blamed herself in the worst way that something was wrong with the food. I'm about to give her the good news, that you're a little better. Also Miss Fergusson has…"

"Moira was here? Did she see me in this state?"

"No, sir. I did not let her see you. We didn't know what was wrong with you. She just came by several times a day, and inquired about your condition. We were all greatly concerned for you. Would you like to have anything else? If not, I'll leave the bell here."

Relieved that Moira had not seen him in his miserable condition, he realized again how weak he felt.

"Are you hungry, Sir?"

"No, right now I'm just thirsty."

"Then finish the glass and after that you should continue to rest. Your body needs to regain its strength. I will check on you later. Shall I put on some more wood?"

"It's warm enough. Thank you Albert. I have to talk to Samuel. Please send him to see me."

"Shouldn't you wait until tomorrow? You'll feel a little better then."

"No. I've been out of action long enough and I need to see him urgently. Send him up to me, please."

"Very well."

Later, when Samuel knocked at the door, Robert had already dozed off, but the sound of the door opening woke him up again.

"Oh, did I wake you up? I can come back later."

"No, that's all right. Come on in, I need to talk to you."

Samuel came closer and stopped at the foot of the bed.

"You look awful and should get some rest a while

131

longer. Every walking corpse looks better. If Moira sees you like this, she'll run away from you. The poor thing is completely beside herself, since she found out about you. She seems to hold herself responsible for your condition. Every day she comes here several times to inquire about you."

"Thank you for the pep talk. He who has the damage doesn't have to worry about the ridicule, does he?", returned Robert sardonically to Samuel.

"You'd better tell me how, during the last two days, the work has been going on. How are the mares doing, and were the sales negotiations that should have taken place yesterday postponed?"

"Everything is fine. The mares are ok. One of the workhorses got hurt on one of the fences. It's in the barn now, it's been patched up and the spot on the fence has been repaired. The negotiations took place yesterday. I think that I have concluded it in your interest. Lord Bratley's administrator bought the two breeding bulls and immediately looked at two more that he also wants. He will be in touch with you when you are back on your feet."

Acknowledging, Robert nodded. He had known that he had a capable collaborator in Samuel and thus replied:

"You've done well. It seems to me that I am completely superfluous."

"Well, I can manage without you for a few more days, but then you should help out again."

Samuel joked.

"Seriously. You should take it easy now. That was not just a little indigestion, and it doesn't help anyone if you get up too early. You don't have to worry, I've got everything under control and now I can ask you, if any problems arise."

"Thank you Samuel, I knew I could count on you. I'd like to give you a raise and give you a piece of land to build a house on. I've had it in mind for a while and wanted to tell you, but somehow it was never the right opportunity. Also, I have to tell you that the other day I involuntarily witnessed a conversation between you and Eileen. I know how much you would like to marry her and I hope that it is possible now. I am so happy and grateful that I found Moira and I would like to facilitate the happiness of others if it is in my power to do so."

Samuel couldn't believe what he was hearing.

"Are you serious?"

"I don't joke about such things. The raise takes effect this month, and when I get back in the saddle, I'll show you that piece of land I have in mind for you."

"I don't even know what to say. No one has ever done anything like this for me before. Eileen's going to be in for a real treat when I finally get to ask her that long-awaited proposal of marriage. Thank you, Robert. Thank you so much. You should get some more rest now and above all, take good care of yourself."

"What do you mean?"

"It's just a feeling. The way you've drained the life out of your body in the last few days. It has nothing to do with an upset stomach or bad food, in my opinion. It reminded me much of your uncle's last days. The symptoms were the same. Maybe you just handled it better than he did. Think about it."

Two days later, he was on his feet again for a few hours. Although he was still not fully recovered, with the diet that Gwyneth had cooked for him and the light exercise in the fresh air that he had been prescribed for himself, things were visibly better. His stomach, which was still rebelling a little after the first solid food intake, no longer caused any problems and day by day he would regain his old condition.

Yesterday afternoon he had seen Moira again for the first time. He had received her in his small reading room and had been totally surprised when she had fallen sobbing into his arms.

"It's all good again, Moira. You don't have to cry," he had wanted to reassure her. But it had taken quite a while and several kisses before she was actually reassured that everything would be all right again.

"I almost couldn't stand it because of worry. All Albert kept telling me was that there was no improvement. I'm sorry, Robert, but I didn't mean for this to happen."

"What are you talking about," he tried to calm her down.

"You can't help it. Who knows what I caught. It's just good that you didn't get it, too.You know, weeds don't die."

Grinning, he clasped her chin and gave her such a passionate kiss that her head buzzed.

"Let's talk about something else now instead. The wedding is two weeks away and I'm counting the days."

"Do you really think you'll be fully recovered by then? Or would you rather postpone it?"

"Postpone? Under no circumstances am I going to wait any longer for you to finally become my wife, even if they have to drag me into the church on a stretcher. The date is fixed. You'll see, by then I'll be back to my old self."

And he was. The day before his wedding the guests arrived and in the evening there was a reception, that was held in honor of the bride. Since it was already the end of May, spring flowers were blooming in the garden and the weather allowed them to set up tables and benches outside to welcome the party there.

Small lanterns hung from the trees and flower garlands decorated the paths. A small band played soft music and everywhere there was laughter and joking. It was a relaxed atmosphere, but this mood could not hide the fact that each of them had been worried about the illness that Robert had overcome. He had to confirm, more than once that evening, that he had returned to his old strength.

Moira had tried to push all this into the background in the last few days, but with the curious questions of the guests, everything came back to her. She had also been glad that Sir Dumfrey was not among the guests, and yet she could not shake the feeling that she was under observation. Someone in Robert's household had to be his informant, but who was it?

She had been willing to confess to Robert the day she saw him in his reading room. If he had continued to ask her questions that day about her remark, which she had made by mistake, then she would have told him the truth. But she had not mustered the courage to do so herself. Tomorrow she would become his wife and move into this house.

How beautiful everything could be, if not for the lie between them. Maybe Dumfrey was right. As long as he didn't find out about it, everything would be wonderful. He was the most loving man she knew, and she would be happy with him.

Chapter 16

A storm, such as Scotland had not seen for a long time, swept over the country during the night and left a trail of devastation in its wake. The next morning, Moira cast a horrified look out into her front yard.

Was this to be taken as a bad omen? It was supposed to be the most beautiful day for both of them and now it looked horrific outside. Everywhere were broken branches and twigs in the beds and on the lawn. Leaves had been torn from the trees and covered the paths. Yesterday evening they had celebrated in the garden of the castle in beautiful weather.

What would the garden look like now. Although the wedding was to take place in the ballroom and they were therefore independent of the weather, still one wished for such a day with the brightest sunshine. She felt as if her wedding was not under a good star and that God had already sent his gloomy harbingers to earth. Eileen looked in at the door.

"Moira, it's time to get ready. Robert's coachman will pick you up in two hours and we still have to do your hair."

"Oh Eileen, look what the weather has done outside. Did it have to be such a storm last night of all nights? The paths are soaked and everything is wet. The guests can't use the garden. It is a disaster."

"Yes, it's mean, but don't take it so hard. Everything

went great last night and today everything is planned in the castle anyway. The priest is coming to the little chapel and and I think Robert will have taken care of it: you'll get from there to the castle. Everything else does not depend on the weather.

You will see, it will be a beautiful wedding and now we'll make you pretty for Robert. Cheer up and who knows, maybe the sky will clear up."
Encouragingly, she nudged Moira in the shoulder. Moira began to smile and gained new hope.
"You're right. We won't let a little wind like that spoil the beautiful day. Let's go."

Robert had ridden out with Samuel in the early morning hours, before everyone else was awake, to inspect the first damage of the pastures and fields. Although he had experienced such violent weather changes in his homeland, it annoyed him very much, since God knows he had other things to do on his wedding day.

The house was full of his guests and actually he needed to take care of them. But he was also responsible for a lot of people and animals on his land and this had priority now. In the afternoon, however, he stood punctually dressed in black pantaloons, an elegant black tailcoat and his full plaid, which was thrown over his shoulder and hat a pattern in the colors of his clan, in front of the chapel of the castle.

He was waiting impatiently for his carriage, which was sent to pick up Moira at her home. While he nervously paced around outside, the voices of his crowd of guests drifted out to him. They all were waiting for the bride. Then she came and behind her a cart loaded with the children, all dressed in Sunday best. Robert had to smile. Even on her wedding day she could not be without her protégés.

The carriage stopped, and immediately he helped his bride and Eileen out. Eileen gave a wave to the children who spread out on two sides behind Moira to carry the long train of her dress. She looked gorgeous in her glamorous wedding dress. The tight top and the skirt accentuated her narrow waist.

A wide collar which was lined with small pink florets, fell loosely over her bare shoulders. A matching ribbon was tied around her waist and the ends of it fell over the whole train. The florets and the ribbon were the only color accents that she had set, otherwise she was all dressed in white. Eileen had her hair artfully pinned up and a veil covered her face. Robert grabbed her hand, which was in white long gloves.
"You look breathtaking and now I can hardly wait to get you out of all these clothes tonight."

Mischievously, he winked at Moira and saw the blush rise to her face. He squeezed her hand, for he noticed how suddenly unsteady she was.
"Nervous?"
She just nodded.
"Me too. Are you ready?"
Again she nodded and squeezed his hand a little tighter.
"Good, let's go."

It was a beautiful wedding ceremony and when the priest had taken the couple's vows and pronounced them husband and wife, the wedding party let the young couple celebrate.The celebration that followed, began with a sumptuous dinner in which Gwyneth and her maids had displayed truly masterful cooking skills. The small band, from the day before, played for the dance and the hours passed quickly. When the bride and groom retired well after midnight only a handful of guests were left in the hall. Robert led the beaming bride up the stairs to his bedchamber. At the door, he paused briefly and suddenly took her in his arms, which she acknowledged with an astonished laugh. Robert, however, gave her a fleeting kiss and replied, "It is the custom to carry the bride over the threshold."

Thereupon he pushed the door open with his foot and carried her inside. Slowly he let her slide down his body, which he visibly enjoyed, then he closed the door behind him. Finally he was alone with her. The whole evening he had thought of nothing else.

She was now his wife and from now on she would share his bed every night. Every morning she would be the first thing he would see and he was sure he would never get tired of the sight of her.

Moira, however, had gone quiet, she seemed tense. It was the first time that she had entered his bedchamber. Nervously, she looked around and her gaze lingered on the large, dark bed which dominated the room. The interior was absolutely masculine, she thought, it was kept dark and nowhere could she see that a woman had left her feminine features within these walls.

In time, perhaps, she would give the room a different touch, but now she worried more about what Robert would do. What was a wife supposed to do? He seemed to have noticed that she had become quieter and quieter, because he tenderly stroked her cheek, took her by the hand and led her to the small seating area by the fireplace, where there was a small table with a bottle of champagne and two glasses, waiting for them. He poured them both and then handed her a glass.

"Finally we are alone. The whole evening I wanted to toast with you without being interrupted - to your health

Lady MacIntyre."

He toasted her and watched her take a sip, too, then he put down his glass and pulled her into his arms. His lips were soft as they closed her mouth. Tenderly, he nibbled on her lower lip until Moira gave up her resistance and opened her lips a little.

She snuggled tightly against him. He tasted of the champagne he had just drunk and she noticed how his kisses became more demanding and passionate. A warmth rose in her, but she couldn't quite tell if it was from the champagne or if it was Robert's presence.
She didn't care either way. Everything seemed so easy to her that she simply let herself fall and thus handed over the lead to him. But Robert was not in a hurry, after all, they had the whole night ahead of them.Slowly he pulled the pins out of her hair and ran his fingers through it. Her brown, wavy hair fell over her shoulders.

In the light of the fireplace her eyes sparkled like little emeralds. Passion flared up in him and so he quickly got rid of his tailcoat and vest and threw the clothes heedlessly over the back of the nearest chair. With a quick grip, he grasped Moira's waist, pulled her close to him and began to slide his mouth over her body. He kissed her forehead and cheeks, her neck and collarbone. Again and again he paused briefly and watched his wife.

His wife - the word sounded strange and yet so good. Moira, on the other hand, had her eyes closed and purred in his arms like a little kitten. He felt his desire growing stronger and stronger. Tonight they would continue where they had left off back at the pond and the very idea of it made him moan. Without stopping his caresses, he fiddled with his fingers at the fastening of her dress, until he had loosened the small hooks and the dress slowly fell to the floor.

With nimble fingers he pulled the ribbons from

the corsage, so that it too slipped down, then he carried Moira over to the bed, where he laid her gently onto the soft sheets. He knew he had to proceed slowly and carefully if he did not want to frighten her, but the sight of his young wife lying on his bed in heralmost transparent underwear, and looking at him nervously with big green eyes, demanded an immense restraint from him.

"Moira, you are so beautiful. I love you."

Without taking his eyes off her, he brushed off his shoes and laid down on his side next to her. At length he looked at her. Her petite figure with a narrow waist lay stiffly on the white sheet. Her firm breasts rose and fell and her breathing was intermittent. She was so innocent and had no clue about what the sight of her was doing to him.

Smiling, he let his eyes roam over her body. Her slender legs were encased in long white stockings attached to a waist band and inwardly he pictured how he was about to free her from all those obstructive garments. His blood began to boil and he felt himself getting hard at the thought. He would have liked to tear the pieces off her body, but only an amateur would do such a thing to his inexperienced wife. He wanted her to enjoy the act as well and that required all his restraint at the moment. Moira seemed to misinterpret the silence between them, because in an uncertain voice she turned to him:

"Don't you like me? I know I'm not exactly well-built."

"Don't like you? God, Moira, you're the most stunning woman I've ever met. The sight of you drives me crazy and I want to hold you in my arms forever and love you. Don't be afraid. Let me show you tonight what love means."

He tenderly caressed her cheek and kissed her passionately on the mouth. Spontaneously she put her arms around his neck and pulled him half on top of her. She felt his hard muscles against her breasts and his touch made her shiver. The blood pulsed in her veins, she pulled him even closer to her and let her hands slide over his back.

The coolness of his shirt was a great contrast to the heat that was rising in her, and growing bolder, she pulled the ends out of his Pants and let her fingers rest on his skin. Moira's hands on his skin brought Robert's blood to such a boil that he gave up his restraint and boldly slipped his hands under her chemise to cup her breasts.

Moira gasped and dug her fingers into his flesh. Her passion was further stoked when he began to play with the hard bud. As he changed his position a bit and took off her chemise over her head, she drew in her air heavily. Robert, on the other hand, tore off his own shirt in such a way that the buttons popped off and scattered around the room.

He had to laugh so hard at his wife's horrified face that for a moment it was difficult for him not to pounce on her immediately. She was so delightfully innocent, but after this night she would know what fun they could have together and so he closed her mouth with a kiss before she could make a remark. But Moira was no longer being reserved. She had admired his upper body at the pond and now she let her eyes roam over his chest appreciatively.

With her fingers she traced the contours of his muscles, which nearly drove Robert out of his mind. It was hard for him to keep still, but he let her do it. Moira's gaze slowly slid down to the point that was pulsating strongly. Robert began to sweat. She had no idea what her looks did to him. Slowly he bent over her and buried her body with his.

His weight pressed her into the soft mattress. Teasingly, he ran his hand along her thigh until he touched her most intimate place. Moira clung to him and called his name. She had never experienced such feelings. Only vaguely she remembered how Robert took off the last of her clothes before she lay completely naked under him. Ashamed of her nakedness, she closed her eyes.

"Moira, look at me. You are so beautiful."

Slowly she opened her green eyes, which were now dark with passion.

"Robert, I can't do this."

He grabbed her hand and placed it on his chest.

"Can you feel my heartbeat?"

Speechless and surprised at how wildly his heart was beating, she just nodded.

"That's you! You're driving me crazy, and my body is craving you. Let me make love to you tonight. Trust me."

Without another word he took possession of her mouth and kissed her so passionately that Moira forgot to be scared. His hand touched the sensitive spot again and it didn't take long until Moira's body was jerking wildly under him. But Moira could not think clearly anymore and no longer wanted to. The feelings she was experiencing right now were the most beautiful she had ever felt. She no longer wanted him to stop, on the contrary, there was something that demanded more, and so she instinctively bent toward him.

Robert knew that she was ready for him. He quickly removed the rest of his clothes and carefully penetrated her. Moira moaned and so he remained motionless for a moment, so that her body could get used to him. Just as Moira was about to say something, he pushed his body deeper inside. A sharp pain ran through her body.

She cried out and a small tear ran down her cheek. Tenderly he kissed it away before he slowly began to move inside her with a rhythm. The initial pain was quickly forgotten and she had the feeling of floating. Something indescribably beautiful inside her became stronger and stronger and when she thought she could no longer stand it, her body exploded wildly jerking under him. In their ecstasy they climaxed together.

She called his name, curled her fingers into his flesh, and let the tremors of her body subside until she fell back exhausted into the sheets. Robert, on the other hand, still breathing heavily lying on top of her, rolled to the side and pulled her into his arms. Exhausted, but happy, she let her head rest on his chest and played dreamily with his chest hair.

She listened to his gradually calming heartbeat. My goodness, she had had no idea what wonderful feelings he could evoke in her.

Would it always be like this?

"You're so quiet, is something bothering you?"

Uncertainty was in Robert's voice. He hadn't exactly been restrained at the end and should have been more considerate the first time. Moira had responded so passionately to his touch, that his good intentions had been over. Now he feared that she might be in pain.

"I'm sorry if I hurt you, but it's only the first time."

Moira looked up and looked into those eyes that looked at her with love and concern at the same time.

"Will it always be like this?"

Embarrassed at having apparently caused her great pain after all, he quickly assured her, "No, it only hurts once."

"That's not what I mean. I don't have any pain. I wanted to know if it would always be this nice. That feeling, it was indescribable."

Relieved, he smiled at her and replied, "It will get even better."

Incredulous, she looked down at him and in Robert the fire awoke again. How did his wife manage to bring him to ecstasy with only a look?

"Can I feel it again?"

"Heavens, you are a little glutton – I love you."

Smiling mischievously, he added, "Give me a moment and then we'll see."

Moira laid her head on his chest again and let her fingers playfully wander over his body. Thereby she came dangerously close. She felt him draw in his breath sharply and before she knew it, Robert had her with a nimble turn back into the pillows. The sound of shock from her mouth was immediately smothered with a heartfelt kiss. In an instant their passion for one another was rekindled and so they loved each other that night one more time.

Chapter 17

The gray gelding trotted joyfully in front of the buggy and moved swiftly along the deserted road.

The birds were chirping merrily in the trees and a few clouds passed by in the blue sky. It had become summer, the temperatures were quite high already in the early morning hours and the landscape was in full bloom. Lush green meadows, where her husband's cattle and sheep grazed, lined the path. The grain was thriving and the pregnant mares were getting fatter and would foal for the first time in a few months.

Moira's life had changed in the last few weeks since her wedding. She was now the mistress of Shepherds King and with that many new tasks had come her way.

Not only was she married and enjoying married life with Robert to the fullest, she was now in charge of the household and that had been a big adjustment for her. Robert had a whole court around him and it had not been easy for her at the beginning to find her way around his house.

But he had supported her in word and deed. In the early days, he had always been near her to help her when questions were asked about her wishes and changes. But except for lighter curtains and a dressing table with a mirror in the bedroom, she hadn't made any changes so far. Now she took a deep breath of the fresh air with relish and looked forward to the visit she was about to make.

"Eileen!"

Eileen looked up when she heard the voice. She was just outside with the children in the garden, weeding, when the little carriage pulled up in front of the house.

"Moira!"

Joyfully, the children and Eileen ran to meet their friend. The boys and girls welcomed Moira stormily.

"Oh how I have missed you all. Come here and let me hug you."

Moira pressed a big kiss on each of their foreheads. She understood only half of what the children were saying to her, because they were all talking at her at once. Laughing they jumped around in a circle.

"Eileen, I need you to free me. Help!,"

Moira joked, casting a pleading look over at her friend. But Eileen stood with her arms folded with an amused expression on her face slightly off to the side, watching the scene.

"No, no, no. That's the punishment for not showing your face for so long."

But she took pity on her friend and clapped her hands.

"All right kids, now let me say hello to Moira. Go play, we'll continue later."

With a loud roar, the group of children ran around the corner of the house. Moira had to laugh.

"I almost forgot how lively they can be."

Eileen and Moira hugged each other warmly.

"Yes, they can be quite exhausting at times. Come on, let's make a cup of tea and then you can tell me all about it. And I really mean everything."

With that, she nudged Moira knowingly in the arm, who rolled her eyes in amusement. A little bit later they were both sitting on the porch of the orphanage, watching the children playing and sipping the hot drink.

"Is everything okay with you here, Eileen? I feel so bad that I'm leaving you alone with all this work."

"You don't have to. Everything is well taken care of.

Robert has offered to help Samuel and me, but as long as we still live here it's a good solution after all."

"Really? Does Samuel feel the same way? He'd probably much rather live alone with you in the new house instead of having the kids around all the time. You know what I mean by that."

"Of course it would be nice if the house was finished and we could live there, but it will only take a few more weeks and then it will be ready. We are so grateful to Robert that he gave us this piece of land and is building us a house on it. Samuel is a little ashamed that we can never repay him."

"You don't need to do that. A gift is a gift and I think Robert knows what he has in Samuel. He appreciates your husband very much and I'm glad that Samuel took the opportunity to propose to you. You look well, Eileen. Married life seems to be treating you well."

"Yeah, I can't believe it's been two weeks since we were married. It all feels so nice and every morning, when I wake up, he's lying next to me. I can't believe he's there. But I always talk about me and Samuel, when I would much rather know how you are? You look exhausted. Robert shouldn't put so much strain on you. Everything's all right between you, isn't it?"

"Why, yes. The last few weeks have been the most beautiful I've ever experienced. Robert cares a lot about me and I feel his love for me every day. When he looks at me in the morning, beaming with his blue eyes, my heart opens. We try to spend every free minute together and I count the hours in between, until we meet again in the evening. I miss his closeness when he is busy during the day and I know that he often leaves work on the desk in the evening so that we can spend at least a few hours together. I should not complain and yet I wish that he had more time for me."

"He has large estates to manage, which is a lot of work. If you love him, you'll find a way to free up time for yourselves. It is also not easy for him to adjust. I think he feels the same way and I'm sure it's important to him that you are happy."

"I am, Eileen. I love him so much. I would give my life for him."

"Well I know, from personal experience, that the gentlemen can be a little too passionate at times, but he shouldn't put so much strain on you. You look a little pale. Are you really well?"

Concerned, Eileen looked at Moira. Was Robert overdoing it a little with his marital duties? Moira's face flushed and quickly she replied, "No, it's not that. I think I'm getting sick. I haven't told Robert about it yet, because I don't want him to worry, but for the last two weeks I have been constantly nauseous and have no real appetite. Sometimes I suddenly can't smell certain things and yesterday my eyes went black for a moment. Thank God no one has noticed this yet, but I'm starting to get a little bit scared."

"I think I can put your mind at ease on that. These are the same symptoms that a friend of mine described when she was pregnant."

Astonished, she looked at Eileen. She had never considered this possibility. She had only been married three months.

"You mean I could be pregnant?"

"I not only mean that, but I am almost convinced of it. You're having a baby."

"But, so soon? It can't be."

"Well, it doesn't take long, and I imagine Robert is a healthy husband and attends to you regularly."

Thoughts rolled over in Moira's mind. The initial shock slowly turned into fear of what was coming. How was she going to tell Robert? Should she tell him right away or wait a little longer until she was more sure that she was really pregnant? How would he react to that? They had never talked about children before. Eileen, who was watching her friend closely, could guess what was going on in her mind right now.

"He'll be happy, I'm sure of it. You're going to have a child, and that's the most beautiful thing you can crown your love with. Give yourself a few more days to get used to the idea, and then tell him. You'll see that he'll be happy to hear it."

Despondent, Moira said, "Do you really think so? I'm going to be a mother, I don't know if I can do it."

"Oh, Moira, if you can't do it, who can? You have kept up this house with all its children for the last few years, so you can do it easily. Believe me, everything will work itself out. I'm so happy for you."

She hugged her friend and the fear in Moira disappeared. She regained her old strength.

"You're right. I have to take care of the garden party this weekend. That is my baptism of fire as a hostess and after that I'll be ready for the things that are to come. You two are coming this weekend too, right?"

"I wouldn't miss the party for the world. and see you in action as Lady MacIntyre."

Laughing, they sat on the porch and drank their tea.

Satisfied, Moira looked around. Her first social assignment seemed to go well. The gardeners had implemented her wishes. Colorful lanterns hung down from the trees and bathed the neatly trimmed lawn beneath them in a warm light. Tables and chairs were

festively set and a long table was laden with the most
wonderful delicacies. There were pies, roast venison and
beef, salads, vegetables, casseroles, bread and many
dishes more. In addition to Scottish desserts, they had
also prepared cakes and petit fours. Proud of his perfect
little housewife, Robert took Moira in his arms and
kissed her passionately.

Somewhat embarrassed that the staff could see
her like this, she tried to keep him at a distance but she
was unsuccessful in doing so.

"Robert, don't. We are being watched."

"So what! Let everyone see how happy I am with you.
You've done well. Everything looks great. Come on, our
guests are arriving."

One hundred and twenty guests were expected this
evening and most of them came from the high and
landed gentry.

A few distinguished merchants and business
partners were present as well as Samuel with his wife,
who as administrator of Robert's estate, had the honor to
attend the feast. One by one the carriages drove up and
the couples were greeted by them. The women were all
dressed in the most beautiful robes, while the gentlemen
had mainly chosen the social black tailcoat, which in
some cases were worn by the clan chiefs with a plaid
over the shoulder.

Robert also had chosen his black tailcoat for this
evening and wore the plaid over his shoulder, which
was held by a clasp that showed the coat of arms of the
family. Moira, on the other hand, wore a ravishing
ensemble of a crinoline skirt in dark blue silk, which she
wore together with a dark green short-sleeved velvet
corsage and a red sash.

They were the colors of the MacIntyre clan.
They had already greeted most all the guests, when
Moira suddenly lost her breath. In front of her stood

Dumfrey and looked at her with a smile then he turned to Robert.

"Lord MacIntyre, it is an honor to attend your feast today."

"Sir Dumfrey, I am pleased that you have accepted my invitation. I need not introduce you to my wife."

"Lady MacIntyre, it is good to see you again."

She could not allow her annoyance to show, and forced herself to offer him her hand. Dumfrey accepted it and gave her a kiss on the hand, then he joined the other guests. Moira, however, found it difficult to concentrate on the rest of the guests. What did he want here? She had hoped that he would not bother her anymore. He had left her alone for months. That he now appeared again, could not mean anything good. Robert, sensing that something was wrong, whispered to her.

"What's wrong? Is there a problem?"

"Why is he here?

She pointed her head at Dumfrey. Robert followed her gaze and replied:

"Well, I invited him. He belongs to a number of distinguished businessmen and I thought you'd be pleased to have him here. After all he was a friend of your parents. Is something wrong?"

"No, everything is fine, I was just a little surprised to see him here."

She was a bad liar. Something was very wrong, he could feel it, but he couldn't dwell on it now, because the guests were waiting for him to open the party with a speech and so he left his wife's answer as it was and led her to the others in the garden.

Over and over again, she caught herself following what Dumfrey was doing that evening and who he was talking to. But nothing in his behavior indicated that he had another villainy in mind. He gallantly entertained the ladies and joked with them, while a little later he was engaged in a political debate with a group of gentlemen. Moira tried to relax.

Actually, this was supposed to be a cheerful, informal evening for her, but with him here, she could hardly keep her anxiety in check. She noticed that he was watching her closely. She could feel his eyes on her back when she tried to be a good hostess and talked boisterously with her guests.

How she wished that Robert knew about it and would expel him from the party. She had been able to suppress the memories of her deeds well in the last months, but now they all came out again and she felt sick. What was he up to? He was not here to have a good time, he had come to remind her of her sacrilegious deeds and that she was at his mercy. Moira noticed the nausea was increasing, she apologized to the ladies she had just been talking to and fled in the direction of the house. Just as she reached the steps to the terrace Dumfrey stood in her way.

"Where are you going in such a hurry Moira? You have so far done very well to avoid me this evening, but it won't do you any good."
"What are you doing here?"

"Why so rude? I am here because your husband invited me. I must say, I am proud of you. You took my adviceand didn't tell him. Very wise decision and that it will stay that way, that's why I'm here. I just wanted to make sure that you haven't forgotten me in all your marital bliss."
"Why don't you leave me alone? I'll be able to pay you back soon."
"Oh, are you now among the businessmen? Good for you, but I've already told you before that I don't care

about money anymore."

"I've done everything you asked."

"Well, we are far from finished with each other and you will continue to be at my disposal."

Desperation and anger welled up inside her. She wanted this to end. She loved her husband and with him the life she was now leading and under no circumstances did she want to put him in danger again.

"I will no longer lie to my husband and I will do nothing more for you. It's over, Sir Dumfrey."

Moira was about to hurry up the steps when he angrily held her back by the arm.

"Not so fast, my dear. We'll be through with each other when I tell you we will be and until then you will do as I command. Or do you want me to say here and now, in front of all these people what a criminal you are?"

Horrified, she gave up her resistance. Would he really accuse her of a crime? Here in front of all her guests?

"I think you understand me. Now go and powder your nose before you go back to playing the carefree and affectionate hostess again. Have a nice evening."

With that, he left her standing and walked away. Moira, on the other hand, dragged herself up the stairs and disappeared into the house.

Robert, who had been watching this scene from the other side of the garden while he was talking to his business partners, wondered. He recalled that he had witnessed a similar scene between the two of them the night he met Moira. Something was going on here.

All evening long she had given him the impression, as if something was bothering her. Just like on their first evening at the ball.

What was going on between Dumfrey and Moira? He thought about asking Moira directly, but then decided against it. Maybe she would tell him tonight what the scene was all about. But the night passed without Moira bringing up the conversation and he did not follow up.

Chapter 18

Something had awakened him. When he opened his eyes, it was still dark in the room. How late it might be, he did not know. He looked next to him and saw the empty side of the bed. Immediately he was wide awake and sat up.

Was that it? Had he woken up because Moira had left the bed? Where was she? He put on his robe and went barefoot to the bathroom. But it also was empty.

He could not say exactly why, but suddenly he had a bad feeling. He hurriedly ran out of the room and down the stairs. He searched the downstairs rooms and the kitchen, but he could not find her anywhere. When he glanced out of the window in his office, he couldn't believe his eyes. Moira was standing out there, barefoot and dressed only in her robe.

Quickly he hurried to the back door, circled the house in seconds and saw her standing in front of him in the darkness. She did not seem to have heard him, for she was terribly frightened when he gently put his hand on her shoulders.

"Moira, what are you doing out here?"

Gently, he turned her to face him and saw the tears on her face. She was trembling all over, and instinctively he picked her up and carried her back into the house. Without a word she snuggled tightly against his chest like a child. She seemed so fragile at that moment that Robert brought her back upstairs to the bedchamber where he carefully lowered her onto the bed and then sat down on the edge of the bed next to her.

"What's wrong Moira?" he asked gently. "Why are you crying? Did I do something wrong?"

She struggled with her tears. She didn't want him to see her like this. How was she supposed to explain to him what the reason was? It had been a terrible night.

At first she had not been able to fall asleep, because she had searched frantically for a solution. She had not found it and when she finally had fallen asleep, she had had terrible dreams. Dreams in which first Dumfrey and then she herself did bad things to Robert. She had woken up and felt the need to get some fresh air. How easy it would be if she could confide in him. He would know what to do, because she could always count on him. He was the strong shoulder on which she found new strength.

But she also had the words of Dumfrey buzzing in her ear, who had told her that if Robert ever found out, she would be dead to him and in danger of going to the gallows herself.

"Moira, please talk to me. What's wrong with you?"

In a voice choked with tears, she tried to form her words. "I'm sorry, I didn't mean to wake you. I had a bad dream."

"A nightmare? What was it?"

"If I did something that was worse than I was aware that it was, would you leave me? Stop loving me?"

"I don't understand what you mean. Why would you have done anything bad? Moira, you're scaring me. What's the matter? Does it have something to do with Dumfrey?"

"With Dumfrey?"

She was terrified. Did Robert suspect something?

"I saw you talking to him this evening, and it seemed to me that you were having a disagreement."

Relieved that he seemed to have no idea after all, she quickly added.

"No, there was nothing. I just got a little staggered and he grabbed my arm to support me. I just had a nightmare and needed fresh air, but I'm better now."

"Are you sure?"

"Yes absolutely, but maybe now is the right time to tell you something important. I've only known for a few days myself and I can't really believe it yet."

"What is it?"

"I'm having a baby."

Anxious to see his reaction, she looked him in his eyes and hoped to see the joy of the news there.

"Is it true? We're going to have a child? Moira, that is the most beautiful thing you could have told me. I love you!"

"Really? I was so nervous to tell you."

"I guess that's why the nightmare. My God, we're going to be parents."

Passionately he pulled her into his arms and kissed her. Relieved that the message about the pregnancy had pushed the other topic to the background, she pulled him down to her and returned his kisses with the same devotion. She snuggled up to him, because she had to make sure he wouldn't let her go.

Like a drowning woman, she clung to his body and arched toward him. Their bodies melted into each other and together they found fulfillment. The love they felt for each other tonight was worth doing everything in the world not to lose it. Even if it meant living with a lie for the rest of her life.

Robert sat dreamily at his desk. Actually, he had plenty of papers to sift through and correspondence to conduct, but he could hardly concentrate on his work today. His thoughts were constantly drifting to the past hours. It had probably been the most incredible night they had spent together in their short marriage.

After he had put Moira to bed again they had made love to the point of exhaustion. Moira had been more passionate than ever before. And now she was expecting a child - his child. He had nothing against children, quite the opposite, but that it was already happening so quickly was something he had to think about. Was he really ready to become a father?

Not that one could change it now, but he was still allowed to ask himself the question. He ran his hand through his hair and kneaded his neck. Boy oh boy, his parents would be happy to become grandparents, and he himself still had a little time to get used to the idea. It was something great coming their way.

Robert was called back to the present when there was a knock at the door.

"Come in."

Samuel appeared in the doorway and came straight towards him.

"Good morning Robert. Here are the papers, you asked to see."

"Thank you, have a seat. Did you get home okay yesterday?"

"Yes, thank you again for inviting us. It was a lovely party."

"Yes, it was. What I wanted to say. I hope it meets with your approval. I have agreed with Moira that when your house is finished and you've moved in, we'll hire a governess to live at the orphanage and take care of the children when Eileen is not there. We think it's a good solution for all concerned. What do you say?"

"I agree, and I'll share that with Eileen later. She's already thought about it, and I know it will reassure her. Do you know yet whether you will lease the fallow fields again to get the costs for the house or will you use them for breeding?"

"I had thought of leasing, for the same reason as you, but it is Moira's inheritance and she has to decide about it. However, we haven't had much opportunity to talk about such business matters lately."

Samuel grinned mischievously as he opined:

"Yes, I heard that. You don't waste any time do you?"

Robert leaned forward and addressed his opposite in Mock indignation.

"Who ever gave you permission to speak to me with such disrespect? The one should really be scolded, but you are right. How come you already know about it? No, don't tell me. I can guess who told you. Eileen, is it true?"

"That's right. Congratulations, too. It's great news."

Robert leaned back again, relaxed and propped his elbows on the armrest.

"I admit it scares me a little, about becoming a father."

"Hey, it'll be fine. I have eight siblings and all of them are older than me and have been married longer. With eight married couples, there's always a baby on it's way and I can tell you from experience of a large family, that it all works out. You'll see. Look forward to it."

"Yeah, you're probably right. Now something completely different. What do you know about Sir Dumfrey?"

"Not much, actually. He moved into the Fellow sisters' estate a few years ago. It's this kind of dark castle-like mansion on the other side of the village, heading north."

Robert nodded to show him that he knew which house he was talking about. Samuel continued with his explanation: "The two sisters were never married.

And six years ago the younger of the two died of pneumonia. When, then, I believe three or four years ago, the older one also died suddenly, Sir Dumfrey came here. As far as I know he is quite wealthy.

Where he got his money, whether by birth, inheritance or good business fortune, no one really knows. He has no land or any other business that he calls his own, but he still owns a townhouse in Edinburgh. Your uncle was at his ball just before he died. Why are you interested in Dumfrey?"

"He was here at the festival yesterday."

"Yes, I saw him."

"He was talking to Moira yesterday and it looked to me like she wasn't on good terms with him, so I wanted to know more about him."

"I can well imagine that about Moira; after all, Dumfrey has courted her since her parents died, and made quite a few proposals of marriage, which she has refused each time."

Robert sat up in amazement.

"Dumfrey was going to marry Moira? Do you know that about her?"

"No, Moira would never confide such a thing to me. Eileen told me that Sir Dumfrey often badgered Moira to say yes at last. He also wanted to support her financially, buy her lands or rebuild her childhood home, if she would marry him, but she refused each time until he finally understood that Moira would never marry him."

"She never told me that."

"I only know all this from Eileen, because she is her best friend and Eileen can't stand him. But that's all water under the bridge now. She's your wife now and unattainable for him. So," Samuel stood up," I'm going to get back to work. If you have time later on, you should come over to the stable and take a look at

Majestic's injury. You know better than I do and maybe you can tell me how we can cure it."

"I'll do that, see you later."

Samuel left the writing room, leaving a thoughtful Robert behind. Dumfrey had courted Moira. Why had she never mentioned him in a syllable? And if she didn't why had she appeared in his company at the ball? And how did the scene he had observed between the two of them last night fit in? He had not believed Moira's explanation. What was going on here?

Questions upon questions suddenly arose and he found no answers for them. Of course he could go up and ask Moira himself, but wouldn't he sound like a jealous husband? Besides, he couldn't shake the feeling that he wouldn't hear the truth from her on this subject. No, he would not say anything for now, but he would definitely keep an eye on things and try to get behind the secret.

When he thought about the secrets, he remembered a completely different story that he hadn't bothered about for a long time. It was time to address this smuggling issue as well. Soon it would be full moon again and this time he decided that, come what may, he would wait for the villains at the bay.

Chapter 19

"Robert? Are you here?"

"Yes, in the last stall."

Moira hurried down the stable alley, then stopped in horror in front of the open stall. She saw the pregnant mare lying in the straw, whinnying loudly in pain, and her hooves thickly wrapped with cloth and loosely tied. Samuel knelt by the mare's neck and patted it, while he soothed her. Robert, on the other hand, the hind legs of a foal still in its mother's body in his hands and pulled on them.

Breathless with effort, Robert called out to her:"

"Moira, you shouldn't be here."

"My God, isn't there anything I can do to help?"

"Get some hot water, it's over there in the kettle. The foal is stuck upside down and I'm trying to pull it out before the mother dies."

Moira hurried over to the corner, where a kettle with warm water was ready and filled a large bucket with it. Regardless of her and her circumstance, she lifted the heavy bucket and carried it over to the box. Robert struggled, with each squeezing contraction, to pull the foal further out, but it did not look good.

The mare was getting visibly weaker and the foal was still too far in the belly of the mother. Moira could only helplessly watch as her husband tried with all his strength to save the animal. He cursed angrily to himself and it would have been better if she had covered her ears, because the words he uttered in his desperation were not meant for the ears of a lady. But Moira was at the same time horrified and fascinated by what was happening. She had never watched a birth before.

She suffered with the mare and when she thought all was lost, Robert managed to get the butt out with a last powerful jerk. Then it took only one more contraction and he could pull the little slippery foal out of the mother's body. For a while, none of them said anything. Robert had crashed against the back wall of the barn with the last jerk, together with the foal, and was just getting himself up again when Samuel and Moira came to his aid.

The little foal was sticky and wet and could not yet stand up, but it was alive. Even the mother seemed to understand that it was over, because she lifted her head and looked for her little one.

"Oh Robert, you did it. You saved her."

Moira threw herself into Robert's arms as he stood up and rose. Tears of joy ran down her face.

"Look, I'm dirty and sweaty and..."

"I don't care. You earned this one."

With that, she pressed a long kiss on his lips and Robert returned it passionately. Samuel's clearing of his throat brought them both back again and so Robert detached himself from Moira's embrace and began to examine both animals.

"Rub the foal well with straw. I'm going to take the mother's fetlocks and then we have to hope that the foal, as well as the mother, stand up. Only then did we make it."

A few minutes later, when all three of them were standing in the box, it was the mare that was the first to try to get up. Robert held his breath. He knew this was the moment of truth, whether the mare would make it or not and whether she would accept her foal. It took the mare three tries before she was back on her feet again and began to lick her foal. Moira's heart soared at this scene. She could literally feel the mare's motherly love for her newborn and again tears came to her eyes.

Then the mother nudged her little one encouragingly and after several awkward attempts the little foal stood on wobbly legs for the first time. Robert exhaled audibly.

"That was close, but we made it. Let's leave these two alone for a while, so they can get to know each other."

Samuel, who had never experienced such a difficult birth, patted Robert on the back appreciatively.

"How lucky you are to know so well. I would have been totally overwhelmed."

"I've only done that twice, too, having a foal situated upside down. This is the first time mother and foal did it together. Hope that the other foals will be born normally. Please put in some fresh straw so that they are well bedded. I'm going to go over and freshen up, then I'll be back. Come on Moira, you don't have to cry anymore. It's over."

Robert took his distraught wife in his arms to calm her down and then led her out of the stable.

"These are tears of joy. That was incredible and the little foal, so cute to look at, lying there in the straw. That was a masterstroke. I love you."

"Mhm, how much?"

"What do you mean?"

"How much do you love me? I think I deserve a reward and you could show me how much you love me." With feigned indignation, she stood up in front of him and dug her finger into his chest.

"Lord MacIntyre, you are a very bad one, and I can't disappear in broad daylight with you into the bedchamber. I wonder what the others will think."

Robert hurried into the house with the laughing Moira by the hand.
"We're married, remember?"

Albert was packing his master's valise when Robert entered his bedchamber.
"Shall I pack your evening suit as well, sir?"
"Yes, that would be good. That way I'll be prepared in case things should go ahead a little more formally after all."
"How long will you be gone, and will my lady accompany you?"
"My wife will not be going. It is a business meeting, and she would only be bored. If everything goes to my satisfaction I will be back in five days."
"Do you really want to go by horse instead of taking your carriage? Wouldn't it be more comfortable that way?"
"Oh Albert, I appreciate that you want to make a real lord out of me, but I'm an outdoors-man and I like to get around on horseback. The carriage I leave to the ladies or the older gentlemen. The horse has clear advantages, because I can ride cross-country, and it saves me a lot of time."
"Then I'll have Gwyneth prepare a good bag of provisions for you, Sir."
"I won't say no to that."
When Robert came to the stable the next morning to fetch his horse, he was wearing the riding clothes that he had worn on his long ride through the American wilderness. It was more comfortable and sturdy than the European pantaloons. Under his jacket he wore around his waist his old gun belt. He had not carried a weapon since he arrived here in Scotland, but

he could not break the old habit of setting out on a journey without some sort of defense.

One could never know if there were any wayfarers along the way and so he did not want to put himself in danger without protection. Robert stowed his luggage and the well bag of provisions and said goodbye to Samuel.

"Take good care of everything for me. If everything goes according to plan, I'll be back in five days."

"You can count on me, and watch out, don't let old Stuart pull a fast one on you. I hear he's a fox."

"So am I. So long."

With that, he mounted his black steed and trotted over to the house. Moira stood waiting there.

"Take good care of yourself and come back safe. I do not like it at all that you want to ride all by yourself. You should at least take Samuel with you."

"He is needed here. Don't worry, I'll be back in five days."

"That's such a long time without you."

Robert leaned down to her. Tenderly grasped her chin, breathed a kiss on her mouth and replied, "You'll see that the time will pass very quickly. I have to go, Moira. Take good care of our little one and don't overexert yourself."

With that, he kissed her passionately on the mouth before he stood up, tapped his hat in salute and gave his horse his spurs. Moira gazed after him until he disappeared from her view.

Chapter 20

Moira strolled through the garden. Robert had only been gone for two days, but she missed him painfully. She couldn't even remember what it had been like without him. In an attempt to distract herself, she had been busy with a number of domestic tasks, had been visiting Eileen and had helped Samuel bring the new foal with its mother to a small pasture, but nothing had really helped. She missed him and hoped that time would pass more quickly. Just as she was about to go back into the house, to get a book from the library, Albert intercepted her.

"Milady. This letter has just been dropped for you."

She accepted it gratefully, put it in her skirt pocket and went into the library. She searched through the many old books, for one that would interest her, found what she was looking for and went to the small reception room. There she settled down in a comfortable armchair near the window. Just as she began to read the first page, she remembered the letter and reached into her pocket to take it out. She froze. Would this never end? The letter now opened in her hand, she read the words written in the already familiar script.

Your husband is out of the house. Meet me the evening after tomorrow at the same time and place as always. Destroy this message.

Angry and desperate, she crumpled the letter into a ball and threw it into the cold fireplace. In that moment she did not care if Robert found it. She knew that if he confronted her and pressed her with words, that she would confess everything to him. But he was not here. Once again, Dumfrey's informant had done a good job. She simply could not escape him. But this time, she would only obey Dumfrey's instructions. For her, it was over. She was no longer willing to betray Robert.

Despite the mild night temperatures she had chosen a black cape. She did not want to be recognized under any circumstances, in case someone came along the way. Right now she stood in the shelter of the old tree and was waiting for Dumfrey's carriage.

This time it had not been as easy as the times before to leave the house unobserved. Too many servants scurried through the corridors of the castle, to ensure that everything ran smoothly, even in the evening hours. When it looked like the last of them had gone to rest, she had carefully climbed down the stairs and sneaked out of the house through the back door.

The fact that she had to sneak out of her own house, like a thief, tugged at her nerves. She had hurried to the meeting place, but Dumfrey was not here yet. Just when she hoped he would not come, she heard the carriage approaching. Directly in front of her it stopped and the coachman, whom she already knew from their encounter at the bay, gave her a sign that she should get in. When, without a word, the hutch was opened from the inside she got in and the carriage slowly started to move.

Robert let his horse trot across the meadow, it was already late, but he had almost made it. His visit to Lord Bratley had been satisfactory. The lord had already bought some breeding bulls from him and wanted to expand further. The gentlemen had quickly agreed on the price and the procedure and so he had been ready to start his journey home late this morning.

He was looking forward to getting home. He had missed Moira the last few days and he resolved to take her with him next time. He gave his horse the spurs, so that it would go a little faster. Tonight he would hold her in his arms again. She was probably already in bed and did not expect his return until tomorrow.

He was just leaving the small forest behind him, which separated him from the main road, when he heard the sound of hooves. At the moment when he was about to turn into the road, a black carriage passed him at a moderate speed. The driver had not noticed him, for he continued on his way until he stopped some distance away. Robert was startled. Even if the coachman had not seen him, he had clearly noticed that it was the same carriage, that had almost run him over the other night. Curious as to why the carriage had stopped in this deserted area, he steered his horse back into the woods and tried to creep closer to it parallel to the road.

When he was almost at the same height as the carriage, he dismounted and tied his horse to a tree. Quietly he crept on. Strange, he thought to himself. The carriage stood motionless and nothing moved. What was going on here? What was the coachman waiting for? Suddenly, the hutch opened and a petite figure in a black robe stepped out. Robert's breath caught in his throat. He didn't need any clairvoyant abilities at all, to know who was hidden there under the cape.

He would have recognized her among thousands of women. Before he could even think about what Moira was doing here, he could see Charles Dumfrey lean out of the carriage and hand her a small box, which she immediately let disappear into her skirt pocket.

"You know what you have to do in two days."

The figure in the cloak nodded silently and then went on his way in the direction of the castle. Robert did not understand what he just observed. Did his wife have an affair with Dumfrey? The door was closed again and the coachman turned the carriage. He cracked the whip and the horses trotted off in the direction from which Robert had come. For a few seconds he stood still.

He could not believe what he had just seen. If he hurried, he could get home before Moira and catch her in the bedroom when she returned. A few minutes later he reached the stable. He hurried into the house and up to his bedroom, driven by the hope that he had made a mistake after all. But when he opened the door to the room, he found himself alone.

The bed was empty and there was no trace of Moira. He closed the door behind him and sat down in one of the armchairs by the fireplace. Without lighting a candle, he waited in the darkness for his traitorous wife. He did not have to wait long to hear the small steps from the hallway. Quietly the door was opened and closed again, and when she was in the middle of the room, he could observe how she got rid of the cloak and expelled her breath audibly.

"Did you enjoy your night's ride?"

Moira wheeled around, startled, and let out a small scream of terror when she heard her husband's voice behind her.

"Robert! You're home already?"

Without rising from his chair, he began his interrogation.

"Where did you come from now?"

Moira was visibly nervous, how should she answer him now?

"I was just getting some air."

"Don't lie to me!"

Horrified at her husband's angry voice, she backed away.

"I know exactly where you came from, because I saw you get out of Dumfrey's carriage. I would have thought you had a little more taste, than to take an old fop like him to cuckold me. How long has this been going on."

"It's not what you think."

"Oh no? Then how is it, explain it to me."

Slowly he rose and came toward her. She saw the anger in his eyes and instinctively she took a step back, but Robert grabbed her arm and pulled her toward him.

"Am I already so repugnant to you that you want to run away from me?"

"No, please Robert you're hurting me."

Immediately, he loosened his grip, but he did not let her go. Desperation rose up in her, how should she explain everything to him. He was so angry with her and she could feel it starting to boil inside him.

"I'm still waiting for an explanation and don't feed me any stories. I can tell a lie from you in a heartbeat."

Was she really so easy to see through or did he just know her too well already.

"Please Robert, you have to believe me, I am not having an affair with Dumfrey. I don't even like him. I love you - only you."

"Then why were you in his carriage?"

"That, I can't tell you."

Furious, he pulled her closer to him until her body pressed against him.

"Can't or won't?"

Astonished, she noticed how he reached into her skirt pocket and pulled out the small can. He let go of her and was about to open the can, when she rushed to snatch it out of his hands. But Robert was faster and kept Moira to within an arm's length of him.

"Please, give it back to me," she pleaded in a final fit of desperation.

But she only had to read the determination in his face to know that she was lost. He would not let up, not until he had gotten the whole truth out of her. Horrified, she watched as he opened the can and was amazed at what he found inside. Apparently it had not been what he had suspected. He held the opened can under her nose.

"What is this and why did Dumfrey give it to you?"

Speechless, she looked at him. But then he thundered the next words down on her.

"Start talking. I want to know what this is."

Moira was at a loss for words. The pure despair was seen to her and she felt the tears well up in her eyes. Robert felt the inner battle his wife was fighting with herself and he was inclined to take her in his arms to comfort her. But if he gave in now, he would never know what was being played here and so he steeled himself against the sight of his distraught wife and looked down on her implacably.

"I think it's a sleeping powder," she said in a low voice.

"You think it is, but you're not sure? What should you do with it?"

"I should administer it to you."

For a moment Robert looked at her in amazement.

"Why?"

"Dumfrey wants to keep you from getting in his way in the bay."

Slowly it dawned on him. Dumfrey was behind the smuggling, but how was Moira involved in all this? Was she part of this gang? He couldn't believe where his thoughts were taking him.

"You've done this before, haven't you? The first night

you were with me, I woke up the next morning at my desk. Why, Moira, why? "

A dam broke loose and in a tearful voice she pleaded with him.

"Please Robert, I didn't mean for any of this to happen, but I had no choice."

"You always have another choice."

"No, he has me in the palm of his hand, and if I don't do what he says, a lot of people are going to suffer."

"Won't you finally tell me everything?"

"Since my parents have been dead, Dumfrey has been courting me. Despite my refusals, he has continued to press me. He wanted to buy the lands and rebuild my parents' house if I married him, but I didn't want that. One day he came with a promissory bill signed by my father. He had owed him ten thousand pounds and Dumfrey demanded this sum back from me, knowing full well that I could not raise it. He then also threatened me with imprisonment and the expropriation of my property, if I didn't work off the money with him. For some reason, he wanted me to keep you away from the bay, and so that we could get to know each other and I could have the opportunity to do that, he took me to the ball at that time."

"So it's all been theater from the beginning? Our getting to know each other and everything that came afterwards until today? I have to say, you're more hard-nosed than I ever thought you'd be. Did you at least have a delicious time at my expense?"

The full contempt towards her spoke from his words and put a stab in Moira's heart. This was no longer just about telling the truth, it was now about fighting for her marriage, because no matter what he thought of her at the moment, she loved him with all her heart.

"It wasn't a game. I really do love you, Robert."

He laughed wickedly.

"Who's going to believe you now? How could I have fallen for you like that? How many times have you slipped me some of that powder?"

"Twice, he had me believe, that it was only a sleeping powder, you must believe me Robert I didn't know. Then when you got so ill, I confronted him and told him I wasn't going to continue. I had no idea what he was capable of."

"I had you to thank for that nausea? God Moira, what was it? Poison, perhaps?"

"Arsenic, but I didn't know anything about it. He didn't tell me until the next day. You must believe me, Robert, please. I wouldn't have given you this otherwise. I didn't know what to do. He kept threatening to put me in the whorehouse, or do something to Eileen or the kids or you. What was I supposed to do?"

She tried to put her hands soothingly on his, but he pushed them away.

"Why didn't you ever tell me anything. Didn't I tell you from the beginning that I want to help you? I laid my heart at your feet and you stomped on it. You are a criminal and should be punished."

Horror and fear erupted in her. Dumfrey had warned her never to tell him what she had done. Now she experienced it firsthand. His harsh words reached her only through a veil of tears.

"Actually, I should hand you over to the authorities, but you carry my name and my child under your heart, if this is not just an act, too. As long as you are pregnant with my child, you'll spend most of your time here in this room. You will only leave this room once a day for an hour to get some fresh air. When I have social duties, you will play the dutiful, loving wife by my side. This should not be so difficult for you, since you have been doing it well all along. The rest of the time, until the birth of the child, you will spend in this house and you will never see me again."

Horrified, she looked at him.

"You lock me in this room here? You can't do this, please Robert I beg you. Don't do this to me."

"You are a criminal and I have every right in the world to treat you like this, and besides, I think this way is better than the wet, damp cellar holes of the local prisons. Tomorrow Albert will get my belongings out of here and take them to the West Wing. You can hope that you are really pregnant, because the child is saving you from the gallows."

Without caring any more about Moira, he left her standing there and went to the door. Once there, he turned to her once more. Now, completely calm and emotionless, he turned to her one last time.

"I loved you, truly loved you. Why?"

With these words he turned, opened the door and went out. Moira heard the door close behind him. Suddenly there was silence in the room, which was still in darkness, but she did not register any of this.

Her world had just collapsed. Sobbing, she fell to her knees and buried her face in her hands. Robert heard her crying outside the door and his heart clenched. He still loved her, but somehow he had to manage to forget her. She had lied to him and cheated on him from the very beginning and he could not forgive that.

Chapter 21

The next morning, everything had taken place just as Robert had predicted. He must have told his household that she was pregnant and not well at the moment, and in order not to endanger the child's life and to give his wife rest, he had moved into another bedroom, for Harried, with a knowing smile, brought her breakfast and had told her that everything would get better with time.

Then Albert had appeared and removed Robert's clothes from the room and in the afternoon Harried had come again to help her into a dress so that she could go out. After that she had been alone in the room again and had seen no one except the servant who had brought her dinner. She had neither heard Robert's voice nor had she seen him herself.

As much as she had hoped that he would talk to her again the next day, she had to realize that in the evening he had put into practice everything he had told her. That evening she cried herself to sleep. The next day did not begin any better. She saw the servant only for breakfast and then again for lunch.

In the time in between she lay listlessly in her bed and thought. She had to talk to him again. Trying to explain to him that she really loved him. He could not really believe that she had been acting for him all those nights. In the evening she gave the servant a letter for

Robert, in which she asked him to talk to her. But the evening passed and Robert did not appear.

"Samuel, I need to talk to you," Robert called out to his foreman and gave him a wave, that indicated he wanted to meet him at the stable. Samuel, recognizing the urgency in Robert's voice, literally dropped everything and hurried after him. Robert was just checking his tack when Samuel came up behind him.
"What is it?"
"I need you tonight. I want you to accompany me to the bay."
Finally there was something exciting to do and so he could hardly hide his excitement.
"Tell me, what's going on?"
"I asked you the other day about smugglers in this area, remember? There are some at work in the bay below."
Samuel patted his hand on his thigh.
"Didn't I know it from the start, that the thing back then with the book was an excuse."
"Okay, I admit it, I just wanted to make sure no one else was in on it.
"You thought I was in on it?"
"Not really, but I had to make sure. Sorry."
"Bygones. So what are you up to?"
"I know the gang's coming back tonight. And I want to know what's going on."
"Don't you think we better get the police if you're going to let them get busted?"
"I don't want to bust them tonight, I want to know who their mastermind is. It's not enough to just get the henchmen. I want the head of the gang, and I want you to help me get him. Will you do it? It could be dangerous."

"You can count on me. Man, then it's probably been going on there for a while, because your uncle already suspected something. I'm sure of it now."

"I think you can go even further and say he knew something and that puts a whole different face on his death. I want the head of the gang, because I want to ask him that very question."

Samuel nodded in agreement.

"When do you want to go?"

"Meet me here tonight at ten."

A few hours later, both men were lying on the cliffs of the bay in wait. Their horses were well hidden and so they waited there quietly until they heard footsteps and voices in the distance.

"They're coming," Robert whispered, and they both ducked deep into the tall grass. A whole horde of men passed them by and disappeared a short time later in the bay below them. Cautiously, Robert and Samuel crawled to the edge to see what was going on down on the beach. Just like the last time he had been up here, some boats came in from the sea to the beach. Tonight they must have been expecting a particularly large load, because four boats were pulled ashore. Immediately the smugglers set about unloading the boats, which were right away lowered back into the water and disappeared into the darkness.

"What do they have in those barrels?" Samuel quietly asked.

"I can only guess, but I think it's rum that they're smuggling into the country to avoid the tax."

"That ought to make a real penny with that kind of quantity."

"It's probably a very large shipment today, too. The first

time, there were only eight of them. Today there are three times as many. We couldn't have done it alone. Come on, let's hide again. They'll be coming up the path any minute now and then we'll go after them."

Immediately they crawled back into their hiding place and waited. When the heavily laden rogues had passed them panting and they had been given a certain head start, Robert and Samuel straightened up.

"Did you also notice what I saw?"

"That William, the Page, was among them?"

Samuel nodded.

"Well, if I catch him. I'll read him the riot act."

"No, you won't."

Astonished, Samuel looked at Robert.

"Why? He's double-crossing you."

"Yes, and he will not escape his punishment, but we may still need him. We now know the enemy in our camp, and that gives us an advantage over the others."

Grinning, Samuel replied, "You really are a fox."

Robert patted Samuel on the shoulder.

"Come, we don't want to give them too much of a head start. Grab your horse and then follow me."

Surprised that Robert did not follow the group but rode inland, he turned to him again.

"I thought you were going after them?"

"Don't worry, we will, but I know where they come out on the road, and that's where we'll wait for them."

A few minutes later, as they hid in the bushes opposite, they could see two carts fully loaded driving from Moira's property onto the road and from there towards the village.

"They are using Moira's property for their deeds and she doesn't know about it?"

You bet she knew about it, Robert thought, but he kept it to himself and let the cart get another larger lead before he and his horse slowly followed. He was not surprised that the tracks led to Dumfrey's property, but now it was no longer a guess, but certainty. The bastard was the head of the gang.

"This is the property of Sir Dumfrey's. It can't be."

Samuel looked at Robert and was surprised to see that he wasn't as surprised as he was.

"You knew that, didn't you?"

"Didn't know, but suspected, and now I have confirmation."

"How did you know?"

"That's a different story, maybe I'll tell you sometime."

"What do we do now? We can't let him get away with it."

"I don't intend to. We have William, he'll know when this shipment is going to be shipped out, and then we'll strike."

"Genius."

Chapter 22

Impatiently he tapped his fingers on the upholstered back of his seat. He hoped for the messenger that his information was really important, because if it wasn't, he would make him a head shorter for depriving him of a well-deserved night's rest.

Already last night he had stayed up to wait for the delivery. His men had done a good job and now his cellar was filled to the brim with good Jamaican rum. The customers were already waiting for it and it was up to him to distribute the goods to them as quickly as possible. Unfortunately, the transport had to be delayed for a while, because his contact person had informed him that the police had raided some of his buyers.

Now some time had to pass before completing the transaction. He could well have been lying in his bed instead of waiting here for his informant. Suddenly there was a knocking from above against the roof of the car. His Coachman signaled him the arrival of his informant. Dumfrey stuck his head out of the window and saw the young man standing in front of him.

"I hope for your sake that the message is important."

Somewhat nervously, his counterpart indicated:

"You said yourself that you wanted to be informed about anything new right away."

"Yes, yes it's all right. So what do you have to report?"

"Milady is pregnant and does not seem to be well.
At least she's been in bed."

"Well done, and now go, before you'll be missed."

"Isn't the information worth at least a few Shillings?"

The boy held out his open hand toward him, but Dumfrey ignored it.

"Get out of here and don't be so greedy. You get enough yet."

With that, he gave his driver the command to leave, leaving the young man standing there.

William was nervous. Never before had the lord summoned him. What could possibly be the reason for it. With wet fingers he knocked on the door of his writing room, when a "Come in! from inside sounded and he entered the room. He was surprised to see not only his master but also Mister Summerton in the room. Not knowing how to behave now he stood awkwardly at the door.

Samuel stood at the window with his arms folded and watched the arrival. Robert, on the other hand, was sitting behind his desk, looked up and gestured to his bellboy to come closer.

"Please close the door behind you and come over here."

He did as he was told and then stepped in front of the table.

"How old are you, William?"

"Sixteen, sir."

"And how long have you been working here?"

"A little over two years. Lord Dunbar, your uncle, employed me."

"Do you live in this village?"

William secretly wondered at the lord's questions. Never before had anyone taken an interest in him. Dutifully, however, he gave the information.

"Yes, I live there with my mother and my siblings."

"How many siblings do you have?"

"There are six of us at home, I'm the oldest."

Robert looked at him in silence for a while and William became visibly more nervous. What did the lord intend by these questions.

Robert however, was completely elsewhere with his thoughts. What a bastard Dumfrey was, that he used a child for his crimes. How could he reconcile it with his conscience, to bring this boy to justice. He had been guilty of a misdemeanor, and he didn't even know that the noose around his neck was slowly tightening.

A quick glance over at Samuel signaled that he seemed to be thinking the same thing, then he turned back to his page.

"Where is your father?"

"He died in an accident a little over two years ago in the field. Since then my mother has been trying to get us through."

"What does your mother do?"

"She works at the bakery. But the money isn't enough, and that's why I took the job here and put in my wages."

It was getting better and better, Robert thought. He couldn't have the second earner of this family locked up.

"Are you satisfied with your wages?"

"Oh, yes, my lord. It helps my mother very much."

"Then I ask you now, why do you deceive me?"

William turned pale in the face. He tried to defend himself.

"Who, me?"

"Yes you. You needn't deny it, because Mr. Summerton and I saw you working with smugglers in the bay last night. Smuggling is punishable by prison, as I am sure you know."

184

The boy now looked hurriedly from one to the other. The trap had snapped shut. Robert rose from his chair and came around the table. He stood up in front of the frightened boy. The latter, however, pleaded with him.

"Please sir, don't throw me in jail. My mother wouldn't survive it. She doesn't know anything about it, but we could use the money so well. It was easily earned. I just carried the barrels to the wagon, that's all."

"Don't forget to mention, in your confession, that you are also a spy for Sir Dumfrey."

Horrified, the boy backed away. With bowed head and shaky voice, he asked, "How do you know that?"

"As I told you before, we have seen you. We have followed everything and we know that Dumfrey had to have an informant here. Until the day before yesterday we didn't know who it was, but you've just confirmed our suspicions. I'll take that as a confession. The only thing I'm interested in now is, the how. How do you get in touch with Dumfrey when you want to send him a message and how does he contact you?"

William was silent. How could he save himself now? The revenge of Dumfrey, when he would learn that he had been found out would be terrible. Robert gradually lost his patience with this boy. Didn't he understand that only full cooperation would help him now to protect himself from a severe punishment.

"Boy, you should start talking. I want to know how this operation works."

The words just thundered down on him. Lowly, he finally gave in.

"Please sir, if Sir Dumfrey finds out that I have given you this information, he's going to do something bad to my family. He can be very mean."

Robert was convinced of that.

"Tell me what I want to know and I will protect your

family from him."

"There is an old oak tree at the entrance to the village, that has a small hole in its trunk. There- I put a note in it when I want to see him. He, on the other hand, sends me a letter when he needs my help. Please, I have told you everything I know. Will you protect my family for that long, while I am in prison?"

"That won't be necessary, because I'll let you go..."

William couldn't believe his luck.

"Thank you sir, I also promise that I will never do it again."

"I'll let you go only on one condition, that we don't get it wrong. I deeply disapprove and despise what you have done, but I credit you your young age and your inexperience and hope that you will not make me regret my good nature towards you. You will continue to work here and pretend that nothing has happened.

You will stand by for Dumfrey, and you will report to me immediately when he's contacted you. Do you know when the load is to be moved from his property?"

"Not exactly. He said last night that he would need us again in about two weeks."

"Well, let's wait for him to let you know, and until then, be warned. One wrong move from you and I won't hesitate to inform the police about you. Are we clear?"

"Yes sir, thank you. You will not regret it. Thank you."

"Good, then back to work."

When the boy had left the room Robert heaved a sigh. Samuel patted him appreciatively on the shoulders.

"Tell me I did the right thing. I hope the kid understands what's at stake for him."

"I think he does. It's his second chance. We will keep a close eye on him. What are we going to do when the transport starts?"

"Then we grab them. I'll ride to Fort Williams in a couple of days, and I'll tell the police there. I don't want to leave anything to chance that night."

"Well, what does Moira actually say about all the events? After all, the gang is acting under her nose."

"I didn't bother her with it. She's not doing so well at the moment and I didn't want to upset her further."

"I hope it's nothing serious?"

"No, the baby is bothering her."

"Would you like me to send Eileen over to see if she can help?"

"No, right now rest is best for her."

"Whatever you say."

Samuel sensed that there was more than Robert was telling him. But he accepted that he didn't seem to want to talk to him about it.

Chapter 23

How long she had been here in this room she did not know. The days came and went. The first few days, she had still gotten ready in the morning because she had always hoped to see Robert again, but over time she had to realize that she was waiting in vain. She had also stopped her daily walks in the park.

She simply lacked the drive to do so. Three times a day she saw the same servant, who would only hand her the food tray and then leave again. Several times she had given him a message for her husband, but she had never received an answer from him. He wanted to punish her with disrespect and he had every right to do so.

She had sinned against him and deserved to be punished. But did she not also deserve to defend herself? All she wanted, was the chance to talk to him again, try to explain to him, that she really loved him. She didn't know what offended her more, the accusation that she wanted to poison him or that she had never loved him. She knew it wasn't so, because her heart still beat for him and so she had cried herself out in the first days, until she had no more tears left.

ometimes she had even thought she could hear his footsteps in the hallway, as they paused in front of the door, but that could only have been a dream. Robert had never come to her again after that ominous night, and so she finally had to face the truth. He didn't want her around anymore.

She had died for him, just as Dumfrey had prophesied to her. Moira laughed bitterly. She had believed the power of love could overcome everything. Now she had to bitterly realize that she had been mistaken. She had once been very happy with him and had never thought it would be possible that things could become different.

But now - what kind of life was it to vegetate here, to give birth to a child she would never see grow up and to know that the man she loved would never find his way back to her? Moira had lost her will to live, and one day she lost her appetite and would not touch the food that was brought to her.

When Robert came home dirty and drenched Albert was already running excitedly to meet him. He had been on the road for the last week to talk to the police in Fort Williams. They would be on their way in the next few days to be on standby in the vicinity. After he had spent almost all the time in the saddle and now it had started to rain, he was glad to be back home. He was tired, but a hot bath and a good meal would revive his spirits again. However, when he saw Albert approaching with a worried face, he was sure that it could not bode well.

"My lord. Thank God you are back. My lady is not well."

"What's wrong with her?"

"We don't know, she's locked herself in, please come."

Robert jumped off the horse, left it to itself and hurried up the steps, two at a time. Forgotten was his exhaustion. He stormed through the vestibule and up the

next staircase. Albert followed after him. At the top he took a deep breath to calm his pulse again, then he pressed the door handle, but the door remained locked.
"Why did she lock herself in?"
"We don't know. She did it three days ago, and won't let us in, nor does she respond to our calling."
"Three days - my God Albert. Step aside."

Robert had to throw himself against the door three times before it gave way and the wood splintered on the doorpost. The room had been darkened with the curtains and he tried to get his eyes used to the darkness. The smell that came out of the room took his breath away. It smelled of stale air and food and the smell of a full chamber pot. He found Moira huddled on the floor. She was dressed in a nightgown standing with dirt and did not respond to his touch. Fear befelled him, he would never forgive himself for this, if she died- thank God he felt her pulse. Quickly he lifted her up and laid her in bed.
"Albert, tear open the windows, light the lamps and bring out the extras. Send your wife up. I need her help."
"Very well sir, she's not..."
"No, she's alive. She's unconscious. Hurry."

Robert clapped his hand lightly in Moira's face, but it was not until the third time that she began to move. Slowly, she opened her eyes.
Robert exhaled audibly with relief. A slight smile played around her mouth, when she caught sight of him. Her lips were brittle and torn and her voice would not obey her, when she tried to speak. Croaking, she heard herself say:
"Is it really you? You finally came."

Robert could hardly bear to see her. She had always been a strong, good looking young woman and now here on the white sheets lay a figure that emaciated and filthy and he had to answer for this. He had been angry and hurt, had wanted to forget her. She deserved a lesson and punishment, but he had punished himself with it. Night after night he had not been able to sleep, because in his thoughts were only her. After all she had done to him, he still loved her.

"Save the power of speech until you are well again."

"I...I didn't mean for any of this to happen."

"We'll talk when you're better."

"My lord - oh my child. What are you doing."

Harried immediately hurried over to the bed, picked up the chamber pot with vomit in it and emptied it in the bathroom. Robert called over to her.

"Bring me a glass of water, please."

Harried hurried to hand him a full glass of water. Since Moira was too weak to hold the glass by herself, he helped her drink. Sip by sip, she drank the glass empty.

"Harried, would you please prepare a bath for my wife and help me bathe her?"

"Very well, my lord."

"Oh, and let the maids know, to clean up in the meantime and make the bed fresh."

She nodded, then dumped the water into the tub and hurried out to fetch maids. A few minutes later, Robert had Moira undressed and placed in the warm tub. He held her tightly so that she would not sink, for her body was too weak to hold itself upright in the tub. Harried washed her body and her hair.

Robert, however, looked at the emaciated body and his gaze remained on the now already visible roundness of her belly. In this respect, she had not lied. She was pregnant and it angered him, that she had not only put her life at risk with her hunger strike, but also that of his child. Half an hour later, Moira was lying in a clean nightgown in the freshly made bed. The maids had removed all traces and the room smelled fresh and pleasant again. Robert lit the fireplace and looked up as Albert came in.

"Will you please tell Gwyneth to send up something hearty to eat in half an hour? Some bread, water and strong tea to go with it. I'm going to have dinner with my wife up here, only I want to quickly change and wash myself."

"Very well."

Thirty minutes later on the dot, Albert brought a fully laden tray into the room and placed it together with plates and cutlery on the table by the fireplace then he withdrew. Robert, whose empty stomach growled loudly from the delicious smell of the roast, filled his plate.

He took some potatoes, roast and gravy and a thick slice of freshly baked bread, cut it all into bite-sized pieces and sat down next to Moira, whom he had bedded in a sitting position against the headboard of the bed. Apathetically she sat there and that frightened him mightily, because apart from the two sentences, she had not spoken to him or otherwise shown a reaction. She was awake, following with her eyes what he was doing, but she didn't speak.

"Come Moira, you must eat something."

Dutifully like a child, she opened her mouth and he was able to feed her. He pressed a piece of the bread in her hand and brought both to her lips. She bit a small piece, the size a sparrow would eat, from the slice. While Robert took turns eating something himself and then fed Moira again, her spirits seemed to slowly return.

He gave her the hot tea sip by sip, which seemed to be good for her, because she seemed to become more lively again. When he was full and Moira had eaten several mouthfuls, he got up to put the empty plate away. He felt her hand on his arm. Surprised by her quick reaction she tried to hold him, and with a croaky voice she cried out, frightened, "Don't go. Don't leave me alone." The startled look on his wife's face made him pause.

"I'll stay tonight."

Seemingly relieved, she lowered her hand. Robert, however, put the used dishes outside in the hallway and closed the door behind him as he re-entered the room. He undressed and then slipped into bed with Moira, whom he took in his arms. Without another word between them, she snuggled tightly against him and let her head rest on his chest. Robert closed his eyes.

The strong feelings that her closeness aroused in him, were not expected. He had thought that he had gotten over her. How could it be that he was still attracted to her? She had lied and betrayed him from the beginning, and yet it felt good to feel her now.

Robert had thought that he had freed himself from her in the last few weeks, but many a time he had walked down the hall outside her room and had to force himself not to enter. Now, too, he told himself that he was only here because someone had to watch over her tonight. He realized that Moira must have fallen asleep, because her breaths were regular. His exhaustion, which he had felt when he came home was now taking its toll, Robert's eyes also fell closed and he fell asleep.

The next morning Moira awoke and instinctively sought Robert with her hand. But she reached into a void, because the bed next to her was empty. She woke up with a jolt. Had she only dreamed that he had come to her last night and had slept in her bed? Sad that it must have been so, she sank back into the sheets again. The door opened and instead of the servant who always brought her breakfast, Robert appeared, fully dressed with a tray in his hand.

"I see you are feeling better today. That's good. Here's your breakfast."

He put it on the table by the fireplace, then turned back to his wife.

"Why did you do that? I mean the refusal to eat."

"I can't stand being cooped up here anymore. Please Robert, I want to talk to you."

"You're not locked up. You can leave the room at any time and stay in the house. Once a day you should go for a walk in the park. I had allowed you to do that. So why?"

"What difference does it make whether I stay here in the room or in the house. It is and always will be my prison."

"That's right, and nothing will change."

Angrily, she hissed at him.

"How can you do this to me?"

Robert, whose composure was gradually turning to anger, took a threatening step toward her. The veins on his neck stood out throbbing.

"You hardly have the right to accuse me of anything. Contrary to what you actually deserve, this is still very nice of me. I am not the one who lied. I'm the idiot who let you deceive me. How could I have fallen for you?"

Moira tried to speak in a more conciliatory tone. She had to talk to him, but as upset as he was right now, he would only stonewall.

"Please, let me explain."

"I don't see what else there is to clarify. You stay here until the child is born and you will be under more surveillance from now on. What happened yesterday doesn't happen again. You have a responsibility to our child and you will eat and drink to keep him well. Always remember that the child is keeping you out of prison right now. Do we understand each other?"

She nodded silently and tried to blink away the tears that were stinging her eyes. As Robert turned away and headed for the door, she launched one last attempt. "Please, I beg you, don't go. Let me explain to you that it wasn't like that. Please, Robert."

He stopped at the door. Without turning to her, he replied in now a completely calm tone, "We'll talk when this is over. First I will take care of Dumfrey, then it's your turn."

His words sounded like a threat. Harsh and impersonal, and Moira saw her chance fading that he could ever forgive her.

Chapter 24

Robert found Samuel with the sheep he was feeding. Four days had passed since he had come from Fort Williams and found Moira in her bedroom. He had not seen her since. He had been told, however, that she was eating regularly and also walking in the park again. She complied with his instructions, he could not and would not do more for her at the moment.

He had other things on his mind to take care of. William had just informed him that the removal was to take place in two days. and that is why he was looking for Samuel.

"Here we go."

Samuel placed the trough on the ground and devoted himself entirely to Robert.

"Finally. I was beginning to think he had changed his mind. Do you think you can trust William?"

"I hope so for his sake. I told the police commander that he was Dumfrey's spy, but that William has agreed to help us catch the gang. William is lucky that the commander himself is a father of three boys and has accepted my proposal to grant him immunity if he delivers the gang to us. It's his second chance, and I hope for the boy's sake that he doesn't blow it. That's all I can do."

„That is more than fair. Anyone else would have had

him locked up."

"The boy is almost a child. I can't put a kid in jail. He's done something stupid, and he'll have a chance, to correct it the night after tomorrow."

"How do we proceed?"

Robert briefly explained to Samuel what he had planned, then he set off to meet the police and inform them so that the hunting would finally be over on the night in question.

Dressed all in black, with his face soot-blackened, Robert crouched behind a large tree near the estate of Sir Dumfrey and checked his gun for the last time. He had his revolver strapped around his hips and now held himself ready for its use. Robert looked around and tried to spot the others in the darkness, but he saw no one. He knew they were there and hoped that everyone knew what they had to do.

The police had surrounded the property so that no one could escape, but so far the house was quiet and there was nothing to suggest that a gang of smugglers was up to no good here. Robert checked his pocket watch. It was already late. Where the hell were they? Had they smelled a rat or had William warned them? Then he suddenly heard a horse snort. He ducked even more and saw a little later three carts, on which quite a few men were sitting, coming down the driveway.

Off they went. Quietly, he could watch as the carts passed him and drove unimpeded around the house. Then they disappeared from his view. He cautiously straightened up and spotted a policeman some distance to his right and Samuel to his left, who was just poking his head out of a bush. He gave them both the sign to approach cautiously and then crept up to within a few meters of the house himself. There they waited and listened. From their position they could not see what was going on at the back of the house. There the commander was positioned with his squad and waited to give the signal for the assault. Robert and Samuel had the task of cutting off the escape route from behind.

With that they hoped to be able to arrest the gang without a shootout. Robert signaled to the policeman to his right to continue watching the front entrance, while he and Samuel continued to creep around the house. Gradually, both could hear barrels being rolled across the ground in the distance and loaded onto the carts with great effort.

When they had progressed so far that they were squatting in a bush at the corner of the house, Robert peered cautiously around the corner and saw the crooks with the carts ahead of him. Several barrels had already been loaded. The smugglers formed a human chain to get the removal done as quickly as possible. If he hadn't miscounted, there were twenty men there. The police had arrived with twenty-five men and with the two of them they outnumbered the thieves.

He saw William standing in the cellar hole and passing the barrels to the next man, but nowhere did he see Dumfrey. Where was that son of a bitch? He was so hoping to get his hands on him personally, so that he could slap him in the face in his anger. But probably he supervised the removal in the house and so he turned quietly to Samuel.

"Samuel, listen. Dumfrey is nowhere to be seen. I don't want this guy slipping through our fingers when the police strike. I'm going to go look for him."
Samuel grabbed his arm.

"What are you going to do? The commander said that we shouldn't take any risks and that we shouldn't work on our own."

"I don't care. The guy is nowhere to be seen and if it gets loud here, he might get away from us. I'll sneak into the house and keep him there."
"That's too dangerous. You don't know the floorplan or how many employees he has. I'll go with you."

"No. You have to make sure that no one gets out of here. We want the whole group. We can't let anyone get away. I'll be fine."

With that, he tore himself away and quietly slipped away. He was lucky, because he found a window on the lower floor, which was ajar and he slipped through it unnoticed. The room beyond was in darkness. He looked around briefly and realized that he was in the library. The realization did not help him much, because he did not know the house. Cautiously he opened the door a crack and listened. The hallway behind it was lit by a few wall lamps, and the rooms that led from it were all in darkness. Not a soul was to be seen.

Dumfrey must have given his maid the day off. Cautiously, Robert crept further into the back part of the house, where the cellar stairs had to be. Then it got loud outside. Screams and shouts reached his ears. The police had initiated the raid and he hoped that there would be no bloodshed. Suddenly he heard hurried footsteps from somewhere. One door was torn open and another one was violently pulled shut. Then it was suddenly as quiet as a mouse. Robert listened to see if he could still hear the footsteps anywhere, but the house lay quietly.

Also no more sounds reached his ears from outside. The silence was eerie. Just as he was about to set off again to search the house for Dumfrey, the front door was pushed open and the commander, followed by Samuel and five other policemen appeared in the hallway.
"Do you have them?"
Robert hurried toward them.

"Yes, except for Dumfrey. He wasn't there. A couple of men have confirmed that he is supposed to be here in the house," the policeman replied.

"I heard footsteps in the back the moment you arrested the gang outside, it must have been him. Let's hurry to find him."

"He's trapped. All the exits are guarded. Men, start searching the house. I want every corner checked. He's got to be here somewhere."

The policemen poured out together and it wasn't long before they had searched every room on the first floor. But the rooms were all empty. Then they split up. Half took over the upper floor, while the rest, together with Robert and Samuel took over the basement. An hour later, they were disbelievingly disappointed to discover that Sir Dumfrey had vanished off the face of the earth. Nowhere had he been seen, nor had they discovered any trace of him escaping. Robert was stunned.

"Damn it, how did he get away from us? The house has been surrounded and I was in here."

Samuel placatingly put his arm on Robert's shoulders.

"The police will find him all right. He can't have much of a head start. The commandant wants to telegraph his colleague in Edinburgh to guard Dumfrey's house there. They'll get him. First of all, be glad that the whole gang has been apprehended without bloodshed and the merchandise. We've given Dumfrey a run for his money."

"I guess you're right. We probably won't be able to do anything tonight. Thanks for your help."

"Do you still need me, otherwise I will ride home. I don't like to leave Eileen alone for so long."

"No, that's all right. Go. I'll stay a moment. I'll see you tomorrow."

Samuel left the house and Robert strolled through the

rooms once more. He still did not understand how it could happen that Dumfrey had escaped. He went down to the basement, but except for a few shelves on the wall, the room was now empty.

He looked around again. There was nothing conspicuous to be seen down here and yet he had a feeling that he might have overlooked something important. Outside the house again, he said goodbye to the police and thanked the commander for his help. Then he saw the whole troop depart. In front, the three carts, fully loaded with the rum barrels, now driven by the police, left the driveway and behind them the smugglers, tied up and held in check by the rest of the police.

A long prison sentence awaited them all. Left behind was young William, who now came to him excitedly.

"He was there, sir, you have to believe me. I didn't rat you out."

"It's all right, William. You've done your job and you'll go unpunished. Always remember that today could have turned out differently for you. Better yourself and now hurry home. I'm sure your mother is already worrying about you."

With a grateful smile, he took Robert's hand and squeezed it.

"I will, sir. You will have no more reason to complain to me again. Thank you."

With those words he hurried away and Robert left the place where he had hoped to bring everything to a close.

That had been close. Where had the policemen suddenly come from? Had one of his people turned him in? They had all been there tonight and it had looked as if everything was going smoothly.

So what had gone wrong? His entire merchandise of almost a year was now gone. An immense amount of money had slipped through his fingers. Also his buyers would look elsewhere. In this business, reliability was everything and he had fluffed.

His well-functioning smuggling ring was broken. How could that be? Where was the hole in the system? Had the young bellboy perhaps lost his nerve? Or was it Moira who had told her husband everything? Did he think she was that stupid?

In Moira's favor, however, was the fact that the police were superior in numbers. The boy could not have done it so quickly. It would have taken more finesse and he trusted Moira, as well as her husband. It was time to take care of the two. Robert had been a thorn in his side for long enough now.The time was ripe for him to become master of Shepherds King and take Moira with him. Unfortunately, the good girl already had a brat but there was also a solution for that.

Dumfrey sat back and relaxed. The police or MacIntyre could search as long as they wanted, they would not find him. He was as safe here as a bird on the roof,and so he began to make his next plans.

Chapter 25

Thoughtfully he looked out to the garden. Despite the many clouds in the sky the weather was much too nice to sit here in the room and have to take care of the paperwork. But he had to do it urgently, because lately, he had criminally neglected it.

Too many things had taken up his time and, if he was honest with himself, he had looked for every opportunity to get out of it. But after last night, there was nothing that he could have taken care of at the moment. The gang had been arrested and Dumfrey was on the run, but the police were looking for him and they were sure that he would be caught soon.

Especially since his townhouse in Edinburgh was already guarded. So there was only one more thing for which he had to find a solution. Moira - he spotted her, as she sat alone in the back part of the garden, taking her lonely walk. Just a few weeks ago, he would have dropped everything to go to her. They would have hugged and kissed, joked and laughed. Robert closed his eyes sadly and remembered the many wonderful hours he had spent with her.

Could it really all have been faked? She had wanted to make him believe that Dumfrey had forced her to repay ten thousand pounds. Why should her father have borrowed so much money from Dumfrey, when he had just bought the expensive horses with his uncle.

He would not have gone into debt for it. Robert had never met him, but he didn't think he was that stupid and therefore, it didn't make sense to him. Maybe he should talk to her again, to learn a little more about this matter. But the conversation would have to wait until he was finished here. He glanced out into the garden again to catch one last glimpse of her, but Moira was no longer there. She had probably long since gone back into the house. He heaved a long sigh and went back to his desk. He was just about to sit down in his chair when there was a knock at the door.

"Yes, please?"

Albert appeared in the doorway.

"Excuse me, my lord, Inspector Jennings is here with some of his people and would like to see you urgently."

Hope sprouted in Robert. Had the inspector and his squad already caught the fugitive?

"Show him in, please."

A few moments later, the police commander entered the room. In his hand he held a package.

"Lord Macintyre, I'm sorry to disturb you, but I must have a word with your wife."

Astonished and suspicious at the same time, Robert carefully investigated the inspector's request. Could it be that someone had denounced Moira to the inspector? But who else knew about the matter? Afraid that he had found out about the poison attempt on him by her, he tried to react calmly and level-headed.

"May I ask what this is about, since my wife is not feeling very well at the moment? You must know, we are expecting our first child."

"Oh, congratulations. I'm sure I won't keep her long but she would have to confirm something for me. It is correct, isn't it, that your wife is a Fergusson by birth?"

"Yes, that's right. She's from the neighborhood here, and

her parents were killed in a fire about two years ago."

"Yes, I remember that. Quite a tragic thing back then. We were never able to determine the cause of the fire. However, we always had doubts that the investigation was not done properly. This theory was also supported by Miss Fergusson, I mean your wife, by stating on the record the very next day, the family jewelry and a lot of cash had disappeared from the safe. At the time, we didn't make a big fuss about it, and your wife didn't know about our suspicions either. But this matter from that time is the reason I'm here today."

"I don't quite understand."

The inspector came closer and put the package on Robert's desk. He unwrapped it and out came a jewelry box.

"Lord MacIntyre, I'll explain in a moment, but it would be nice if we could have your wife join us."

"Why, yes – of course."

Robert rang for his butler, and when Albert appeared in the room a moment later, he turned to him.

"Albert, will you tell my wife, please that I need her here. The inspector has a few questions for her."

"Very well."

When Albert had left again, Robert turned his full attention to the inspector.

"You've got me curious now. What is it about this jelwery box?"

Robert offered the commander a seat in the armchair across from his desk, while he himself took a seat in his chair. Inspector Jennings leaned back, relaxed and crossed his legs.

"The box is a strange thing. We just came from Sir Dumfrey's estate and spent the whole day turning the house upside down, trying to find any clue to where he might have gone. In the process, his safe fell into our hands and when we opened it we found this box in there.

As you can see," he opened the lid of the jewelry box and turned it over to Robert, who whistled through his teeth in amazement, "it is filled with several pieces of jewelry and, on top of that, with a chunk of pound notes. To be precise, a small fortune. In addition, there was a letter containing a will naming your wife as beneficiary which was signed by her parents. So you can see that it is very important for me to speak to your wife to find out what she knows about this box and if she can imagine how it came to be in Sir Dumfrey's safe."

Silence fell for a moment. Neither man said anything. Robert thought about what the inspector had just told him, then he said, "If my wife reported these things missing two years ago and they have now turned up at Dumfrey's, doesn't that mean he must have had something to do with taking them? Because otherwise it would mean that you would suspect my wife of complicity."

"Oh, please, no. I in no way suspect your wife. In fact, I'm of the same opinion that Charles Dumfrey must have had a hand in it. Especially since he was a guest in the house the night before. But I need to talk to your wife to make sure it's the family jewelry, as I assume it is."

"Well, I'm sure she'll confirm it in a moment."

Albert appeared in the doorway.

"My lord, I'm sorry, but we can't find My Lady anywhere. She is not upstairs in her room, nor anywhere else in the house."

"She's probably still in the garden, Albert, I saw her there earlier. Have a look please ."

But when Albert came back a short time later he could only report that Moira was not to be found in the garden either. She had disappeared from the grounds. Also an inquiry with Samuel resulted in nothing. Neither a horse was missing nor had the carriage been used.

Gradually Robert became very worried, and the inspector, who had not failed to notice, immediately offered his help, with his men to search the estate for her. Robert gladly accepted the help and also mobilized his men to search the entire property for her.

He couldn't shake the feeling that Moira might have witnessed the arrival of the policemen and had become frightened. Perhaps she had believed that he was going to hand her over to the inspector and was now hiding from them. But after an hour of intensive search, they still had not found any trace of her and gradually it was getting dark outside. Worried, he looked at the setting sun, the darkness would not make their search easier. Where on earth was she?

"We need to widen our search," he turned to Samuel.

"Robert, it's almost dark, we won't be able to do much more. She could be anywhere. Maybe we should wait until morning."

"No! I'll ride out in any case, and you ride over to your wife's place and see if she might be there, and then you meet me on the cliff trail. I will ride from here to the cove and then take the Cliff Path there. The inspector and his troop has streamed out in all directions, and the rest will continue to search for her here."

"Okay, but we should definitely take torches with us. I'll get some and have the others carry them, too."

"Hurry up, I don't want to waste any time. I'm very worried."

The rose garden had been her favorite place. Now at this time of year it smelled of all the beautiful flowers, because not only rose bushes, which had given the place its name, grew here. The gardeners understood their work, because the bushes, shrubs and perennials were in perfect bloom and so she drew in one after the other the fragrance from them. She admired the variety of colors and how masterfully they had been planted to create a varied picture. Behind this garden was the small pond, on whose park bench she had once sat with Robert. She thought back wistfully to that evening.

It had been her first evening here at the castle, on which he had almost shown her what physical love meant. Just the thought of him caressing her and kissing her naked breasts, her heart beat faster. She missed him so much and wished she could turn back the hands of time, to do many things differently, because it was also the evening, where she had sealed her fate by giving him the sleeping powder.

Moira turned around, because she suddenly had the feeling that she had to leave this place and hurried away in the direction of the house entrance. Just as she was about to turn the corner of the house, she saw six uniformed horsemen arriving in front of it. Immediately she retreated, so that she would not run into the hands of the gentlemen. Panic overcame her. The fact that the police were here, could only mean one thing.

Robert wanted to hand her over to the authorities, forgetting his promise that she would have nothing to fear until the birth of her child. He was probably tired of having her in the house. What should she do now? She could no longer go in. The sheer fear of the gallows influenced her thoughts.

Frantically, without a clear thought, she hurried away as fast as her condition allowed. She had to get away as quickly as possible to build up a great distance from the house. Once her absence was discovered, Robert wouldn't hesitate another minute and have the police hunt her down. But where would she go? She had no money and only the clothes on her body. Maybe she should rush home to Eileen. She would tell her friend the truth and hope she would hide her for a while. At least until she could feel safe from Robert's revenge. Would he ever give up? No matter, it was the only hope she had at the moment, but she would not take the shorter route along the village road. This would be too dangerous.

Far too easily for someone to come along the way who recognized her, and therefore she hurried off in the direction of the cliff path. Scared, she constantly looked around for possible pursuers, but everything remained calm and she continued her way along the narrow path by the cliffs. Today the sea lay quiet and peaceful under her, which was a rare sight.

A few gulls were circling in the sky, looking for prey, but Moira had no eyes for the beauty of nature. She had just looked around again fearfully, when she suddenly collided with Sir Dumfrey.

"Oh, where are you going? To see you here is my good fortune."

Moira uttered a gasp of shock as he held her by the arms.

"Let me go. I have to go, the police are after me."

Astonished, Dumfrey looked at her, but did not let her go at all.

"The police? Then come with me, I can hide you."

"No! No, let me go. I will not go with you. You've caused me enough trouble."

"I did? Don't make me laugh. Your husband has ruined my business and thwarted my plans and now you're going to come with me, and pay for not doing your job. I ordered you to keep him away from me. Now he will pay for it and you will marry me."

Angrily, Moira replied: "Have you forgotten? I am already married and I will do nothing more for you."

"I have not forgotten at all that you are married. On the contrary, my dear, for I need you as the widow of Shepherd's King. I'll take care of your husband. He won't be with us much longer."

"You can't scare me anymore. My husband knows about everything..."

Suddenly, Dumfrey tightened his grip on her arms so much that she almost fell to her knees in pain. His eyes seemed to want to pierce her and like a madman, he shouted at her, "What have you done? YOU set him on my business? For two years I have pursued my plans and I will not allow everything to be destroyed by you shortly before the goal is reached. You will see where this leads you and now you will come with me!"

On the narrow path he tried to pull Moira along behind him, but her fear of him gave her strength he had not expected. With a jerk, she was able to tear away from him, but the energy with which she had freed herself from him, now gave her such a backwards jolt, that she stumbled and thereby came too close to the edge of the abyss. She flapped her arms in the air, to avoid the fall, but she lost her balance and fell with a look of shock and a bloodcurdling scream into the depths. Dumfrey, who witnessed the inconceivable event with wide eyes, walked slowly to the place where Moira had been standing just a few seconds ago.

Cautiously he looked over the edge and could not believe what he saw there. His whole plan was gone, but Robert MacIntyre would pay for it – terribly - and so he hurried away.

Chapter 26

Robert drove his horse forward despite the darkness that had set in. He was on the way to the bay, to take the cliff path. With the burning torch in his hand, he illuminated the path, hoping to spot anything that would tell him he was on the right track. But so far he had not found any evidence that Moira had been here.

With a worried face, he reined in his horse and dismounted. From now on, he would have to lead his horse. It was too risky to ride along the narrow path, because it was too easy for the horse to misstep and fall into the depths together with the rider. Before he could set off in the direction of Moira's old childhood home, he wanted to inspect the path down to the bay.

Although he did not believe that Moira had been here or that she would have been so reckless as to climb down in her condition, he did not want to leave any place not searched. A few minutes later he turned back with the knowledge that no one had been here for a long time. Where was she?

There had to be a trace of her somewhere. No one could simply disappear and so he took his horse by the rein and searched the path with the torch. He shone the light on every bush and shrub that grew along the trail and called her name, but except for the soft clapping of the waves below him, everything remained silent. The more time went by without him finding anything the more his hope that he would find her here disappeared. Maybe she was somewhere else and he was wrong with his assumption.

Cautiously he went on, when a flickering light in front of him caught his attention.It came slowly towards him and it could only mean that Samuel was coming towards him. Robert wanted to know what he had to report, so he waited for him and in the meantime he continued to point the torch on the floor. Suddenly he discovered a small footprint in the sand in front of him. He crouched down and held the torch close to the ground. There he could see it. Robert took courage as he directed the light onto the path, and could now clearly make out the footprints of a human being.

With large steps he pursued the trace, until he reached a point where the trail stopped and another one from the opposite direction had joined it. These prints were now much larger and rather those of a man. Had Moira met with someone? Robert tied his horse to a bush and lit the way. At this moment, Samuel arrived, accompanied by Eileen, who was leading Samuel's horse.

"So you haven't found her yet either?"

"No, unfortunately I haven't. She wasn't with me, but Samuel has made out footprints, that have walked along here."

"Yes, but they belong more to a man. However I found smaller ones that run right up to here. It could be, that if it was Moira, she met up with someone here."

"But then we should have found her prints as well, or you should have found his. Somehow they both had to get out of here."

"That's the strange thing. I only found the men's prints that disappeared over there," Robert pointed inland.

„If we just had more light."

Something wasn't right here. Robert could feel it, so he shone his light on the bushes along the precipice and then he saw it. At a bush, not far from him, was a small piece of cloth. When he examined it more closely, he was sure that it was from Moira's dress, which she had worn in the garden.

"Come here, I think I found something."

Immediately they both rushed to Robert. He had begun to examine the bushes to the right and left of him. Samuel also illuminated the area with his torch, but there was no further sign of her. Eileen began to call her name and the men joined in. But everything remained quiet. Following an inner intuition, he stepped closer to the abyss.

"Be careful, the cliffs are treacherous and the edge can easily crumble off."

But Robert turned a deaf ear to Samuel's warning to the wind and stepped right up to the edge. He shone into the black abyss. He was just about to turn away again when something caught his attention. Immediately he lay down flat on his stomach and held his torch far down into the darkness.

"My God! Moira! Samuel, come here and shine your light. I think she's down there."

"What!"

When Samuel also shined his light down into the abyss, they could see her. Her body was lying on a small ledge several feet below them and was not moving. A thicket that grew out of the rock seemed to have broken her fall.

"Moira! Moira!"

But Moira gave no sign of life in response to Robert's calls. He quickly straightened up and ran over to his horse. He pulled a rope from his saddlebag that he hoped was long enough and returned. Samuel and Eileen, who were slowly recovering from their state of shock, saw him tying one end around his waist and pressing the other end into his hands .

"Tie it up somehow and then you can help me. I'm going - down there."

"That's way too dangerous. You could fall yourself. The stones are loose and it's too dark. You can't even see where you're stepping. In a few hours it will be light, then we can help with more people."

Upset, Robert yelled at Samuel.

"I'm going down there now. With or without your help. She's my wife and I have to help her."

Samuel tried to calm Robert down and to make it clear to him that any help was too late, but he saw the determination in his eyes and nodded silently. Then he turned to his wife.

"Eileen, grab my horse and ride back to the castle as fast as you can. Round up everyone you can. Tell them to bring ropes, blankets, and a cart on which we can bed her."

Completely distraught over what had happened to her friend, she answered in a tearful voice, "I will." Samuel lifted her onto the horse and said to her in a softer tone, so that Robert could not hear him, "You should hurry before there is another accident here. The situation is not letting him think clearly. I hope I can prevent something worse from happening here."

"Yes, I will hurry. Take care of him. Such a terrible thing."

Samuel gave his horse a pat on the butt and watched his wife ride off, then turned his attention to Robert, who was already busy attaching the other end of the rope to his horse's saddle. When Samuel came closer and looked at him anxiously he replied:

"I know you think I'm crazy, but I have to get down there. Will you help me?"

Samuel nodded. He had no choice anyway. He just hoped the help came quickly.

"Listen, here's my plan. The rope is tied to the saddle, that's my belay. I'm going to try to go down a little farther to the right because of the loose rocks and then work my way up to her. You will hold the rope from up here and guide me. When I'm with her, you pull us up with the help of the horse."

"Robert, we should wait until the others arrive. Eileen will bring them here."

"I can't wait for that," he drove at Samuel, "If she's hurt, she needs help."

"You don't really think she's alive, do you? I'm sorry to have to tell you this so brutally, but no one has ever survived a fall from the cliffs."

Angry and upset, Robert's eyes sparkled.

"I'm going down there now, and I don't want to hear about her possibly being dead."

Before Samuel could say anything else, Robert turned and readied himself. Slowly and carefully he let himself backwards down the abyss. Feet and fingers sought a foothold in the crevices and he was anxious not to hit any loose stones. He had chosen a spot to the right, so that if any stones started to roll, they would not hit Moira. Samuel had in the meantime made himself ready to support the insane plan.

He hoped fervently that Robert's advance would not end just as badly. A misstep could also mean the end for him. But Robert proceeded cautiously. He was well aware of the danger he was in, but Moira was in even greater danger. If she were still alive and all his action revolved around this one thought, he had to get to her quickly. Any movement by her could mean that the bushes that held her, could give way and she'd plunge completely into the depths. Continuing to creep forward, he cursed the darkness.

The sparse light from the torch that Samuel held at the precipice was by no means sufficient to see his next steps. But he simply could not wait for the help of the others and sit idly by, while his wife was down there on the cold stone needing help.

It seemed to take an eternity, but while Samuel called out to him from time to time where he should step now, he gradually came closer to the ledge. Finally he reached it and saw that the danger to Moira was even greater than he had thought. The ledge on which she lay, was so narrow that any movement on her part would cause her to fall further. Her fall was stopped by only a bush, which grew out from under the ledge.

Robert pushed up to her and held her at bay with his body.

"I'm with her," he called upward.

Samuel exhaled in relief. The first hurdle had been cleared. Then he heard behind him voices and a horse-drawn cart coming down the path. Help was approaching. Thank God. Now they could get them both up.

"Robert, is she alive? The help is here. We'll get you right up."

Robert, was busy examining Moira. Through the darkness he could not make out her injuries and she showed no signs of life. She reacted neither to his voice or his touch. She lay on her stomach and her face was turned away from him, yet he tried to feel her pulse.

At the wrists he could not feel anything and so he tried her neck. Had a small pulse been felt there? Yes, very faintly, he could feel something.

"Moira, can you hear me? I'm going to get you to safety, do you hear me? Hold on."

Then suddenly several ropes were thrown over the precipice from above, torches and lamps illuminated the ledge. At last Robert could see the full extent of the catastrophe. Blood ran in a rivulet from the stone and her arms were also covered with deep abrasions. His heart almost stopped at this sight.

"My lord, take the ropes and tie them around her body and we will pull her up first," sounded down from above and Robert began to tie the first rope under her arms. He tied another rope around her waist, then he tore off her hoop skirt, as it was an obstacle to her recovery. He tied a third rope around himself so that two men could pull him up at the same time.

"We're ready to go, but slowly and carefully", he called upwards. Then the ropes were tightened and Robert pulled Moira to her feet. Held by the ropes, her body hung limp against him, because while Robert himself was pulled up, he tried to support her body as well. When the cliff edge appeared in front of him strong arms pulled first Moira and then him up.

Once he reached the top, he immediately untied the ropes and turned to his wife, who was now lying motionless on the ground. It was a picture of horror. Her face was smeared with blood and she had abrasions on her hands and arms. The petticoat was also soaked with blood and so he did not hesitate and carried his wife over to the cart, where he immediately turned to Samuel.

"Ride to the village and get the doctor. I'll take Moira home. Hurry! It's a matter of life and death."

He didn't have to tell Samuel twice, and before he had even finished the last sentence, he was already on his horse gallopping off. Eileen climbed onto the cart with Robert when he started the horses. She squatted down next to Moira, wrapped her in the blankets, held her hand, and prayed to God that she would survive.

Chapter 27

Robert drove to the castle as quickly as he could. The morning was already dawning and it would not be long before the sun would rise, but Robert's thoughts only circled around Moira's condition. So far she had not regained consciousness and he fervently hoped that the doctor could help her.

Eileen had padded her head and body with blankets so that he could drive quickly, but it still seemed like an eternity until he finally reached his house. No sooner had he brought the carriage to a halt, when he jumped from the coach box and lifted Moira from the loading area into his arms. Effortlessly, he carried her with great strides up the front steps. Eileen hurried ahead of him to open the heavy front door, when Albert came to meet them in the vestibule.

Quite contrary to his usually impeccable appearance, his condition was somewhat deranged that suggested he had been sleeping in his clothes. Before he could say anything about the situation Robert called out to him: "The doctor is coming, send him up right away , call your wife that we need her, and tell Gwyneth to put on some hot water. As much as she can."

Without another word he saw with horror Moira lying lifeless and covered with blood in the arms of her husband. He hurried to his wife and woke up Gwyneth. Robert carried Moira swiftly up the stairs to his bedroom. In the room Eileen had already taken the blankets and pillows from the bed so that he could lay Moira on the mattress. While Robert was still carefully bedding her, Eileen began to light the lamps in the room and to light the fire in the fireplace.

They needed light and warmth when the doctor arrived. Carefully, Robert began to undress Moira. Again and again, he tried to talk to her, but she still showed no movement. Once again he checked her pulse and was relieved to find that it was still there. Weak, but he could feel it. Harried appeared with a pile of clean sheets and bandages on her arm and laid everything out on the table by the fireplace, then she and Eileen carried the table over to the bed. Horrified, she looked at Robert.

"My lord, what has happened? We were up all night hoping your wife would come home. Then when Eileen came here and called everyone together, we didn't know what had happened. Did she have an accident?"

Before he could say anything, he heard hurried footsteps on the stairs and Albert shouted to someone that it was the room to his left. Then he caught sight of the doctor, who was standing with his bag in his hand, followed by Albert and Samuel. Dr. Simmons was a handsome, middle-aged man, and he owned a practice in the village. During years of practice, he had seen many things, but the sight of this young woman lying on the bed covered in blood, made even him stop for a moment. Robert immediately approached him.
"What happened, can you tell me?"

Dr. Simmons hurried to the bed, placed his doctor's bag on the table and took out a stethoscope.

"I found my wife on a ledge by the cliffs. She must have fallen down there. I then brought her here. Please Doctor, you must save her."
Carefully he opened Moira's blouse and listened to her heart. Then he pushed up her eyelids and examined her

eyes. He examined her head and neck and carefully felt her chest. Then, as he felt her abdominal area, he paused. "Is your wife pregnant?"
"Yes, how bad is it?"

"I can't tell for sure right now. She's alive, but the blood loss worries me. She is losing too much blood and has to be treated immediately, so I'm going to have to ask you to leave the room so I can work in peace."
"Under no circumstances will I leave my wife here alone," replied Robert firmly.

The doctor stood up in front of him. He knew this situation well enough, when the relatives stood in his way rather than let him do his work. With the necessary objectivity, he enlightened Robert.

"My lord, I have to concentrate and need quiet to work. If you are here in the room, it's more of a hindrance, and it doesn't benefit neither you nor your wife. So please leave now and wait downstairs until I'm finished. Harried and Eileen will stay here and assist me. Albert, I'm going to need a lot of hot water. Please have it prepared as soon as possible."
"It's already ready for you."
"Very well. Then if I may ask you gentlemen to leave the room?"

While Albert and Samuel went to the door, Robert didn't move a bit. He had brought Moira here and he did not want to leave her alone now.
"Please, my lord," the doctor urged him again, "you are wasting important time."

That's when Eileen intervened and gave her husband a wave, that he should take Robert with him. Samuel understood and tried to influence Robert.

"Come on, let the doctor work. It doesn't help Moira if you keep him from doing it. We'll wait downstairs."

And as he said this, he pushed Robert out of the room in front of him. Relieved to finally be able to begin his work, Harried, at his behest, closed the door behind the men and began to give the doctor a hand. Outside, Samuel turned to Albert, before going into the writing room with Robert.

"Albert, bring him a double scotch, I think he could use it right now."

"Very well."

When Samuel was with Robert in his office, Robert's face was written with despair. He was sitting slumped at his desk and had his head in his hands, while Samuel stood at the window, lost in thought watching the sun as it rose. What a night lay behind them. When he turned around, he saw Robert sitting with his eyes closed. He could well imagine what was going on inside him. One floor up, his wife was fighting for her life and he was supposed to wait here idly. But it didn't help anyone if he made the doctor nervous.

How had it ever come to this? Had it been an accident or did Moira intend to take her own life? Something was no longer right in their relationship. He had this feeling for weeks, but he didn't know if he should bring it up. Eileen said he should ask why Moira no longer came to visit her, and so he took it to heart and spoke his thoughts.

"I know it's none of my business, but what's going on between you and Moira? For weeks I've only seen her from afar, if at all and she doesn't visit Eileen anymore. Something has been bothering you for a long time, too and then tonight. Why was she out there alone? Won't you finally explain to me what's going on?"

Robert looked up and Samuel was almost a little startled.

He had never seen him like this before. Tired, bloodshot eyes looked at him in despair and in a low, resigned voice he began to talk:

"I think she tried to kill herself today and it's my fault."

"She tried to kill herself? Why?"

Horrified, Samuel moved closer.

"She must have seen the police here and thought I was going to turn her in."

"Police? Turn her in? I don't understand, what you mean. Why would she be afraid of the police?"

"Moira was working with Dumfrey and I found out about it."

"What, Moira, a smuggler? I can't believe that. Are you sure about that?"

Gradually, something stirred inside Robert. And how he was sure. It was time he got the whole mess off his chest.

"I saw her myself one night getting out of Dumfrey's carriage. When I confronted her, she confessed everything to me. From the very beginning, she lied to me, deceived me and even tried to kill me.It was thanks to her that I was in such a bad state. Dumfrey had given her a sleeping powder, which was mixed with arsenic. That's why she's been under house arrest for weeks."

Samuel couldn't believe what he was hearing.

"This is all unbelievable. Why would Moira do something like this?"

"She must owe Dumfrey a lot of money and he's asked her to make a pass at me, to keep me away from his activities in the bay. It was a setup from the start and when the police showed up here yesterday, she must have thought I was going to hand her over and fled."

"And you think she tried to take her own life?"

"Yes."

"That's really an incredible story. I've known Moira longer than you have, and Eileen knows her even better, and I can only tell you, I can't understand that. Moira is sometimes quite gullible. She sees only the good in everyone and after the death of her parents, she had to grow up very quickly and take responsibility. Everyone put their problems on her shoulders and I can imagine that she was overwhelmed and easy prey for Dumfrey. But that she should be calculating and ice-cold, I just can't believe."

"She herself told me that she had Dumfrey's orders and what she was supposed to do. Although she claims that she only ever thought it was a sleeping powder, as it was the first time. You remember the morning you found me here? That was her doing. But who would believe her after what she did."

"But I've seen you two interact. The way she looked at you. Boy, that wasn't acting. She really loves you. Maybe she was fooling you at first, but in the weeks before and after your wedding, her feelings were real. No one can fake that and then the baby. She was so happy about it. It doesn't add up when you're supposed to be so calculating."

"I know. I believed that she was fooling me about the baby, too, but she's really having one and that's why I haven't turned her over to the police yet. I can't bring the mother of my child to the gallows, so I told her that she would be under house arrest until the birth."
"And what were you going to do with her then?"

"Honestly, I don't know. When she told me about Dumfrey, I was furious and deeply hurt. I felt taken advantage of and betrayed. I had laid my heart at her feet and she only used me. I punished her and try to banish her from my life but I just couldn't do it. I am a fool because I still love her in spite of everything. I miss every day, the hours we spent together, talking and laughing. I can find no rest, because my body longs for her. I want to hold her in my arms and now I'm scared as

223

hell that I might lose her. Many times I have asked myself if I could forgive her, but how could I ever be able to trust her again?"

Samuel ran his hand through his hair. It was an outrageous story that Robert was telling him and if Moira had really committed all these acts, she had taken on a heavy guilt, but somehow it did not sound like her at all. He knew, through Eileen, that Dumfrey had been badgering her. Could it be that her desperation had been so great that she had agreed to such a pact?

"What puzzles me about the whole thing, is why she didn't ask for your help, if she owes Dumfrey money. Why was she doing this anyway?"

"I don't understand it either. Moira told me that Dumfrey has a promissory bill from her father and that he owed him ten thousand pounds."

Samuel whistled through his teeth.

"A lot of money."

"She said that he had blackmailed her with that sum of money, and that if she told me anything about it, he would hurt Eileen or the children. According to Moira, he even wanted to put her in a whore house in Edinburgh if she didn't work off the money for him."

"What a son of a bitch. It's about time he was caught.

I'm sure even Eileen doesn't know anything about it, because she would have told me. So Moira was desperate because she didn't have anyone to talk to about it."

"She still should have told me. We would have found a way to protect your wife and the kids. I offered to help her from the beginning. I knew that her finances weren't doing very well."

"Maybe there's more to it than that, something that you don't know. If you really still care about her, then you should talk to her again, calmly and without anger. I don't want to defend her, she committed a crime, but it's up to you whether this crime is ever made public. It is in your hands. Only you are the injured party."

Becoming thoughtful, Robert took a deep breath.

"I know what you mean by that. Except Dumfrey, Moira, me and now you, no one knows anything about the attack. So if we don't tell anyone, only Dumfrey could do it, and he'll be guilty as well."

"Right. So it's up to you how far you want to go. If I'm honest, I don't know what I'd do either if this whole thing had happened to me. But as a friend, my advice to you is to talk with each other."

"I should have done it a long time ago, but I wasn't ready to do it yet, and now it's maybe too late. Jesus, is it a good sign or a bad sign, that we've been sitting here for hours and haven't heard anything? I can't stand this waiting anymore."

Robert had jumped up and was wandering through the room. Finally the door opened and Albert appeared.

"My lord, the doctor wishes to see you."

Hastily he hurried up, and as he entered the room, he was met by Eileen, who was carrying a pile of blood-soaked sheets in her hand. The sight did not bode well, but before he could think about it further, Dr. Simmons approached him.

"What about my wife?"

"Please come outside the room with me. I need to talk to you undisturbed."

Robert tried to take a look at the bed, but Harried stood in his line of vision and blocked his view. Thus he went with the doctor in front of the door, who immediately had his say.

"Your wife is alive. I was able to stop the heavy bleeding, but she is very weak due to the high blood loss. On top of that, she has a severe concussion and a number of abrasions and bruises. Your wife was very lucky because she did not suffer any broken bones or internal injuries. However, I have to give you the sad news that she has lost her child."

Robert had feared it, but now hearing the unsparing truth stung his heart. He had just gotten used to the idea of becoming a father, and now this. Suddenly he was overcome by an unspeakable sadness, because this meant that an important reason for not having to hand Moira over to the police had disappeared. How had she taken the news?

"Does my wife know about this yet?"

Dr. Simmons shook his head.

"She was conscious for a short time, but I haven't told her yet. I think it's better, that she regains her strength a little first, before she learns the truth. Otherwise she could go into a deep depression and that would get in the way of her recovery."

"Will she be able to have children again?"

"Yes, she is young and as far as I could see, no irreparable damage has been done. She will be physically well in a few weeks, the psychological damage after a miscarriage is unfortunately impossible to predict. Some women cope better than others.

At the moment she has severe abdominal pain, which on the one hand is caused by the loss of the child and the high loss of blood and on the other hand from the fall in general. I have given her some laudanum for this.

Just in case I'll leave you some more if the pain becomes stronger again. However, you should only give it to her if there is no other way. My lord, your wife should be under constant observation for a few days.

If her condition deteriorates, call me immediately, otherwise I'll check back in two days. Until then, she needs a lot of rest and no excitement. You can go to her now. I will excuse myself."

"Thank you very much, Doctor Simmons."

"Don't thank me. Pray to God for keeping his hands

protectively over her tonight."

As the doctor left, Robert re-entered the bedroom. Harried was the only one left in the room.

"My lord, I'll prepare you a bath. We have enough hot water left for me to fill the tub. Albert will bring you fresh clothes, and you can lay yours at the door for me to take."

Harried looked a little sheepishly at his shirt and Robert followed the look. He hadn't even registered yet, that he too was wearing his wife's blood on his clothes. His shirt and pants were stained with blood. But he cared little about it and went over to the bed.

Wrapped in fresh sheets, Moira lay there. Her face as pale as the sheets themselves. Around her forehead she wore a white bandage and her face was littered with blood-encrusted scratches. In some places, a slight blue tint was visible. There would be colorful bruises in the next few days. Her eyes were closed and her breathing was calm.

It was the second time in a short while that he saw her so helpless and weak in that bed, and he wanted her to regain her strength, wanted her to become his Moira again. Here and now he decided that he didn't care what had been. He wanted a new beginning with her and he would fight for it. Robert drew the thick curtains to darken the room.

It was after eight o'clock in the morning and the hot bath had done him good, but the events of the night had also left their marks and so he had decided to give himself a few hours' sleep. Cautiously, he sat down on the edge of the bed at the side of Moira. She had not moved or woken up in the last half hour.

Carefully, he stroked her cheek with his finger. He had almost forgotten how soft her skin was. Carefully he breathed a kiss on her bandaged forehead. The doctor had advised him to keep her under constant observation and that is exactly what he would do. So it was best if he slept with her, because he would notice any change immediately and so he lay down next to her in bed. For a while he listened to her regular breaths until he himself fell asleep.

Chapter 28

When Moira woke up, the room around her was in semi-darkness. It took her a while to register that she was back in her bed in Robert's bedroom. It worried her, hadn't she run away from him and the police? She had tried to evade arrest, but there seemed to be no escape from him.

Should she try again? But she was tired of running, felt weak and her limbs refused to obey her. A sharp pain immediately ran through her head when she tried to sit up in bed. Groaning, she sank back into the pillows. Then suddenly, seemingly appearing out of nowhere, she saw Harried running excitedly to the bed.

"Oh, my lady, you mustn't move. You had an accident and are injured. We have been very worried about you, but now that you are awake, I'll bring you some food and drink right away. You need to regain your strength. I'll just open the curtains a little so you can see better. Please lie still, until I get back."

Without waiting for a reply, she opened the curtains a small crack to let the daylight in, then she disappeared from the room and Moira was alone. She tried to think, but her head ached too much.

Harried had mentioned that she had been in an accident but no matter how much she thought about it, she could not remember it. The last thing she knew was that the police had shown up and she had run away, but she could not remember where to. The dull pain in her head was sharp and came at intervals and just as she was trying to massage her temples with her fingers she realized that she had a thick bandage around her forehead.

The door opened and instead of Harried, Robert entered the room. Standing tall, he stood for a moment in the door. Dressed in black pants and a white shirt, in which his muscular torso was tucked in and whose sleeves he had rolled up to the upper arms, he looked very virile.

A few strands had come loose from his neatly coiffed black hair, which gave him a daring expression. He looked so outrageously good, that she could not take her eyes off him, and her heart began to beat faster. Without moving, she followed him with her eyes as he came closer and placed a tray he had brought with him on the table next to her bed.

Then he sat down on the edge of the bed with her and looked at her in silence. Moira had to swallow. She didn't seem to be able to escape her punishment. There they sat now, each seeming to assess the other, and neither knew what to say. The gap between them seemed too wide to make a start.

Moira tried to read Robert's face. What was going on inside him, but he controlled himself too well. The fact that Robert said nothing at all worried her so much that she became frightened. Robert, on the other hand, had been relieved when Harried had told him that Moira was awake.

He had immediately dropped everything to check on her. She was still very pale in the face and probably still in a lot of pain, but she bravely tried not to show it. Actually, he had wanted to talk to her as soon as she was awake, but at the sight of her, he inwardly postponed the conversation to the future. He was about to stroke her cheek tenderly and had already raised his hand when

Moira suddenly got a panic stricken expression. Startled, he lowered his hand immediately. Then Moira began to speak in a weak and fragile voice:

"Robert, I beg you, please don't send me to prison. I will do anything you say. I will obey you or go away forever, if that is what you want, but do not send me to prison."

She put her hand on his arm and looked at him with a pleading and desperate look. Instinctively, he sensed her fear - of him, and that was the last thing he wanted. Soothingly, he said:

"Let's talk about it when you're feeling better. You're sick and you should get your strength back."

"No!"

Her violent reaction surprised him and he paused.

"I don't want any more lies and misunderstandings between us. I wish I could undo everything. In my naivety I thought I could deal with Dumfrey myself. If it hadn't been for that promissory bill from my father, everything would have been different. Shortly after the funeral of my parents, Dumfrey asked me to marry him, but......"

Robert saw how the talking was exhausting her and how she could hardly keep her eyes open. She desperately needed the rest that Dr. Simmons had prescribed for her, and so he cut her off.

"Moira, let's wait until you're feeling better. You can hardly keep yourself awake."

But she was determined to get everything off her chest, so she mustered up the last of her strength and continued: "No, please, I have to tell it now. Just listen to me."

Robert, who heard the urgency in her voice and understood that it was important to her, let her. Silently, he sat on the edge of the bed and listened to her words.

"As I said, Dumfrey asked me to marry him quite soon,

but I refused, as I did the countless times after that. He simply did not want to understand that I did not want to marry him. Then, last summer he came one day and proposed again, and I politely declined again.

This must have infuriated him so much, because he suddenly pulled out my father's promissory note and told me that I should pay back the money in installments. But they were prohibitively expensive for me. I was able to pay back the first few installments with savings but at the beginning of the year I could no longer pay. That was the time when he started to blackmail me. Marriage was no longer an option and, strangely enough, he was no longer interested in money. He wanted me to keep you away from the bay. If I refused, he would hurt Eileen, the children and me. He threatened to send me to the brothel, then another time he threatened that there might be a fire at the orphanage, like at my parents.

I know none of those are excuses why I gave you that sleeping powder, but - I didn't know what else to do. He told me that if I told you, you would break up with me and that's what I was afraid of."

Robert listened intently and suddenly felt bad since Dumfrey had known him so well, for he had done just that. He had dropped Moira when he learned of the betrayal. He wanted to say something, but Moira continued.

"I thought that if I gave you the powder. I would have fulfilled my debt to him, but he kept coming back. I told him that I could pay him back the money, but he was not interested in the money any longer. It had also occurred to me to let him think that I would do it, but he knew about every move of mine and of yours. Robert, he has an informant here in your house."

"I know it's William, my bellhop. I caught him in flagrante delicto the other night."

"William? No wonder he knew about everything here."

"What exactly is his plan?"

"I don't know. At first it was to keep you away from the bay. The second time I gave you the powder, I went to the cove myself because I wanted to know what was going on, but unfortunately they caught me."

"That was very dangerous of you," Robert shook his head in disbelief.

"Maybe, but I wanted to know, what was happening there, and also wanted to know if it gave me a chance to get him off my back. I admit that it was very amateurish of me."

"Why didn't you ever confide in me? You knew from the very beginning that I was offering you my help."

"I know, but it was my problem, not yours. It's my father who owes him money. When this whole thing started, I didn't even know you, and that's why I'm accepting my punishment, whatever it may be, but please don't send me to prison. I'll do whatever you say."

"I don't want you to do things for me, just because I tell you to, nor do I want you to stay with me because you think you have to.Tell me one thing and I want to hear the truth, even if it does not turn out the way I would like to hear it. How do you feel about me?"

Without having to think about it, Moira answered in a clear voice:

"I love you. Even on our first night, at the ball outside in the garden, I thought you were very nice. I enjoyed that evening with you very much, but I had also seen the effect you had on the other ladies and I didn't think it was possible that you could be even remotely interested in me. I was therefore happily surprised when you came to visit me a few days later. In all the time that we've been married, I've never once betrayed you. I had the best and happiest days of my life with you and every time I thought that Dumfrey would leave me alone, he showed up again and entangled me deeper and deeper in something I wanted nothing to do with. Robert, I know I've hurt you deeply, and I'm sorry, but can't you feel my love for you?"

Desperation was in her gaze. He seemed not to believe her. Was it a surprise? She had played nasty tricks on him. Robert didn't know what to say. On the one hand he wanted to believe her when she said she loved him, but then there was the night he had found her on the cliffs.

"If you love me, then why did you try to take your own life?"

Horrified, she looked at him.

"Take my life? I would never do that, that would be sinning before God. How could you think such a thing?"

"I found you up on the cliffs. You jumped over the precipice. Lucky or unlucky for you, there was a ledge below you that broke your fall."

Robert watched closely to see what her reaction to his words were, but Moira did not feel caught, she was genuinely horrified by what he told her.

"It can't be. Harried said that I had an accident."

"That's what I told them, so that there wouldn't be gossip. But the fact is that you ran away and wanted to put an end to your life. Was I that repugnant to you?"

Moira's mind was working at full speed, if only she could remember exactly what had happened.

Her head was pounding, not making it any easier for her, but she had to convince Robert here and now that she was not a suicide threat. This idea was absolutely absurd.

"I ran away from the police because I didn't want them to arrest me. I remember panicking."

"Why would the police arrest you? They don't know anything about what you did."

"You didn't tell them?"

"No, except Samuel, who I had to tell two days ago, because he helped me get you off the cliff. Only you and I know what really happened. And I also told you that I wouldn't do anything as long as you were carrying our child."

He winced inwardly at the thought of the baby. It saddened him that it was no longer there, but he could not let on to her.

"I thought you had changed your mind and they had come to arrest me. Without a clear thought, I just started walking, and I think I was going to Eileen, to ask her to hide me for a while."

Images began to form in her mind. Then the fog in her mind cleared and she remembered what had happened.

"Yes, I was trying to get to Eileen and in my panic I kept turning around because I was afraid you would come after me, and then suddenly there was Dumfrey. I literally ran into him."

"Dumfrey was there? Up on the cliffs?"

"Yes, he held me down and talked something about how you were going to pay for ruining his business and that he was going to take me away because of it. When I told him that I had confessed everything to you and that there was no way I was going, he got so angry that he grabbed me and tried to drag me along. I was able to tear myself away, but I somehow lost my balance and then fell down the precipice."

"My God, and the son of a bitch didn't help you? Who knows how long you'd been lying there. I discovered you there more or less by accident. He would have let you die."

Tenderly he took her hand and led it to his lips.

"I'm sorry, I really thought, you had wanted to end your life. And I'm glad you didn't."

"I would never do our child any harm because I'm looking forward to it so much."

Robert was fighting with himself. Maybe he should tell her now. The doctor had mentioned that it was not a good time to tell her,but could he continue to let her believe that the child was doing well? Moira suddenly cramped up painfully. Groaning, she closed her eyes.
"What is it? Moira?"

"I have such severe abdominal pain. There's something wrong. Robert, the baby! Something's wrong with the baby!"

He could not stand by and watch his wife worried about the baby, who was long gone, and so he pulled her onto his lap and cradled her in his arms. She nestled her head on his shoulder and tried to breathe away the pain.
"The doctor left you a painkiller. You should take it."
"No, it could harm the child. It will be fine, but I'm afraid that there's something wrong. These pains, I don't think it's normal. Please get the doctor."
Robert struggled to keep his composure. He had to tell her, but it was the hardest thing he ever had to do.
"Moira, there's no baby. You lost it. I'm sorry."

It took a while for the meaning of his words to reach her, but then her inner tension of the last weeks discharged in a violent scream. Again and again she screamed out her despair and hammered her fists out of sheer desperation against his chest. He grabbed her hands, held them tightly until she had calmed down to some extent, and then pressed her tightly against his chest. There he let her be, as she cried her sorrow out of her soul. Her tears flowed in streams and wetted his shirt. Her reaction didn't leave him cold. His eyes became moist and he was not ashamed of his own reaction to the loss of their child. For a while they sat like that on the edge of the bed. She on his lap, her face leaning against his shoulder and he, holding her tightly against him with his eyes closed, gently rocking her back and forth. They had not been so close for a long time and it awoke feelings in them, which they had long thought to have lost. She listened to his calm heartbeat and slowly she calmed herself. The horror of the loss turned into a deep sadness. Quietly his words reached her ear and it was those words , that caused the first glimmers of hope to sprout in her.

"We will have one again. When you are well again, we will try again. I love you Moira and I'm so thankful to God, that he didn't take you away from me. I could not have borne it and I promise you that I will finally put a stop to Dumfrey once and for all."

"No, not you - we'll put a stop to him. We'll do it together. He has done so much to me, I want to be there too, when he's arrested."

"That's way too dangerous."

"You won't be able to stop me from doing it. I don't have to take my condition into consideration anymore."

Struggling, she looked him in the eye and a smirk flitted across his face. There she was again, his Moira. Strong and stubborn. He loved her so much.

"Okay. But we're going to need a good plan, to track him down and lure him out of hiding. But until that happens, you're going to make yourself get better. Now you should eat something and then rest again."

"Will do, but not until you administer something vital."

"And that would be?" asked Robert, visibly astonished.

With a timid smile on her lips, she said.

"A kiss from you."

This request he fulfilled with pleasure and so he closed her mouth with a long overdue passionate kiss. Many more followed that afternoon until they gave in to reason and Moira finally allowed herself the rest Dr. Simmons had prescribed.

Chapter 29

Moira awoke briefly when she felt a movement next to her and perceived a kiss on her cheek in twilight sleep, then immediately fell back into a deep restful sleep. When she woke up in the morning again, the headache had subsided and the abdominal pain had disappeared. She had the feeling of feeling better and therefore tried to sit up carefully in bed. She looked beside her on the mattress. It was empty, but when she ran her hand over it, she felt that it was warm.

The pillow was still flattened by his head. Robert had spent the night with her and this made her overjoyed. Her stomach began to growl, another sign that her body was recovering. Just as she was wondering whether she should eat something, there was a soft knock on the door and Albert entered. Seeing Moira sitting up in bed, he approached. He was laden with a handful of Robert's clothes and immediately headed for the closet.

"Good morning, my lady. Your husband tells you that he is sorry to have left, but he had urgent work to attend to. He has been on the go quite early. Are you hungry? Can I get you something? I'll just tidy up your husband's clothes back into the armoire, and I'll bring the rest over later, if that's all right."

"Did my husband arrange for this?" Moira asked

curiously.

"Yes. He said you're getting better and there would be no more need for him to spend the night in the other wing."

"I'm very glad to hear that, Albert."

And it actually pleased her that Robert had apparently decided to return to a normal married life again.

"Yes, my lady, I'm pleased, too. You two are well suited to each other, and you should not begin your young marriage with so much grief."

So he had had a hunch that something had been wrong with their marriage lately, and so she smiled gratefully at him. But if she had hoped to get more marriage tips from him, after all he had been married to Harried for over thirty years, she would be disappointed; she soon realized he had nothing more to say.

It was the only personal response from him she would ever get to hear. Immediately he went back again to the proper distance from her, which he was entitled to by his work as a butler. In the afternoon, Dr. Simmons appeared at her house. He had been informed by Robert that his wife knew about the baby and that he could talk to her openly. The doctor had not been enthusiastic about it, since he had warned him about a depression and that Moira's condition was not stable enough. But when he saw the young woman sitting in bed, he was relieved to see that she was already in a much better condition than two days earlier.

"I see you are already feeling better. That's good. Your husband told me that you've got your appetite back, too, so that's even better. If you don't mind, I'd like to examine you again, so we don't miss anything unpleasant."

Moira told him about the fear she had of never being pregnant again and that she sometimes had the feeling that the child was still there. After the exam, Dr.

Simmons was able to reassure her and said everything was fine. The reason that she felt she was still pregnant would have to do with the fact that she wanted to be pregnant and that she had not yet processed the whole thing. He advised her to give herself time to talk about the loss with her husband whenever she felt the need and then one day she would be ready to get pregnant a second time.

"Enjoy the time together. Once the children are here, it's over for the two of you to have quiet togetherness. I can tell you a thing or two about that, because I have five of them and my wife says, that we should make it half a dozen. Moira, you are young and you have a young, healthy man. I can assure you, you'll be pregnant again faster than you can count to three."
They both had to laugh at his joke and before he left, he assured her that there were no health concerns.

That evening Robert came to bed earlier than usual. He undressed, crawled under her blanket and took her in his arms. He told her about his day, about how he had succeeded in concluding a profitable contract with one of the barons from the neighboring county and that he had therefore been on the road early this morning. Moira, on the other hand, told him about the examination and the doctor's findings, that everything was fine and she could have children again.

Robert pressed a kiss on her mouth, which she immediately returned.
"It's going to be okay, sweetheart."

She snuggled closer to him and let her fingers playfully doft through his chest hair. It felt so good to be able to touch him again, to feel his closeness and apparently he felt the same, because she noticed how his breath suddenly went intermittently. She paused and wanted to pull her hand back, but Robert whispered in her ear:

"Go on. I have had to do without your touch for so long. I long for you."

"Robert I - I can't do this yet..."

"Ssh, I know, but when you touch me...I can dream about what it's going to be like, when you're ready again."

And so they fell asleep, snuggled close together.

Two days later Moira had recovered so much that she could take a little walk in the garden. Eileen had come to visit and Moira had felt the need to tell her friend everything. She wanted to close this chapter and that was only possible when there were no more lies.

So she also confessed to her that she had drugged Robert with an arsenic-laced sleeping powder without knowing it. Eileen was horrified and couldn't help but give her friend a good talking to, but was reconciled when she learned that the two of them had talked things out and now everything seemed to be okay again. At the sad news about the loss of the child, she took her friend in her arms, but expressed her confidence that her condition would change again quickly. They sat in the garden until early evening, when Samuel and Robert joined them, and the four of them talked for a while until Samuel left with his wife to go home.

Two more days had passed, when in the afternoon Inspector Jennings rode onto the property again. Once again he was led into the writing room, where this time he found Lord MacIntyre and his wife.

"I am glad to meet you in person today, My Lady, for I have come for you."

Moira's heart almost stopped at these words. Robert, sensing what was going on in her mind, took her hand and gave it an encouraging squeeze. Before she could say anything, he greeted the inspector, offering him a seat in one of the armchairs by the window and led his wife over with him.

"You told me the last time that you wanted to show my wife something."

"Yes, I have it here."

He pulled out the same jelwery box that he had shown Robert at the time, opened it, and turned it toward Moira so that she could see what it contained. Wide-eyed, she looked incredulously from Robert to the inspector and back into the small box. In front of her was her mother's jewelry. She touched it reverently with her fingers and carefully took out a necklace.

"This-this is my mother's jewelry. Where did you get this? It disappeared from the safe."

"So you're confirming for me that this is your parents' jewelry box?"

"Yes, some of them are heirlooms, like this ring, for example," she took out a signet ring, "which bears my grandfather's initials."

Somewhat wistfully, she spotted a silver necklace with a small sapphire on it, and the ring that went with it. Robert, who was watching his wife closely, noticed how the whole thing was affecting her. Her eyes began to shimmer wetly.

"My mother wanted to give this necklace to me as a wedding present. It had been a gift from her mother to her. Where did you find these things?"

Robert intervened.

"Before you tell my wife what you told me, you should tell her what else was in the box."

"Of course. Besides the jewelry, there was a large sum of cash in it, which I didn't bring with me today because it's better off in the safe at the station. There was also a letter addressed to you containing the will of your parents. We found the box in Sir Dumfrey's safe, on his estate and I wanted to know if you have an explanation, how these things came to be there."

"No, I can't explain that. Last time I saw these things was several years ago. I knew that my parents kept cash and jewelry in the safe, but after the fire the safe had been empty. If they turned up at Sir Dumfrey's, it can only mean that he somehow stole them. He was a guest of my parents the night of the fire.

They had dinner together. I remember that so well, because I left the house after dinner to take care of the children in the orphanage. A few of them were sick with the flu and I was worried about them. I stayed there for the night and did not return to the house. What happened there after dinner, I cannot tell you. But I know from a reliable source that Dumfrey, in order to achieve his goals, manipulates people and anesthetizes them with sedatives."

Robert inwardly drew in his breath. Why did Moira tell this to the inspector? Didn't she know that she was putting herself at risk when she told him everything. He tried to find a solution as quickly as possible but Moira was already talking.
"So could it be that he did something like this to my parents?"

"To rob the safe and disguise the crime, set the fire? Well, that I can imagine, and it's very probable that it took place in the same way. But unfortunately it is only conjecture, we can't prove it, and as long as we haven't arrested him, we can't question him. Where did you get this information that he likes to drug his victims with sleeping pills?"
The inspector was surprised by what he had just heard. Nothing escaped him and Robert sweated. How would Moira answer now?

"I want to tell you something, Inspector. My husband has known about this for some time, but I want to clear the air..."

Robert couldn't believe it. Now it was all too late. The inspector would show no mercy if she were to reveal the poison plot, but Moira was determined to confess what she had done and so she began her story.

She told the inspector every little detail of what she knew and what Dumfrey had asked of her and why. The inspector listened intently to her report, interrupting her only rarely when he had questions, but otherwise letting her continue her narrative.

When she finished, Robert's heart was lifted, for she had concealed an important detail from the inspector. The arsenic. Nevertheless, the policeman got straight to the point.

"My lady, what you have done is a crime, even though you were blackmailed. I also give you credit for your confession, although of course I am not thrilled that you have long since informed Lord MacIntyre about the matter, but he did not hint at it to me during the last visit. You should have enlightened me at once."

"Should I have turned in my own wife? And after all and at last, except for me no one was harmed by it. I did not see the need to make a big fuss about it. My wife apologized to me and that was the end of it."

Well, it hadn't been that simple, but that didn't matter here.

"However, what my wife just told you, gives a completely different picture of our Sir Dumfrey. There seems to be more to it than we suspect. It's not just the smuggling. Why did he steal the contents of a safe if he then kept it for years? Or why does he commit a double murder, and we have to assume that's what happened, and then blackmail the daughter with a promissory note that was probably never real? In addition, he had these attacks carried out on me, with the reason to keep me away from the bay where his contraband arrives, but I've come to believe that there's more to it. There's something else I want to tell you."

"And that is?"

Somewhat miffed that he had been kept in the dark for so long, he now looked at Robert promptingly.

"My uncle died in a strange way, if not from an unexplained cause. He developed violent stomach and intestinal problems, after being a guest at a banquet given by Sir Charles Dumfrey in Edinburgh. It was suspected at the time that he must have eaten something bad, but he was the only one to show these symptoms. The doctor who was called in could find nothing and my uncle got worse day by day until he died shortly after. Isn't it strange that this Dumfrey is always where people die?"

"It's a strange thing, and when we catch him, he'll have to answer to us. Unfortunately we have no trace of him so far."

"Since my wife saw him on the cliffs a short time ago, he must still be in the vicinity and must be hiding somewhere. You should check his house again for clues."

"This my men have already done and found nothing."

"Maybe they missed something?"

"I don't think so. He's probably long gone."

When the inspector had left, Robert turned to Moira.

"I don't agree with the inspector that Dumfrey has disappeared. I could almost bet that he is still in the area, and I'm going to take another look at his house tomorrow."

"All right, then. We'll turn the whole house upside down tomorrow."

"We?"

"Have you already forgotten that I said we'd bring him down together? I'm coming with you, of course."

Chapter 30

Robert stood at the foot of the staircase and waited for his wife. It was already late afternoon and it was time for them to get going. Impatiently he paced back and forth. Why was she taking so long? She knew that he wanted to arrive at the house in the light of day and had only gone upstairs for a moment to change in more comfortable clothes. In the meantime, he had fetched his gun belt from his office and strapped it around his waist. The small leather strap on the holster was buckled around his left thigh.

He had practiced a few times with nimble fingers to get his revolver out of the holster and had been pleased with himself and his form. In his old home, he had carried it every day, but here it had been lying in a drawer ever since. Today, however, he would not go without it and had therefore loaded it with the cartridges. With the summer temperatures that prevailed outside he had also decided not to wear the frock coat that he normally wore, because it would only be a hindrance when drawing and so he wore only a gray shirt next to his black trousers.

He heard her footsteps from above. Finally it could start, but when she appeared at the top of the stairs, his eyes almost fell out. She couldn't possibly be serious. Unable to say anything, he stood there with his open-mouth until she had almost reached him.

Somewhat embarrassed, she smiled at him.

"I know it looks a little funny and it's unusual, but for today's task, yet much more practical."

Funny - the word did not quite describe, what he thought of it. He had quite different words on the tip of his tongue. But the one that described it best was the word provocative. He could not believe that she really wanted to go off like that. Every contour of her lovely body he could see in his old pants she was wearing. Likewise, she was wearing a white shirt of his, which she had loosely tucked into her pants.

The dark pantalongs were held by a pair of suspenders that stretched over her breasts. As she walked past him, he could make out her small firm rear end and he felt a completely different feeling.

His mouth became dry and he noticed how his body started to react to the hip movements of his wife. At that moment he was just glad that they were going to ride unaccompanied, because in this getup she would drive any man crazy. Moira paused and turned to face him, when she realized that he was still standing by the stairs and staring after her.

"What is it? I think we want to go. Do you know how to use that thing?"

She pointed to the revolver at his hip, not letting him see that she found him extraordinarily dangerous looking with the visible weapon strapped on, which made her strangely aroused. Lasciviously, he just returned:

"Let's wish I never have to prove it to you."

Smiling, he put his arm on his wife's shoulder and as he directed her out, he thought to himself that his wife seemed to always be good for a surprise and marriage with her would never be boring. Another surprise was waiting for him outside when he saw Samuel there, with three saddled horses waiting for them, and who got googly eyed at the sight of Moira. Moira didn't seem to register any of this, for she was heading straight for her horse, while Robert turned to Samuel.

"Don't say a word."

"I - I just wanted to ... boy, what a getup. I should give Eileen my pants to wear, too."

Robert gave him a nasty and annoyed look.

"What are you doing here, anyway?"

"I thought you could use some help, or should I stay?"

"No, it's probably just as well if you come along. Three can see more than two."

And so Robert lifted Moira into the saddle, mounted himself and they galloped off.

It was quiet at the house. Dumfrey's employees had probably already looked for other employment or were at his home in Edinburgh. The front door was locked, no one had thought of that. Of course, the police had locked everything when they had left here. But Robert did not want to give up so easily.

He walked around the house and examined the windows and doors on the first floor. With such a huge property, it was easy to miss an open window or door, and he was right. The window, through which he entered the evening when they had arrested the gang here, was not locked even now. He climbed in a second time and ran straight to the front door to open it for the two others. Despite the sun still outside, it was already dusk. The many trees around the house gave not only shade from the summer heat, but they darkened the areas also prematurely. So they were forced to light kerosene lamps, which they found in the kitchen.

"When I was standing over there at the time I heard

hurried footsteps. They came from the back of the house and then disappeared through a door, because it was slammed shut. I thought at the time it must have been Dumfrey. That's why I think we concentrate the search of the first floor and basement."

"There's not going to be a lot of rooms in the back down here. There are mainly the utility rooms and reception rooms. Maybe his writing room, but most of the rooms are upstairs."

"We'll split up. You take the rooms on the right. Moira and I will take the ones on the left."

"Wouldn't it be better if I went alone, too, then it would go faster."

"No, if Dumfrey's in here somewhere, I want you near me, it's safer," he said to Moira. They went to the back of the house and then split up. Apart from their footsteps, there was no other sound and Moira, who at first had bravely wanted to run off on her own, now thought it was not a bad idea at all to inspect the rooms together with Robert.

Empty buildings somehow created an oppressive feeling. Robert concentrated on the walls and floors. Perhaps there was a secret door somewhere in the walls or a recess in the floor, behind which a cellar corridor could be suspected. But no matter how long he ran his hands over the wallpaper or lifted the carpets on the floor, his search came to nothing. Samuel also reported no success when they met again in the hall.

"Then we'll take on the basement now. There must be something in there somewhere, otherwise how could he have escaped with the house surrounded?"

There were noises in the house. Quietly he listened and tried to locate the voices and footsteps he heard. They seemed to be in the back of the house. Had the police come again? They would not find him this time either, he was sure of that. Twice they had already tried and had left again, perplexed.

He was just too clever for them. Here he could hold out for eternity and no one would ever find him. The older of the Fellow sisters had shown him this cellar vault and had been proud to tell him several anecdotes connected with this room.

He had immediately recognized the potential of such a room and had known that he had to own this house. It had been easy for him, one day during a visit to pour some arsenic into the lady's tea. Unfortunately, she was not well and had died a short time later, so that the way to own this house had become free for him. No one but he knew of the existence of this secret room and so he leaned back relaxed. Probably the police would be gone in a moment.

Quietly they went down the cellar stairs. The entire part of the house seemed to be a basement. They discovered four rooms. One of them was the coal cellar, which Robert immediately ruled out at once, for it was filled with charcoal and anyone entering it would have left black shoe prints on the floor. But there were none to be found there. The next room they entered was the supply room. They examined it a little more thoroughly, because it had several shelves on the walls.

A wooden box filled with potatoes stood in the corner. Jars of preserved food stood on the shelves next to fruit crates filled with apples and pears. A ham hung on a hook from the ceiling. Dumfrey would not have to suffer if he were here, Robert thought to himself, but they also found no bump on the wall, a hidden door or a locking mechanism. Frustrated, they walked on. They went through the large storage room where the smugged barrels had been.

Now this room was totally empty making it easier for them to investigate. While Samuel and Moira set to work of scanning the walls with their hands, to feel for a possible secret door, Robert stopped in the middle and thought. The last time he had been here, he had had the same feeling as he felt again now.

He was very close to the solution, he felt, but he could not see it. Following a sudden inspiration, he took his kerosene lamp and quietly crept across to the fourth and thus last room. It was the wine cellar. On the left and right of the walls were several wine bottles on shelves, stored horizontally. He carefully illuminated the entire room, ran the lamp along the ceiling and the shelves on the sides. Then he held it close over the floor, crouching down to look under the shelves.

Then, suddenly, he stopped. At one place it seemed to be a little brighter than on the other walls in the room. Making an effort to move silently, he crept directly to the spot and shone again. Now he was sure that light was coming from a small crack in the floor.
A smile flitted across his face. I found you after all.

He straightened up, ran his hands through the shelves attached to it and could feel an elongated crack in the wall. He ran his hand along it and found that it was a small door. Only how to open it, he could not see immediately. When he carefully examined the shelf in front of it, he noticed that there was a bump on one of the posts from behind. He stuck his head into the shelf and shone the lamp into it. There he could feel a small tilting mechanism. This had to be the switch to open the door. Probably the shelf folded out with it.

Just as he was about to take a closer look he

heard Samuel appear in the doorway.

"So this is where you are, do you have anything...."

Samuel immediately broke off when Robert signaled to him with his finger on his mouth to be quiet. He shined another light under the shelf, but the light had disappeared. So there had to be someone behind this door. Moira appeared behind Samuel in the doorway and he quickly turned to her to give her the quiet sign. Tensely they followed how Robert had apparently found something, but he suddenly said loudly:

"Nothing here either, I'm afraid," he approached both of them, signaling as he spoke to follow them quietly, and continued to say, "it seems to be as the police have already suspected, that Dumfrey is long gone."

Robert said no more until he was outside the house with the horses. Then he turned in a low voice to his two surprised companions.

"He's down there. A secret door is in the wine cellar and I saw light coming, but he could hear you. When you entered the room, the light was extinguished."

"Then let's catch him!" said Moira excitedly.

"Yes, there are two of us, we can overpower him."

"We don't know if he's there alone. We don't know if he has any weapons with him either. I think, he's still feeling safe, and that's our advantage. I'll notify the inspector and tomorrow, together with his people, we'll storm the hole and then we'll have him."

Somewhat disappointed about not being able to catch the bastard tonight, the three rode back unaccomplished. Halfway back, Samuel said goodbye until the next morning and rode home. In the meantime it had become dark and the stars were in the sky. It was a clear night that was falling. The search had taken longer than he had expected, but Robert was satisfied. At last they knew where Dumfrey had gone. He was in the trap that would snap shut tomorrow.

Dumfrey held his breath when he heard the voice. He quickly extinguished his lamp and listened at the door. Was it really possible that the police had found him? Beads of sweat formed on his forehead.

No matter how hard he tried, he could suddenly hear nothing more from outside. Did that mean that they were already gone again, or were they already working on a plan to get him? For the first time he was no longer so sure that this hiding place was untraceable, but then he heard the voice that told the others, that they had found nothing and he breathed a sigh of relief.

Ha, he was the best after all. He was a genius. No one would be able to stop him and so he continued to forge his plans for revenge.

Chapter 31

For today the work ended. The stable boys had already retired, horses in the stable had been cared for, and so all was quiet when they arrived at home.

"Go on into the house, I'll take care of the horses and then I'll follow. Maybe Gwyneth might have something tasty in the kitchen for us."

"I'll help you, it'll go faster."

Together they led the animals into the stable. While Robert hung the saddles on hooks on the wall, Moira watched Robert furtively. Since they had set out that afternoon, she had not been unaware of this underlying tension between them, and now, as they rode home alone under the starry sky, a longing had set in that she had almost thought lost.

Now she stood here and followed his every move, and she became hot with longing.The play of his muscles under his shirt made her heart beat faster and the look of his narrow hips and firm buttocks took her breath away. The air around her seemed to charge magically. Driven by his attraction, she walked toward him, and when he turned, she threw herself into his arms. Surprised, he caught her and held her tightly. Moira wrapped her arms around his neck and kissed him with such passion, that Robert forgot everything around him.

"Touch me, love me, here and now."

She did not wait for the answer, but began to ruffle his hair with her fingers, covering his face with kisses and nibbling on his shirt buttons with her fingers. Breathless and overwhelmed by the fact that his wife seduced him here, he tried to get a last clear thought between two kisses.

"Moira, do you really think we should? The doctor has...".

She paused and put her hand on his mouth, which made him fall silent and looked at him tenderly. Black strands of hair hung in his face and while she gleefully ran her fingers over his half-exposed upper body, she breathed towards him.

"I don't want to wait any longer. I want you to touch me, show me that you love me. I want to feel you inside me, tonight."

How long he had waited for these words. He pulled her into the only empty stall, which was laid out with fresh straw and kissed her hard on the mouth. His tongue played with her lips and when she opened them a little, he conquered her mouth.

She moaned out while Robert ran his hands in her hair and deftly untied the knot she was wearing. Immediately her long brown curls fell down over her shoulders, and he buried his hands in them. Moira touched her lips to his naked torso. The kisses she left on his skin seemed to set his body on fire.

Breathlessly, he uttered her name and pushed the suspenders off her shoulders. Moira pulled the rest of his shirt out of his pants and slipped it off his arms. Carelessly it fell to the ground. She clung to his steel-hard torso and ran her mouth up his neck until she came to his twitching Adam's apple.

This was too much for him. He undid his gunbelt with one hand and let it slide with the gun to the ground, then he pulled Moira closer to him. He grasped her buttocks with both hands and pressed her tightly against him. Through the fabric of her pants, she could feel his arousal and felt how the heat of his body seized her. Slowly, he ran one hand up her thigh until he stopped between her legs. Moira closed her eyes and threw her head back. The feelings that Robert released in her were indescribable and when he stripped off her pants and she felt the cool air against her legs, she dug her fingers into his back.

His shirt she was wearing was so long that she could have worn it as a nightgown and Robert couldn't help but smile. She looked so seductive in his clothes. He hoped that Moira was really ready for him, because he no longer had the strength to stop. His body ached with every fiber. He had already had to do without for too long. He had not been able to touch her like this for weeks and now these pent-up feelings burst out of him. Passionately and wildly he kissed her.

His hands nibbled at the buttons of her shirt and finally laid the corset free. He covered the firm base of her breast with his lips. Then with practiced grips he opened her corset and removed the last hurdle. At the sight of her firm breasts he drew in the air sharply. She was so infinitely beautiful. He buried his face in her skin and Moira pulled him closer to her. He kissed her breasts and nibbled her buds. Moira could not form a clear thought and called out his name.

She closed her eyes and gave in to the feelings he evoked in her. Half naked she stood before him here in the stable. At any moment, someone from the service staff could come in, but they did not care about that. Here and now there were only the two of them.

She wanted to feel him, deep inside her. For too long she had had to wait for this. She gasped when she felt his hand on her most intimate spot, felt how he stroked her tenderly. A tremor went through her body and she felt her legs give way, but Robert held her tightly, with his hand pressed against her, while he sealed her mouth with his lips.

He couldn't wait any longer. His body was longing for release and so he removed the last hindering pieces of clothing and lifted her onto his hips. Moira immediately wrapped her legs around his body to have a better hold, because only his upper body held her against the wooden wall.

When she felt him inside her, she reared up to meet him. She wrapped her arms around his neck and kissed him passionately, then began to move. Slowly at first, then faster and faster inside her.

Her ecstasy determined the rhythm and led her higher, higher and higher, until her feelings discharged in a violent explosion.

Their bodies trembled and twitched and only gradually the waves of ecstasy subsided. Exhausted, they remained in their position for quite a while. Their sweaty bodies clung to each other and Robert smiled happily at Moira. She breathed his name and snuggled against his neck.

"Who would have ever thought that my wife would seduce me in the stable. You are really good for surprises," he whispered into her ear and played with a lock of her hair. Somewhat ashamed, Moira straightened up and looked into those incredible blue eyes that had captivated her from the very first day.

"Oh, I probably shouldn't have done it, but it just came over me. I've missed your closeness so much."

He lifted her chin with his hand and pressed a deep intimate kiss on her lips.

"I'm sure I'm the last person who would complain. I just didn't know what a wonderfully passionate woman I had married. I love you, Moira."

She beamed happily at him.

"I love you, too, and actually I learned all this from you."

Playfully startled, he smiled at her, and her heart warmed.

"Really?"

"Do you want me to prove it to you?"

"Well, I think we'd better continue this conversation in a more comfortable place."

Chapter 32

That very night Robert had sent a messenger to the inspector to inform him of the latest state of his investigation and to ask him to come by the next day with a strong team. Now Moira, Samuel and Robert awaited his arrival. While the two men put their heads together over Robert's desk, trying to to come up with a battle plan, Moira stood pensively at the window.

She looked up into the cloudy sky. Behind her she heard Robert tell how he imagined the arrest of Dumfrey would go. It all sounded so simple and yet she knew that it would be not without danger. It was her fault that Dumfrey's machinations had come to light so late. She had played wickedly with Robert and had almost lost the man who meant everything to her.

But he had forgiven her and was now fighting for her. What had she done to deserve his love for her? Last night had shown them both how much they loved and needed each other and she realized it was a gift from God that she had met him. Her thoughts turned to her dead parents, and she knew that they would have been very pleased with her choice.

Moira turned around and as if Robert could feel the glances from her, he raised his head and looked over at her. It seemed as if he wanted to say something to her, but he was interrupted by Albert, who came into the room and announced the inspector.

"Send him in, please, Albert."

A few seconds later, the policeman appeared and greeted those present.

"My lord, you have already written to me in your letter what happened yesterday. It was absolutely right to leave this matter to us."

Robert, who felt he had to set the record straight, replied: "Inspector Jennings, I have no intention whatsoever of withdrawing now. We will, of course, accompany you, because without me you will not find the place in the cellar."

Appeasingly, the inspector raised his hands.

"I didn't mean it that way. I already realize that you want to be part of the game, and I welcome it. Without you, we would still be under the assumption that he had long since disappeared. I'm assuming, that you have already thought of something?"

"That's right. We could do it like this..," and Robert began to explain his plan to the inspector.

"Seems to have been well thought out," declared the policeman, after Robert had finished with his plan.

"I'll brief my men."

"Let's go then, what are we waiting for."

Three pairs of eyes were now focused on Moira, who was getting ready to leave.

"My lady, you're not going, are you?"

That was all the inspector needed, that he should have to take care of a woman. Women had no place on the battlefield, but Moira looked at him challengingly.

"Do you mind? I made a promise to my husband that I would be there, and I will be. Dumfrey has done harm to me as well and I want to see him arrested."

Puzzled, the inspector looked over at Robert, when he only shrugged his shoulders and said,

"You don't know my wife, she can be quite stubborn", and gave Moira a wink at that.

"Okay, I get the point, but my lady, you stay in

the background."
"That's what I had to promise my husband."
"Then everything is settled. You inform your men and we'll get our horses."

Robert reached for his gun belt, which was hanging on the back of his chair and strapped it around his waist. Samuel also grabbed a hunting rifle from the gun cabinet. Samuel left the room with the inspector in front and when Robert tried to follow, Moira held him back by the sleeve. Tenderly, he took her in his arms.
"Promise me you'll take care of yourself."
He pulled her closer to him and gave her a tender kiss.
"Don't be afraid. We'll get him."

Gently, he disengaged from her and let her lead the way. Moira wore a gray riding costume today, which, flattered her figure despite its simplicity.

She had intended to wear his pants again, but he had decided to have that discussion last night. For nothing in the world would he have exposed her to the army of young policemen in that getup. At first she did not understand his objections, but when he showed her what her outfit did to a man, she had given up her resistance with her head up.

Robert noticed how the thoughts of her alone took possession of his body. But now was not the time to indulge in such ideas. Taking a deep breath, he followed his wife outside. The troop of horsemen approached the estate and the inspector's group split up. They would surround the entire house while the commander, along with Robert, Samuel and five other police officers, would storm the basement.

Moira was to stay at a safe distance from the house. When all had reached their positions and Moira was also at a proper distance, the eight men crept to the front door. Unlike the last visit, this time they went directly to the front door, because the inspector had a

key with him. Without making a sound, they crept inside
and down the basement stairs.

Then they listened, but not a sound was heard.
Robert led the troop into the wine cellar. He pointed
with his finger to the hidden door in the wall and bent
down to look under the shelf in front of it. This time
there was no light to be seen and he immediately had a
bad feeling. He quickly rose, groped for the mechanism
that would open the door and gave the law enforcement
officers behind him a signal to stand by.

Quick as a flash, he flicked the switch, the door
opened a crack, and Robert immediately pulled it open
so that the policemen behind him could rush into the
room with their weapons drawn. But the disappointment
was great. The room was empty and there was no trace
of Dumfrey.

"Damn it, this can't be true. He's always one step ahead
of us," groaned Robert angrily.

But the inspector reassured him: "He can't be far
ahead yet. The candle here is still warm and the wax is
not yet dry. Stuart, light this lamp here, so that we can
get a little more light."

"How did he get away? The house is surrounded."

"Sir, take a look at this."

One of the guards had grabbed a tapestry on the opposite
side and was now uncovering a narrow corridor behind
it.

"Well, I think there's your answer, my lord.
Stuart, Weller and Fetherton, grab a couple of lamps and
find out where this passageway goes, but watch out, we
don't know what surprises Sir Dumfrey might have in
store for us. Roger, get Lady MacIntyre over here. I
want her to take a look at it."

Robert and Samuel, who were now looking curiously
over the inspector's shoulder, could see that he had found
a note on the desk at which he was standing. Samuel lit

the candle and now they could see clearly that it was an old letter.

"Is there anything important in it?", Robert wanted to know and the inspector handed him the letter, so that he could read it himself.

"I think this should make a few things clear."

Robert looked around. The room was not particularly large. Apart from a bed and a night table there was only a wing chair, which had also seen better days and the desk, before which they stood now.

On this piled up quite a few letters and documents, which the inspector was already looking through. Otherwise, there was nothing in the room worthy of closer examination. When Moira appeared, he could see her disappointment. He had promised her that everything would be over today and now Dumfrey had slipped through their fingers again.

"My lady, please come over here and look at this letter."

The inspector handed her the old document and Moira's gaze darkened as she held it in her hand. Astonished by the lines, she looked at the Commander.

"It is a letter from my father to Dumfrey. I did not know that he had had any trouble with him at that time. It says quite clearly here that he's giving Dumfrey a pass about the sale of the land at the cliffs and that he should refrain from further visits in this regard. Why was Dumfrey visiting us the night of the fire anyway?"

"I'm sure he'll explain that to us when we catch him, but it's likely he's changed tactics based on the letter. Since we found the jewelry from the safe at his place, we can assume that he tricked your parent into inviting him to dinner and then put his diabolical plan into action. He will have been looking for an opportunity to disable your parents, then rob them and set the fire as a cover-up. I found some more interesting papers here. See for yourself."

He moved slightly to the side so that Moira could have an unobstructed view of the table. Robert and Samuel also came closer to see what interesting detail the inspector was referring to.

"These are all my father's promissory notes", Moira marveled.

"Yes, but it is always the same text about the same amount, also the signature appears to be you father's, but if you look closer, it looks slightly different each time. I think we have the proof that Dumfrey forged your father's promissory note and based on the signature from the old letter he practiced until he was able to copy it so perfectly that you would not have noticed it."

"Then it was all a trap? And I being an idiot immediately believed him. I didn't have the slightest doubt that the appearance could not be real. What a fool I was, I should have at least considered it."

Inwardly agitated, she tried to reconstruct the individual meetings with Dumfrey, but she was interrupted when she felt Robert behind her, who put his hand tenderly on her shoulder. He seemed to understand what was going on. She was about to say something when she heard hurried footsteps coming from the secret passage and immediately the three uniformed men appeared.

"What did you find out?"

"The corridor ends in a bush near the road. It is well hidden and not visible from the driveway . His horse must have been standing there, because we have found traces. Unfortunately, we could not determine in which direction he rode off."

"Damn. This man has more luck than he deserves. I don't know how he realized we were coming, but now he's definitely warned and will never come back here again. Let the others know, we're breaking up here."

Robert couldn't believe his ears and reared up in front of

the inspector.

"Jennings, you can't do that. He is getting away from us. Dumfrey couldn't have gone far, and we should be scouring the area."

"What do you want me to do? The guy is long gone and without any clues, it's like looking for a needle in a haystack. I'm sorry, but we're breaking off."

Dumfrey looked around in a hurry. That had been close. It was just a coincidence that he had left the corridor the moment he heard the horses of the police. But now they knew his secret and it was impossible for him to return.

Once again the lord had proven to be a problem but this time he had gone too far and the revenge would be his. Hastily he drove his horse forward. Every minute counted. The police knew what game he was playing, but he only needed a small head start to realize his deadly plan.

After that he would disappear without a trace for a long time to build a new identity, and then he would return for Moira as her second husband take over the inheritance of her husband, who unfortunately had died young. Dumfrey's eyes lit up at this notion, the plan was ingenious and he knew exactly what he had to do to finally get rid of Lord MacIntyre and get his hands on Moira for himself. All he needed, was a little head start.

Chapter 33

Disappointed at the failure of their mission, Robert, Samuel and Moira rode back with the policemen. Suddenly, Robert reined in his horse and stuck his nose into the wind.
"Do you smell that, too? Something's burning!"
The pack stopped immediately.

"My God, that's coming from the direction of the orphanage," Samuel shouted in horror and dashed off with his horse before the others could follow. The closer they got to the house, the stronger the smell of burning became. First clouds of smoke formed in the sky. Samuel was right, there was another fire on Moira's property. When they arrived at the orphanage, they were horrified to see that one wall of the house was already ablaze. Desperate cries for help rang out to them from within. They had to hurry.

Robert jumped from his horse and shouted over his shoulder to Moira that she had to take care of the horses and stay away from the fire with them. Then he ran toward the fire with Samuel, who called for his wife. The policemen took the saddles off the horses, spread out around the house and tried to fight the fire with saddle blankets. Samuel and Robert hurried to the front door.
"Why aren't Eileen and the children out of the house

yet? There's still no fire yet."

"Maybe the door is stuck. Look at that, the bastard's put brushwood all around the house. It's burning like tinder. We have to hurry. Soon the flames will reach the front as well."

When the two of them reached the front door, they saw why the occupants of the house had not fled.Two wooden boards had been jammed into each other in such a way that the door was blocked. The two immediately set about removing the boards. The flames were already creeping closer and higher.

When the door was exposed, Robert tore the stacked brushwood from the door with his bare hands. From the inside the cries for help grew louder and the fire also increased in intensity. The smoke was black and thick and made breathing difficult, but Robert and Samuel did not give up. In the meantime Jenning's men had rushed to help and were beating the fire with their blankets. They could not prevent the heat of the flames shattering the windows and gave the fire more food as the curtains ignited from inside. In the meantime the two husbands got the door free and rushed in.

Moira, who was watching the scene from the sidelines, became frightened and anxious when she saw Robert storming into the house. She was afraid for him, but she also knew that he would do everything he could to get Eileen and the children out of the house safely with Samuel. She tried not to think of what would have happend if they had shown up just a few minutes later.

It seemed to take an eternity before she could finally breathe a sigh of relief. Coughing and gasping for air, her husband and Samuel took Eileen and the children to safety. She was relieved to see that they were all well, because the three adults led the crying children away from the burning house. The inspector's group was still trying to fight the fire, but it seemed that they were losing the battle. Moira was about to go in a wide arc around the house to join the others, when she felt the barrel of a pistol in her back. Abruptly she stopped and was about to turn around, when she heard Dumfrey's voice behind her.

"Now you slowly get on your horse and come with me."

Panic seized her. How could she escape from his grasp without him putting a bullet in her back. Hastily she looked around. Neither the policemen nor Robert seemed to have seen him. Was the man crazy? Why did he put himself in this danger? All it took was for one of the men to catch sight of him, or did he not care? She had to stall somehow and so she gathered all her courage and asked him: "What are you going to do? If they see you, they will catch you."

"They won't if you mount your horse and come along."

"I will not go with you!"

Moira had not expected the sudden violence that Dumfrey now displayed. With a jerk, he turned her around to face him, and looked down at her with evil glittering eyes. Trembling with rage quivering, he spat the words at her.

"I didn't work for two years on this plan, set fire to your parents' house and poison your husband's uncle, so that now everything would be over. Your husband has been a thorn in my side since he arrived and you had the task to keep him away from me. But you failed and now you will come with me. You will marry me as soon as I put a bullet in your spouse's head. Actually, he deserves a slower way to die but I'm running out of time. He won't even know I've blown his lights out. So let's move forward now."

"You are insane!"

Without another word, Dumfrey grabbed two horses and pulled Moira along with him. Desperately, she thought of how she could draw attention to herself.

Still everyone was busy trying to get the fire under control. She thought about calling out, but the sound of crackling wood drowned out everything and Dumfrey would immediately knock her down or kill her. She didn't have much time left, because they were getting farther and farther away from the house.

When Dumfrey stopped and pulled her to one of the horses, she had an idea. She hoped that the Almighty would give her enough strength. As soon as Dumfrey loosened his grip to lift her into the saddle, she saw her chance. She grabbed his arm with her free hand and bit into his flesh as hard as she could. Filled with pain, he cried out and let go of her. This was her opportunity. With full force she threw her body into his belly and brought him down, then she gathered up her skirt and began to run toward the house.

Calling for help, she ran toward the helpers. Robert, who first heard Moira's voice, looked in her direction. What the hell had his wife...? But then he saw Dumfrey standing behind her and understood immediately.

Even before one of the others had grasped the situation, he ran toward his wife. When he had almost reached her, a bullet struck a tree trunk near him and splintering wood flew towards him. That son of a bitch shot at him. Moira seemed to be oblivious to this because she threw herself breathlessly into his arms.

"Are you all right? I'm gonna get that son of a bitch."

Before Moira could say anything in reply, however, Robert left her standing there and went after Dumfrey. Unfortunately, the rogue had a big head start, but he would now chase him until he had him. Dumfrey had ridden away with his horse in the direction of the cliffs. On the first stretch the path was wide enough for Robert to give his horse the spurs. He sped around the next bend and saw the fugitive a few hundred yards ahead of him. With his upper body bent far above the animal's neck, he chased after him. Robert did not have much time to catch up with him, because he knew that the road would soon narrow and run very close to the cliffs. If Dumfrey reached that stretch of road before he caught him, then he would probably escape, for Robert would not ride recklessly after him.

The danger of falling off was too great for horse and rider. Robert made up yards by yards and got everything out of his horse. Dumfrey looked around in a hurry. His pursuer was getting closer and closer and his lame mare seemed to be slowing down. He could already hear the quick breath of the animal as he rammed the spurs into the belly of his horse.

But nothing helped, he could not shake off his pursuer. Robert steered his horse alongside Dumfrey's and when he was finally on the same level, he started to jump. With a tremendous force he threw himself at Dumfrey and lifted him out of the saddle.

They hit the ground hard. Dumfrey was lucky that he had landed on top of Robert and was thus able to move better. He rammed his elbow into his face and thus bought himself enough time to pick himself up and flee on foot. He ran along the path that brought him closer to the cliffs. Hastily, he looked around for his horse, but it was standing too far away with Roberts and was grazing. It was not possible for him to reach it, so he ran on. Robert, who was getting up in a daze, needed a few seconds to grasp the situation. He heard the sound of hooves. Help was approaching.

He saw Samuel, the inspector and some of his men coming toward him. Probably Moira had mobilized them, but time was passing, he could not wait for them. Dumfrey had already a head start again and so he took up the pursuit again. With his long legs, he had no trouble catching up with the older and much smaller man. When Dumfrey felt his pursuer already at his neck he turned around in a flash and fired another bullet from his pistol at Robert. This time it missed him by only a few inches. Robert threw himself to the ground, drew his revolver and fired. Hit by the bullet, Dumfrey cried out. He grabbed his leg and saw the blood gushing out. Horrified, he staggered backwards. Dumfrey didn't seem to have noticed how close he was to the abyss, but Robert shouted to him, with his gun drawn:" Stand still Dumfrey, it's over. Come here."

"No way, go to hell!", again he laid into Robert, but before he could pull the trigger, Robert shot the gun out of his hand. Dumfrey backed away, startled. Robert, recognizing the danger in which Dumfrey was in, called out to him again to come toward him, but his counterpart only laughed at him. He took another step back and now realized his mistake.

With wildly flailing arms, he tried to regain his balance, but he was lost. Robert rushed forward at the moment Dumfrey lost his balance backwards, but his saving grip came to nothing as Dumfrey plunged down the precipice before his eyes with a terrified scream. At that moment, the others also reached him. Stunned, they looked over the edge.

"We were able to observe everything, he had the choice. Be glad, it's all over."

With that, the inspector turned away and went to his people. Robert, however, was still looking into the abyss. Disappointment and anger spread through him. Why hadn't he been a little faster, he could have saved him. Not that he suddenly felt sorry for Dumfrey. He had gotten what he deserved. Nevertheless, he would have preferred to crush him himself like an annoying insect. For he was not much more in his eyes. Then Samuel stepped next to him and put his hand on his friend's shoulder.

"He didn't deserve it any other way."

"I know, but I would have liked to see him dangle from the gallows and have his brains beaten out of him first. This has been a far too merciful death for him."

"I wish I could have gotten my hands on him for what he did to Eileen, but this is as good as it gets."

"Yes, it's over!"

Epilogue

It had begun to snow. The first snow that Robert saw in his new home. Temperatures had plummeted in recent days and everyone was glad to be inside the warm house today after church services. Thoughtfully he stood in the hall by the festively decorated tree.

Albert and Harried had decorated it beautifully with Moira. In the background he could hear the many voices talking happily in the dining room. Tonight there would be a Christmas feast and Samuel had come with Eileen to celebrate with them. Since the fire at the orphanage, life had come to his house.

Since housing for the children had to be found quickly, he had agreed with Moira that they would be housed and taught in a wing of his house and be educated. Moira knew what it meant to have ten lively children in the house, and credited her husband with immediately agreeing to house them on a temporary basis. She had come to the decision not to rebuild the orphanage and so it had already been torn down.

The new orphanage should be in her parents' house. In the new building, they had more space and could accommodate even more children in the future. Robert was pleased that Moira could distract herself from the events of the last few months. What with everything that had happened this year!

"You once said to me you felt lonely despite the many people around you, is that still the case?"

Robert was jolted out of his thoughts when he heard Moira's voice behind him. Tenderly she put her arms around him and nestled against his back. Robert slowly turned to her and looked into her green eyes.

"Are you happy, Robert? I mean, you said to me once that you might not want to stay here and go back. Is that still the case?"

With a smile on his lips, he answered her:

"I must have said quite a few stupid sentences. Since you came into my life, I am not lonely anymore. You are my family now, only sometimes I wish that my parents had the chance to meet you."

"I would like that very much, too, but it's going to take a while, because you're going to have more tasks to accomplish."

"What do you mean?" he looked at her in amazement.

"I was going to tell you later when we were alone, but I think now, it's also a good time. I'm pregnant again."

Immediately, a little anticipation grew inside him.

"Are you quite sure?"

"I know it's early, but a woman can sense something like this. Yes I'm quite sure."

Happily, Robert lifted her up and twirled her around. Moira laughed in his arms. His kiss that followed made her anticipate how they would spend the night and it made her shiver pleasantly.

"This is the most beautiful Christmas present that you could have given me. I love you."

Tenderly, she caressed his cheek.

"You are the best thing that ever could have happened to me and I hope that someday you will show me your home."

"My home is here with you, and when we make the long journey someday, it will only be for a visit, because I want to spend my life here, with you and our children."

She looked into his eyes in love, into those bright blue eyes that had captivated her from the beginning. Robert MacIntyre was her life, and it would always be that way.

Now Available – Part II

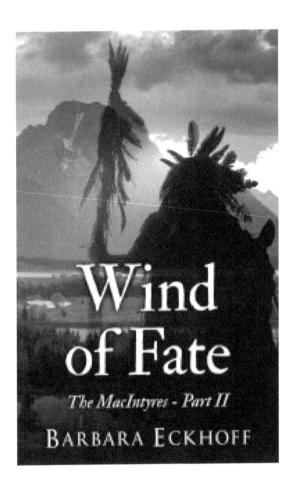

Isabella had exchanged her sunday dress for her riding costume. It was such a glorious spring day that she wanted to steal a few hours and venture out for a ride.

It was the first, since the long winter, and it would do her and her mare Tipsy good to get off the ranch. After the Reverend had been invited not only to the apple pie, but also for lunch, he was now on his way home, and Isabella had a little time to kill before she had to see to dinner. She had agreed with Louisa to be back on time. Quickly she slipped into her brown winter riding skirt, which was made of heavy wool.

Along with it she wore a white blouse with long sleeves and high collar. Against the still fresh temperatures, she put on her moss green jacket made of warm winter wool, which reached her hips and had a longer peplum towards the back. Her appearance was completed with warm, wool-lined, brown riding boots, black gloves, a jaunty lime-green scarf, tied around her neck and a cowboy hat that did not quite match her elegant style of dress, but was very practical and under which she hid her long, chestnut hair.

With a last, satisfied look in the mirror, she left her room and made her way to the stable. Normally, she did not make such a fuss about her appearance, but today was a beautiful day and she was looking forward to her ride. So why not dress up for a change? The opportunities on a ranch were not very often available. With a smile on her lips and a little melody in her head, she arrived at the huge barn.

The stables were part of a large barn complex located near the main house. One barn housed the horses used for ranch work. Just behind it were several paddocks where the horses now grazed and quite a few small and larger paddocks where the cowboys could break in new horses or drive cattle in for branding. In one of these small paddocks, a bit off to the side, stood a black stallion that watched her with attentive eyes.

The ears pricked, he followed every move she made. Isabella thought about it and paused briefly before turning to the animal. Slowly, she walked toward the small paddock. Immediately the animal started to move and ran restlessly around. Her father had caught the wild mustang a week ago and brought him here.

He wanted him for himself and would have long ago ridden him but the animal was the devil in person. As soon as someone tried to approach him, he rose threatening. When Isabella came closer, the stallion started to snort, tossed his black mane wildly back and forth and pranced on the ground. Isabella stopped.
She was only a short distance away from the fence and could see the diabolical eyes of the animal.

It was a beautiful animal, but unfortunately unrideable and she wondered, as she turned around and went back to the stable, what her father was going to do with him. Well, today she was going to spend some quality time with her own horse. Her chestnut mare was already neighing happily when she heard her coming down the aisle.

Tipsy was a good-natured horse, that Isabella had bought as a foal for her fifth birthday. Since then they were one heart and soul and understood each other blindly, when they rode out together.

"Well beautiful? Shall we go for a ride today? It's so beautiful outside. You'll like to let the wind blow through your mane."

The mare joyfully rubbed her nostrils against Isabella's arm and neighed approvingly, as if she had understood what she had just heard. It was not long before Isabella had saddled her horse and left the stable. Skillfully, she swung herself into the saddle and steered her mare in the direction of the main house, since her grandfather had just come out of the front door.

"Do you want to take a little ride?"

"Yes, it's lovely today and I haven't been out for a long time."

"Don't ride too far, though. Did you bring the rifle? Just in case?"

She reached up to her right thigh and pulled the rifle stock out of the holster a little so that her grandfather could see the weapon.

"It's all there, I'll be back in a couple of hours. See you later."

She slid the rifle back into the holster, tapped her hat in salute and gave her mare the command to trot. Joyfully they both trotted off.

The sun was shining brightly from the sky and not a single cloud clouded the weather. First she rode a good distance along the fence of the cattle pasture and had seen several of her father's cowboys at work.

The ranch was located in a kind of high valley. In the distance you could see forests, hills and high mountain ranges to the right and left of the ranch. In between far-reaching pastures. Later she had made a small but sharp gallop over the endless expanse of the adjacent prairie which had led into a stop on a hill. She looked around. From the hill she had a breathtaking view of her home. As far as the eye reached, she saw small black points grazing on the prairie.

hey were her father's cattle. The ranch house could no longer be seen.

"That was lovely, wasn't it Tipsy? Come let's ride on."

Happily, she patted the animal on the neck and Tipsy snorted in satisfaction. She steered her horse into the adjacent forest and rode slowly into it. All too far, she did not want to ride more, since she had promised to be back on time, but they both enjoyed the ride so much that she decided to extend it a bit more. She loved the smell of the forest. The delicate, lime green buds of the new leaves. Her horse carried her safely along the small trail around the trees.

Somewhere above, sat birds singing their spring song. She was briefly startled when two rabbits jumped out of the bushes in front of her, but Tipsy didn't let that upset her. Cheekily, the two rabbits sat down on the forest floor in front of them and watched the approaching hares, before they suddenly disappeared with a leap into the undergrowth. Laughing, she rode on. A deer appeared in the undergrowth and immediately disappeared from her view.

All of nature had awakened from its long winter sleep. She enjoyed the peaceful atmosphere that prevailed here. How gladly she would have stayed longer but she had to make her way home. Isabella knew her way around here well. How often had she come along this path.

Only a short distance, then the forest would open up and a small trail would lead down the embankment, where she could ride along the forest on open prairie back to the ranch. Suddenly Tipsy stopped abruptly and began to neigh nervously. Isabella looked around, but could see nothing suspicious. Reassuringly she tried to talk to the increasingly nervous animal.

"Calm down, Tipsy. What is it that makes you nervous? Come on let's ride on."

But the animal did not move from the spot. Instead, it began to neigh loudly and prance nervously on the spot. Isabella slowly pulled the rifle from the holster and inwardly prepared herself to fire a shot. Whatever was around her, she had to try to steer Tipsy out of the woods. She had not quite finished this thought when, out of nowhere, a cougar jumped on her horse and bit the animal in the neck. Tipsy reared up wildly in pain, shook its neck convulsively and tried to shake off the beast. Isabella had cried out in horror when the cougar jumped onto the horse in front of her.

The moment of shock had lasted until she had recognized the situation, had used the cougar to bite the horse's neck firmly. She couldn't shoot, the cougar was too close for that, but she tried to knock him off his horse with the butt of her rifle. With all her strength she hit the animal, the cougar let go of the horse's neck and now clawed his one paw deep into her thigh, while he came closer to her body with his sharp teeth. Painfully she cried out and panic-stricken she continued to hit the cougar with the rifle.

At that moment Tipsy started to move, to escape the cougar. But the cougar had bitten into her neck again. With great difficulty she managed to stay on the horse and at the same time tried to shake off the beast. Tipsy was going faster and faster. Isabella held at the same time the reins in one hand and the saddle horn to give herself support, while the other hand tried to hit the cougar with the butt of the rifle.

Crouched, so as not to be lifted out of the saddle by the branches of the trees, she saw the end of the forest coming. She had to make it as far as the open prairie, then she would be able to move better, but until then endless time seemed to pass.

Finally Tipsy had reached the embankment and galloped down at a wild pace. Isabella was in danger of losing her footing. She was a good rider and had been in the saddle since childhood, but she had never been prepared for this extreme situation. She clawed her thighs against the horse's body and was glad when they arrived on level ground.

But instead of Tipsy riding toward the ranch, she swept along the prairie in the opposite direction. Now she was able to stand up. She tied the reins around the pommel of the saddle so she wouldn't lose them and took the rifle in both hands. With the remaining strength she still had, she took a swing with the rifle and hit the cougar on the head with full force.

The cougar finally let go of the animal, snarling, and with a second blow immediately following, the cougar flew off the horse in a high arc.

Inwardly, Isabella breathed a sigh of relief. She had managed to shake off the dangerous beast. Isabella quickly stowed the rifle in the stock under her thigh and took up the reins again, while she tried to calm down Tipsy and steer her in the direction of the ranch. But the animal was in such a panic that it did not respond neither to the reassuring words of her nor to the rein aids. On the contrary, now on the open terrain, the animal gained even more speed. They moved away at a murderous pace mile after mile more from the ranch and the environment became more and more unknown to her.

On the hill he reined in his horse. The forest was behind him and now gave him a clear view of the breathtaking landscape below him. He had been on the road for a long time with his mission, but he had not made a single step forward. Somewhat undecided as to, where he should turn now, he stood on the hill and let the magic of nature fall upon him.

Between the small ridge on which he stood and the deep ravine that opened up a few hundred yards away from him lay green prairie. His gaze wandered to the left, where he saw that the canyon widened and the prairie ended. There, he would only get further if he could find a way down and the gorge allowed him to ride in it. To the right, the terrain looked as if he could continue his way. Just as he wanted to steer his horse in this direction, down the hill, a cloud of dust on the horizon caught his attention. What could it be that was coming at him at a seemingly rapid pace?

A herd of buffalo? No, the dust cloud was not big enough for that. He had seen many buffalo herds before, and when they came, the ground shook and the dust clouds were huge. His trained sharp eyes suddenly spotted a single rider, but what drove this rider into this area with such speed? Slowly he gave his horse the command to descend the hill. He did not want to reveal himself too early to the oncoming rider.

When he reached the bottom, he took cover behind a bush and could observe from here that the rider had not reduced his speed and, from his point of view, was dashing along the precipice in an extremely dangerous manner. The rider had to be insane. He could plunge into the abyss at any moment with a misstep of the horse. When the horse was at his eye level, he realized that the rider was a woman, who had apparently lost control of her animal.

Without hesitating, he slammed his heels into his horse's flanks and galloped wildly after the rider. The horse was fast, but it was no match for his mustang and so he made up ground yard by yard.

The rider did not seem to have noticed him, nor was she aware of the danger she was in. At any moment she could lose her balance, or her horse could fall with her, into the ravine. Glancing ahead, he saw that they were nearing the end where the ravine joined the ridge and the grass ended.

The rider's animal continued to dash towards it without stopping. He recognized the panicked look in the horse's eyes and knew that he had to get the woman from the horse. With the Indian words that he whispered into his horse's ear, the animal immediately stepped up its pace once again.

He shifted to the left of the panicked animal and now rode almost level with it. At that moment, the woman caught a glimpse of him and widened her eyes in fear. Just as she was about to draw her rifle with her right hand, he steered his horse right next to hers, bent over to her, wrapped his right arm around her delicate waist and lifted her with a skillful grip from her saddle. He threw her directly over his animal's neck. Quickly he yanked the reins and let his mustang run out for a few more yards before he brought the animal to a halt.

Elegantly he let himself slide off the horse and pulled the woman kicking in front of him off the horse. Because she flailed wildly and he let go of her at that moment, she lost her balance and landed on her rear end. With a cry, she tried to pull herself up, but her legs failed cooperate and she landed on the floor again. Desperate and driven by fear, she slowly crawled away from the frightening Indian, who was now standing calmly next to his black stallion and watching her closely.

Wind of Fate

Now Available

BARBARA ECKHOFF

Born near Hannover/ Germany in 1968, she was drawn to faraway places at an early age.

As a hotel manageress, she worked in hotels all over Germany and spent a year in Canada as an au pair, before settling down with her husband and the two daughters in a small village in Schleswig-Holstein. In 2013, she emigrated with her family to Florida/USA. It was there, when she began to get more serious about writing. In the meantime, more books have been published in German and English. Today, she lives with her husband and their Golden Retriever in the beautiful Shenandoah Valley in Virginia/USA and runs a Bed & Breakfast.

For more Infos:

www.barbaraeckhoff.de

www.brierleyhill.com